MY
NAME
is
MONSTER

MY
NAME
is
MONSTER

Katie Hale

CANONGATE

First published in Great Britain in 2019
by Canongate Books Ltd, 14 High Street, Edinburgh EH1 1TE

canongate.co.uk

1

British Library Cataloguing-in-Publication Data
A catalogue record for this book is available on
request from the British Library

ISBN 978 1 78689 635 3

Typeset in Goudy 11/15pt by Palimpsest Book Production Ltd,
Falkirk, Stirlingshire

Printed and bound in Great Britain by Clays Ltd, Elcograf S.p.A.

For my parents,
who've always told me stories

PART ONE

MONSTER

'I am cast upon a horrible, desolate Island, void
of all hope of Recovery.
  But I am alive; and not drown'd as all my
Ship's Company were.'
                    Robinson Crusoe, Daniel Defoe

When the world is burning, it's easy to forget about ice.

Easy for most people, that is. I knew nothing but freeze for over a year. I lived with the ice, on the ice, inside it – locked on the island as the rest of the world grew desperate with rage and disease. As the missiles fell and cities were blasted by a thousand-degree heat, I struggled to keep warm.

Frostbite and a chill so keen it cuts right through the heart: that's the price of survival.

Then what?

After everyone else was dead, I sat by a window for three days watching the glacier creak and break. When I took off my trousers, my skin flaked away and my legs itched. I scratched at the dead skin until I was pink and sore, then I got dressed again.

I thought about the scientists who had vanished into a crevasse twenty years earlier and were never found, how their little bodies would one day tumble out of the glacier's mouth like babies being born, frozen solid and perfectly preserved in their brightly coloured thermals.

People used to think that ice is white, but it isn't. There is all kinds of history inside it, waiting to be brought out.

*

The beach tastes of skin and salt. Sand clogs my mouth and grinds against my teeth. When I move my hand I can feel the grains shifting beneath it.

Slowly, I lift my head. I sit up and cough. It starts in my throat, in the sand and spume still rattling in my oesophagus – then it expands, rising and billowing until I'm coughing from my stomach up, till my whole body is racked with it. I cough till I vomit on the sand, again, and again, and again, till all I can bring up is bile.

Wiping my mouth on my sleeve, I take several deep breaths.

This is where the sea spat me out.

To the right, a broad belt of sand stretches for miles, into the mist and sea spray of the horizon. In front, following the line of the beach, a low cliff is dotted with trees and seagulls. The gulls nestle on ledges and wheel overhead, screeching. Every rock is covered, streaked white and grey. The noise is horrendous. After the deep quiet of Svalbard, it feels like an assault. I had forgotten how noisy life could be.

Beyond the diving gulls, where the cliff meets the pregnant grey sky, is a line of coarse bracken and heather. Like the trees, these plants look hardy and gnarled, gripping onto the rock face with old men's fingers.

My own hands are red and rough from weeks in the cold, the knuckles inflamed, the fingers sinewy and chapped. When I flex them, I can feel pockets of air clicking between the cartilage. My mother had pianist's fingers, elegant and slender, her nails shaped and painstakingly buffed. My hands are better.

I look to my left, where a cluster of rocks catches the sea

and whirls it around, so the waves come crashing back towards the beach. Which is how I ended up here, of all places.

I turn to the sea and there it is: the boat, my boat, beached and broken on the rocks a short way out, rocking with the swell. Or rather, what's left of the boat.

If I were a nautical person, I suppose I would say *she* instead of *it*. I might stand on the lonely shore and regret that I did not go down with her. But I'm not.

When I haul myself to my feet, the whole right side of my body smarts where the sea and rocks have battered me. I take another deep breath. I have not survived this long only to die on a shit-splattered beach in Scotland.

I wade back out into the undertow. It tugs at my feet, smaller now than the fierce grip of the storm, but still there – an echo.

I expect the boat to be nothing but timbers and a few sodden relics, but for the first time in weeks, lightness fills my lungs like bellows. The cabin is still intact.

I stuff what I can into my backpack and carry it aloft back to shore. I remember seeing a film as a child where a warrior fording a river had to carry his sword above his head to keep it dry, the weapon his most valued possession, raised high like a benediction. This is my benediction: a backpack full of clothes, food, a sleeping bag, two rolls of Elastoplast, a Swiss army knife, rope, a lighter. This is what will keep me alive.

I make four more trips out to the boat, bringing back whatever else I can salvage, reclaiming food then breaking off dry bits of wood. Back on the beach, I kindle a fire above the tideline. Forget mourning her passing – I burn her bones to keep me warm.

Once stripped of my dripping, salt-soaked clothes and changed into ones that are merely damp, I scour the beach for anything else that may have washed ashore. I gather carrier bags, two odd socks that I dry by the fire, a plastic bottle, string. I lay out my collection in military rows in the sand, and the rows become a calendar, marking out the limits of my time. If I do not find anything else, I have only eight days left to survive.

I pull out my sleeping bag and am asleep before the sun has set.

By the time I wake, the fire has died and the remains of the boat have been claimed by the sea. I eat some of the more perishable food, pack my backpack and lace up my boots. As I climb the shallow cliff, the gulls shriek and divebomb, but I ignore them.

I reach the top and start to walk.

*

I walk because somewhere there must be food and water. I walk to seek out shelter. I choose a destination because otherwise the possibility of *anywhere* is too big.

My parents lived around forty miles from Scotland. The Scottish mainland is roughly three hundred miles long. I do not know where I have washed up, but if I manage an average of ten miles a day, I should be home inside a month.

Of course it will take me much longer than that. I will get lost. As much as possible, I will avoid towns and cities. I will avoid their bombed and broken buildings, and their Sickness-ridden bodies lurking like a virus already in the bloodstream.

I will leave the roads, clogged with the cars of all those who tried to flee from explosions or infestations, those who had not already been claimed by the War or the Sickness that rose out of it, those who tried to reach the so-called Safe Centres before they shut their gates. Who knows how many shells are lying unexploded on the tarmac? Who knows what kinds of explosives or gases or diseases they might contain?

I will stick to fields and moorland and heaths. Nature always was a more predictable place – though even then there will be obstacles to overcome. There will be places to stop and search for food, and the unavoidable ritual of living. Survival is time-consuming.

Still it sits somewhere at the base of my belly, this drive to return. I am like a homing pigeon, pulled back to the place it was fed and watered and kept safe from prowling foxes, even though its keeper is no longer there to care for it. I suppose it is a pilgrimage of sorts. A sacrifice meted out in aches and blisters – an absolution. I need to see for myself that my parents are gone.

I dream about it sometimes. Not home itself, but the journey, the perpetual striving. In my dreams, I climb the hill behind my parents' house, or I drag my feet along the lane that leads to their village, but I always wake just before I arrive. There is always further to go.

*

My father called me Monster. It was supposed to be ironic, I think – an affectionate joke.

As I got older, my mother tried to change it, but by then the name had solidified around me. It was a shame, she said, for such a pretty child to have an ugly name.

My mother often lamented that I didn't fit my cherub cheeks and curls. Her name was Beatrice and she wore it like an elegant fur coat. As for me, I grew into my name and out of my curls. I think it takes a monster to survive when nobody else can.

*

I sit on a crumbling rock at the edge of a copse, where the air still smells of sea.

The fields here are wide and flat, and there is a feeling of height. The ground seems to go only as far as the nearest wall, and then into a cold sky beyond. I watch bright clouds scud across the horizon until it feels as though the whole world is moving.

For a moment, I can almost believe there was no War, no Sickness, no inevitable Last Fall. Then my eye lingers on the tangle of weeds growing over the bottom of the five-bar gate, part of the faint air of neglect that has settled over everything, human control succumbing to plant-life as the War forced people into towns and the Sickness swept through what remained of the villages.

A blister as big as a five pence coin has bubbled up on my right heel. I pop it between my nails and a clear liquid leaks across my thumb. I sit with cold air stinging the raw skin, until I'm numb from sitting. Then I stick a plaster on my heel and put my boot back on.

*

When I was five, I started to squirrel things under my bed in my mother's old shoe boxes. Little things, the flotsam and jetsam of daily life: spare plugs, old phones, the toaster that was supposed to be thrown out. I sat straining my eyes by the desk lamp, fiddling and tinkering until they worked again, or until I could piece the parts together into something new. I fell in love with the honesty of objects, how they thrived or failed based on their own mechanical truth. On rainy days, I would lay out all the pieces on my bedroom floor just to gaze at them. I knew their ridges and grooves intimately.

My screws and wires were my company. In the playground, I fought the girls who whispered behind my back and cold-shouldered the boys who prodded me in the side and sometimes claimed to want to be my friend. When Callum Jenkins slouched over one lunchtime to tell me I was 'cool for a girl', I bit his arm until I tasted blood.

As a teenager I became volatile and fierce, snapping at neighbours who asked about my favourite subjects, turning a sullen eye on critical aunts and uncles. I swore loudly at the gaggle of cousins who came to visit. My mother bought me a book: *How to Start Conversations and Make Friends*. I told her to fuck off.

By the time I was sixteen, I had taught myself how to be Monster.

*

For two days it rains. I take shelter in a bothy, by a gushing stream that threatens to burst its banks. The only wood I can find is rotted through and slimy to the touch, impossible to make a fire from. I spend all day cocooned in my sleeping bag, reliant on the scant protection of four walls and a dripping roof. The flaking plaster is black with mildew and there is a smell of dead rats. In the shut-in dark, it's too easy to remember the Seed Vault. It's too easy to think of Erik, wide-eyed and afraid in the pressing underground chamber of the vault. Then the silence, and the world crumbling outside. I close my eyes and focus on the noise of rain.

*

The grass is patchy, the earth wet and cloying. It clings to my boots as I squelch through it, making them heavy with mud. I drop down behind a hill and am confronted by a village. A mean thing – a dozen old stone houses hunkered in a glen. The place still has an air of isolation and hellish winters, and for a while I stand at a distance and just look.

There are no noises except the half-hearted gusting of wind through trees. The village itself is still and huddled as a dead thing. At the furthest edge, a patch of burnt ground like a footprint. If I hold my hand at arm's length, I can block out the whole sorry lot of it.

I have two days left before I run out of food.

Just once, as a teenager, I caught my mother in my bedroom, her flower-printed back to the door, fingers flicking through the pilfered things in my shoe box, turning them up to the light and putting them unceremoniously back.

That is what entering this village is like. I open doors to the houses and inside them I open cupboards and inside the cupboards I open boxes and tins. At every act of opening, I turn the hidden places up to the light and feel part of myself recoil. Everywhere I look, there are books or photographs or withered house-plants – all the flotsam that once made pieces of a life. If places could move, these would scurry from my entering them like woodlice on an upturned rock.

I try not to look too much, to break down these houses in my mind the way I might break down a machine into its functioning parts, so that I see each building only as a series of potential food stores, so I limit my attention to where supplies might be. I do not know how much I succeed, but I emerge from the last house with half a packet of oats, a tub of lentils, some tins and a box of not-quite luxury chocolates I decant into a bag. My pack is heavy, but my calendar of survival grows a little longer.

I follow a road so rough and potholed it is really no more than a track, skirting the bottom of a hill. A small bridge crosses a brook, and I dip down to fill my water bottles. Two of the tins clink together in my pack as I scramble back up the bank.

A few miles further on, my rutted strip of tarmac arrives at a wider road, with grass verges and a dotted white line along the centre. The signpost points to a town in one direction, a nature reserve in the other. I stop to drink from my water bottle, balancing the possibility of food and shelter against the need for emptiness and open space. I think about what a town might mean – like the village but bigger, an unbearable cavity, cluttered with all the paraphernalia of what my mother might have called 'normal people': people who followed the rules, who had families and a community, who stuck so hard to their so-called loved ones they eventually let it kill them.

I think about my parents, like two satellites with incompatible programming, but orbiting on the same trajectory. I try not to think about Erik, his fatal need for human touch. When there is nobody else, it is easier to think about hating people than about wanting them.

In the War and in the Sickness that followed, so many people depended too much on those they cared about. But survival has a cost. It has always had a cost, and the cost is being alone, cutting out friends and family like a cancerous

14

growth and sealing the wound behind them. And if you pay the greatest price, you get to survive the longest – which is why there is only me, and why I must keep walking.

I test the weight of the new supplies on my back, and head away from the town.

*

The ground is icy now. I leave the road and trek across fields. The frozen grass crunches under my boots. All around me, the world is wide and silver, like the painting of winter my parents had in the back bedroom. I walk with my face covered to protect myself from the cold. I can feel it in my toes and the tips of my fingers. Every day I hug my arms around my chest and am thankful for my thermal clothes. At night I light a fire and sleep as close to it as I dare.

When my toes go numb, I stamp the feeling back into them. When my mind starts to wander, when the immense unpeopled emptiness tugs at my thoughts and tries to scatter them, when the wind ruffling the reeds is the sound of Erik's voice echoing in the Seed Vault – I count my steps. I focus on the rhythm and it almost pulls me back.

*

They used to say survival came in threes, that a person could survive three days without water, three weeks without food, three months without company.

At two months and twenty-one days I stopped counting. I didn't want to know the moment that loneliness would mature into insanity. I didn't want to know when I had finally become a madwoman.

Perhaps I am mad now. Perhaps none of this is real, and I'm still trapped in the Seed Vault and this world is all my own construction. I think that only a mind like mine could create such a world. When I look at broken houses baring their pipes and wires and inner workings to the outside world, I think only I could invent such mechanical detail.

When I was a child I did have one friend. Harry Symmonds.

Harry Symmonds built models out of cocktail sticks and cried when other children touched his things. Harry Symmonds, who I smacked on the side of the head one day at school – who decided that a blow to the face was an act of friendship and followed me home.

I made him wait outside on the step until my mother realised and I had to let him in.

'Take him upstairs and show him your collection,' she said.

So I did, because I had to. I unfolded all the wires and rawl plugs and pilfered things onto the bedroom carpet and warned him not to touch any of it, and his eyes shone round.

By that time I had started to create my museum in the back half of the garden shed: a motley gathering of old bones from the surrounding fields. Bird and small mammal bones, mostly, scrubbed clean or left sprouting with moss, each one accompanied by a neat little card documenting the date and location of its finding. Once, for two whole weeks, the museum exhibited a dead rat, damp fur and tail still clinging to its bones, until the maggots broke out and it had to be thrown in the bin.

The pride of this collection was the sheep skull: gorgeous and whole and noble, with elegant curling horns like German braids. I showed it to Harry Symmonds and he looked at it for a long time, scuffing up his shoes on the grubby floorboards. I refused to let him touch it.

Harry Symmonds, who took all the meanness I ever threw at him and never threw anything back, who wouldn't separate himself from me for the next four years, because I smacked or bit any child who came too close, and that protection made it worth braving my battering jibes. By the time we reached secondary school, Harry Symmonds was ignored by everybody, and I had become his hard-shelled beetle with no soft underbelly. Once or twice, some of the boys would call Harry Symmonds my boyfriend and tell me I was pretty, then laugh as they catcalled and pretended to swoon. I spat back. In woodwork, when Robin Fell made a crude joke about nailing, I struck a precise tack through the skin between his thumb and forefinger – and later, Harry Symmonds joined me in insisting Robin had nailed his own hand to the desk by accident.

Harry Symmonds, who I didn't like or dislike, but tolerated, because I found that thinking was easier when there was someone to talk at. Harry Symmonds, proving even then that survival is easier in pairs.

This morning I buried a sparrow. I don't know what made me do it.

It was outside a once-whitewashed crofter's cottage at the foot of a mountain. I thought there could be food in the kitchen – instead I found a table set with two tea cups, each one lined with a fuzzy green and white mould. Upstairs, damp curtains blew at an open window, and something lay sprawled in the middle of the bed. As I entered the room, I upset the flurry of crows that had gathered to steal its softer parts. They cawed and scuffled and scratched at me as I barrelled backwards.

Scarf tight over my nose and mouth, I checked the empty kitchen cupboards and left.

As I stepped back onto the road, I crunched something into the tarmac. A sparrow – a small speckled bump on the wet black road, trying vainly to lift its head and chirrup. I bent down to scoop it up. It was soft and firm, like a tennis ball. It quivered in my hands – a bundle of terrified warmth.

At the end of the last century, London lost three-quarters of its sparrows in just six years – one of those facts I read and inexplicably remembered – and nobody really cared. So what difference did another sparrow make?

But it was as if a cloud had stuffed itself into my throat – I struggled to breathe, felt my eyes go sharp. I fell to the road and clutched this ordinary bird to my chest.

Maybe it was because of the broken wing, or the matchstick feet dangling from its juddering stomach. Maybe because this was the first living body I had touched in weeks.

I put it out of its misery with a rock from the edge of the road, then buried it as best I could in a dip by the wall. I didn't leave a marker – who was there to find it? I carried on walking south.

Growing up, I never understood the need for touch, for desire, for other people's bodies – the way these things gushed into everyday life, unstoppable, till they permeated every layer of people's existence. On television and on the sides of buses, people kissed or embraced or touched parts of their own skin. In my mother's magazines, boys strolled along the beach sporting swimming trunks and superhero muscles. The girls posed in skimpy bikinis and pretended not to look at the camera.

When I was thirteen, my mother sent me into town with money for my birthday. I snuck into a clothes shop on the high street, thrilling with trepidation. The halogen lighting and bulging rails seemed to be everywhere, till they were a barrage, pushing in at me on all sides. As a shop assistant in heavy eye make-up sashayed over, I grabbed the first bikini I saw and ducked into the changing rooms, pulling the curtains tight up to the edges to make sure nobody could see in. With my back to the mirror, I changed.

I cannot remember what I wanted. I do not know what I expected to happen, or what part of me had thought this might be a good idea. I only remember looking nothing like the girls in my mother's magazines.

The top sat flatly over my chest. In magazines, the women always had long hair that cascaded over their shoulders and made everything else look curved and in proportion. My short rough hair made my neck look too long, and there was too much bareness. My skin was pale and mottled. In the shop lighting, it was almost blue, except for my face and arms, which were red from sun and windburn, and made my body look disconnected. The bikini bottom cut into the line around my groin. It made my legs stick out, like those branches that grow too big in the wrong directions and need propping up with wooden stakes to stop the whole tree collapsing. In the gusset, the protective plastic strip was hard and uncomfortable, and crinkled when I moved.

I bought it out of spite. At home, I stuffed it down the gap at the back of my chest of drawers, where it haunted my teenage years like the ghosts of all the women in my mother's magazines.

At school, some of the boys had started to spend their lunch money on newspapers with pictures of topless girls in them. These pictures would end up stuffed in people's lockers, or tucked unexpectedly into exercise books, or shoved at you as you walked between classrooms to raucous yells of 'Tits on your face!'

I hunched over, avoided their eyes. I stopped watching films and I avoided looking at the pictures of models in shop windows. I learned to walk without attracting attention.

*

Open ground has given way to forest. Not the kind of nurturing, ancient treescape found in children's adventure stories, but a sprawling pine farm, all evenly spaced trunks and a dark floor drowning in needles. I follow a dirt path, just wide enough for a four-by-four, although I doubt a vehicle has driven along here in years. Not since the War hit British soil and the construction industry collapsed along with so many others. Now, this forest is turning wild. Ferns and saplings sprout from the earth, while weeds inch their way through the hardened dust of the path. A fallen tree sprawls across it at an angle, its branches and bare twigs brittle. I clamber over it, then stop a few steps later to pick brown pine needles out of my clothes and the cracks between my boots and socks.

About a mile further along, I come to a clearing. It is not big – only a widening of the path, perhaps once meant as a passing place or to park a single vehicle. But the break in the trees means the air feels fresher, and more light filters through to illuminate the scene below. Which is probably why they chose this spot in the first place.

Three tents are grouped across the path, sagging and torn, their poles bent out of shape. In the shelter of the trees beyond, five rusty camping chairs surround a circle of stones that must once have formed the edge of a fire pit. Out here, away from towns and cities and the ferocity of the War, after the Safe Centres were full and shut their doors, these people must have assumed they had escaped. The Sickness could never reach them here, so far from the dispersing bombs and packed communities that allowed it to spread.

I wonder how long they were here before they realised they

were wrong. Was it wildlife that brought it to them? Or did one of the people carry it with them from their old life like a live wire, just waiting to be touched? Or perhaps they managed to outrun the Sickness after all, only to be crippled by starvation.

Five people, sacrificing home comforts in an attempt to survive, but still unwilling to sacrifice each other. Discovering too late that near-isolation and living minimally in the open air was not quite enough to save them.

I hurry through, holding my breath even though I tell myself the Sickness cannot still be here. I do not stop until I am certain there are at least a couple of miles between us. I wonder if this vagabond life will be enough to save me.

My hair has grown long. It brushes my shoulders and catches under the straps of my backpack. It has been months since I owned a hairbrush, and my scalp itches. I could try cutting it, but hair dulls blades and I need my knife to be sharp. Instead, I cut a length of string and tie my hair in a fat clump at the nape of my neck. That will have to do for now.

*

I was eight when I first cut my hair. I stole the kitchen scissors while my mother was on the phone, then locked myself in the bathroom. With the small mirror leant against the bath taps to keep it from falling, I stripped down to my knickers and sat in the empty tub. I cut close to my scalp and the hair tumbled down me and stuck in my creases. I nicked the top of my ear, and blood ran down my neck, flowing freely, the way blood does from the head – but I folded toilet paper across it and continued. I kept cutting steadily, determined not to leave the job half done. I brushed myself off and got dressed, then gathered up the dead hairs into the waste-paper basket.

Only then did I let myself explore my new head. I mapped its contours with my fingertips. It felt cold and shocking to the touch. When I examined myself in the mirror, I saw how my cranium was not round as I had always assumed, but had little bumps and dips like a landscape. For the first time, I thought a part of myself was beautiful.

My mother shrieked when she saw me. Her hand flew to her chest like a startled bird and her breaths came loud. 'Oh, Monster!' she wailed. 'What have you done?'

I ran my hand across my beautiful head.

That night, I sat upstairs with my collection, listening to my parents' voices oscillating through the floorboards as I tried to get to grips with the mechanics of a circuit board stolen from the school skip.

As I entered the kitchen next morning, my father greeted me with a watery smile as my mother banged down spoons and breakfast bowls on the table. She pursed her lips, but said nothing. She kept her silence as she tidied away the cereal and drove me to school, though her eyes and lips were still narrow.

Of course, the children in my class laughed, but that is because children are idiots. I ignored them and they soon grew bored. They went back to their games and glitter pens, and I sat with Harry Symmonds and folded models out of paper.

*

I think about all the people I ever knew. Every day I remember someone else, as if they're all buried inside me like books in a library, just waiting for my brain to pick one out. It's shocking how many people you encounter in a lifetime.

Yesterday, I thought about the woman who ran the roadside café I worked in one summer, whose name I can't remember. She had a flat high voice like a fork scraping across a plate, and she used to raid the table where the surplus cakes were kept. I can still hear her suck and slurp at her fingers as she pushed broken biscuits into her mouth.

Sometimes, I catch myself thinking about Joe. Joe was the school caretaker. When my mother was going to be late picking me up, or when I didn't want to spend breaktime outside with the other children, I would sit with Joe in his office and drink strong tea.

It was not what my father would have recognised as an office – there were no banks of computers or overflowing stacks of paper, no yellowing pot plants. Joe's office was a workshop, a forest of shelves and half-fixed electricals. Tools hung like artworks from the walls, and the only computer was a salvaged Acorn Archimedes he had spent the past twenty years trying to restore. Joe's jumpers were always stretched in odd places where he had pegged them on the washing line, and tufts of grey hair sprouted from his ears and nose. But he could re-assemble a fuse box blindfolded in twenty-three seconds.

When I was a child, first learning to talk, I used to sit on my father's lap and go through all the names I knew: Mummy, Daddy, Monster, Ganny, Alfie, Joan. I used to say them over and over, demarcating the limits of my little world.

As I got older, my world became so huge that I couldn't remember everybody even if I tried. My life is full of people and places that I've let slip down the back of my brain.

When my head gets so cold my face goes numb, I try to run through all the things I can remember. I try to list them, like descending the rungs of a ladder. Sometimes, as I go deeper, I remember things I'd forgotten even existed.

There was a quotation – I forget who said it, one of those things that flitted about the internet with a black-and-white picture and quirky font – that history is just a set of lies agreed upon. Now nobody needs to agree on anything. Now all of it is mine.

This is what I remember:

I remember that the Normans won the Battle of Hastings in 1066 – though what that means I don't know, now that there are no more kings, no more place-names, no more dates.

I remember my fifth birthday with a cake that looked like a lion.

I remember that my mother's birthday was 9 October.

I remember her fingers hovering over the keys of the piano that always needed tuning.

I remember the sounds of a person in the next room – the small eases and beats like a murmuring of the heart.

I remember train stations at rush hour.

I remember how most people lived crowded together, how there was never enough space.

I remember satellites. Sometimes, I remember that they're still above me, tumbling through orbit, all screws and wires and metal.

I remember planting a time capsule in the school garden, sealing it in a Tupperware box to stop the worms getting in.

I remember Luke Denham, who sat next to me at school

and had a birthmark on the bridge of his nose, and whose dad won the village darts competition six years in a row.

I remember Luke Denham wiping his nose on the sleeve of his jumper.

I remember my dad's caterpillar eyebrows.

I remember faces – how beauty was in the petite and symmetrical, and ugliness was in the unexpected.

I remember Erik's face, its drawn-out anguish as we waited, the terrible hunger in his eyes. I remember the helpless desperation of him.

This is always where I try to stop remembering.

*

Sometimes I think I'm being watched. If I sleep badly, I wake to a feeling like a hand grabbing my shoulder and the urge to turn and look. I spend the whole day thinking of eyes – countless unblinking eyes, following my progress along footpaths or staring from the hedgerows. They press me under their gaze like the ghosts of all the people who died in the War and the Sickness, like the ghosts of my parents, or blue-eyed Erik. I have never believed in spirits or an afterlife, but still they swirl around me like a current, dragging at me as if my survival was somehow a betrayal. At night I dream about the vault.

*

The Seed Vault is a metal and concrete blade jutting from the permafrost. Look at it too long and your eyes start flickering from the snow-glare and the sun on mirrored steel. The first time I saw it, I thought it looked like the perfect piece of that icy world, like the final bit of a jigsaw puzzle that suddenly reveals what the picture is supposed to be.

Inside is different. Through the heavy doors, all the elegance of the landscape is gone, and the mechanical insides of the structure are on display. Here is a grey and white world of pipes and covered wires, concrete and corrugated metal, and a long cold tunnel that leads to the vault.

When I was a child, I always thought of vaults as exotic places, secret stashes, stacked with glimmering treasures like Tutankhamun's tomb. Places just waiting to be broken into.

The Seed Vault is not a treasure trove. Instead, it looks more like a warehouse: metal racks stacked with hundreds of uniform black plastic boxes. It is a place of order and purpose. A place where time has no jurisdiction, where everything is suspended. It is a place for waiting out the end of the world.

I was posted to the Seed Vault two years before the Last Fall, when the dying population still believed the Sickness could have a cure, before the Safe Centres shut their gates and left anyone outside them to die. When the vault was still a scientific exercise and not a military target, when people still thought the future might be a thing worth striving for.

When I first got off the plane, the air was sharp and biting. Despite the summer Arctic sunshine, already I could feel it scouring my ungloved fingers. I hesitated at the top of the stairs, taking in this stone and concrete world.

Waiting just inside the terminal building was a blond man holding a homemade cardboard placard which just said: MEKANIKER.

That was me. The woman brought in to fix things.

I walked over to him and held out my hand: 'Monster.'

'What?' His accent was sharp, like an ice shard. He had blue eyes and skin pale as the walls.

'Monster,' I repeated, 'my name's Monster.'

'Monster? What, like a *monster?*'

'Yes. You?'

'Oh.' He tucked the placard under his arm and shook my hand. 'Oh, OK. I'm Erik.'

'Erik.'

'Biologist,' he said, 'up at the vault.'

The vault. I learned later that Erik did not believe in God or religion or spirituality, but the way he spoke about the Seed Vault was as if he had found a higher purpose through which to orientate his own life. He was devoted to it. Cataloguing its contents was his rosary. Putting out calls for unrepresented species of plant-life was his version of prayer, and the Seed Vault itself was his church.

*

It used to be said that walking was good for the soul, that tramping for miles and miles created a rhythm in the body that opened the mind to the unconscious and all sorts of crap.

I have seen too many dead people to believe in a soul. Walking is only good for one thing, and that is survival. One blistered foot in front of the other. Getting through the day one step at a time.

I wake, I eat, sometimes I wash, I pack up my sleeping bag, warm my hands by the dying fire, bandage my feet, lace up my boots, put on my pack and start walking. I walk until my feet are hurting too much for me to ignore. I sit, take off my boots, rest a while, rebandage my feet, lace my boots back up and keep on walking. I avoid the towns, most of them whole and eerily empty, where the Sickness spread through them like a purging fire, leaving only buildings and possessions in its wake. On the outskirts, there is always a patch of blackened earth, marking the bonfires for burning the dead.

A couple of times, I pass towns blown apart by bombs. They hunch against the landscape like unattempted jigsaw puzzles. Here and there, a single street or row of shops is still standing. I avoid these too. When the War constricted everything, the places that survived became prime targets for looting. The people that survived with them became the worst versions of themselves, struggling against their own inevitable collapse.

I stick to scavenging from the smallest villages. Even then, I leave as quickly as I can, and always before dark.

When the light starts to fade, I hunt for shelter, build a fire with whatever I can find, eat whatever I have or can easily get, take off my boots, bury myself in my sleeping bag, and sleep. My dreams are filled with walking. They have a rhythm to them, now, a one-two-one-two circular flow.

*

Here is what I learn about walking:

Walking, like running, is about finding a pace. Stride out too quickly and you soon tire and become disheartened. Stroll too slowly and the journey can sit heavy in the bowl of your stomach.

It is not passing across a landscape. Instead, it is feeling the landscape pass under you, as if the pushing of your feet into the ground turns the Earth further away from you, like balancing on a giant ball.

You do not walk with your feet. You walk with your boots. Bad boots make the walking harder.

When you walk, you notice the details. You notice the colours and shapes and precise movements of everything around you, from blades of grass to birds to creatures scurrying through the undergrowth. It is a way of becoming intimate with the landscape.

Walking on flat roads is too easy. It lets you think too much.

Walking over uneven rocky ground is a way to escape from the mind.

Wet shoes weigh you down.

Walking on a full stomach is like a sickness.

Walking on an empty stomach is worse.

Footsteps do not only make a noise at the point where your boots hit the tarmac. They also sound in your head. They echo like an organ note in a cathedral.

Even when your body sweats, the ends of your fingers are still cold.

Feet can be hot and cold at the same time.

Walking on broken skin is a reminder of everything that is

wrong with the world. With every step, I can picture news footage from the War – the screen wobble as a shockwave rushed towards the camera, the aftermath of Sickness-filled explosives filmed on shaking mobile phones, people on the pavements with empty eyes and a blue tinge spreading from their lips, the slackened jaws and flat expressions that it could happen here, in this county, in suburbs and villages, on high streets filled with shops. With every thought of the Sickness, I remember another person dead. At the ends of the worst nights, I wake shivering.

Every day that I walk, it becomes easier and harder to set off.

*

My mother and father lived in a middle-sized house next to
the church in a middle-sized village surrounded by fields. It
was farm country, or had been thirty years ago, but my parents
were not farm people.

My mother worked at the village shop part-time on weekday
afternoons. She brought my father spare copies of the *Racing
Post*, and he would sit long evenings in his easy chair, analysing
the odds, working out which horse should win and whether
it favoured this or that kind of ground, and what would be
the most effective bet. He never actually bet any money as
far as I know.

By day he was an accountant. He worked in town in a small
upstairs office with no heating, and on winter evenings he
would earn us a little extra money doing tax returns for the
few farmers that the village had left. 'Treat pennies,' he called
it. As soon as the autumn nights drew in, farmers or their
wives would start to appear at our door, bearing carrier bags
of receipts and bank statements bundled together with twine.
My father would scatter these across the kitchen table as he
scanned them for some kind of order, until my mother flipped
and banished him and the mess to the spare room.

By the time the pale spring nights returned, the papers had
gone from the house, and my father was back to his racing
calculations. As for me, I was already counting the days until
the long school holiday, when I could get up each morning to
scour the fields, or tinker with my collection. I would do this all
through the summer, filling my days with creation and invention,
until one day autumn would arrive, and I would be forced to
pack up my bag, put on my clean uniform and return to school.

This was the rhythm of our lives, marked by afternoons in the shop and the closing down and opening up again of the seasons.

As I got older, our rhythms changed – but only on the surface. Underneath, we still turned on the same rotation.

As the War diminished imports and drove the currency down, my mother's hours in the shop were cut, sliced away so thinly that at first it was barely noticeable, until one day she wasn't working there at all. Instead, she would clean the house daily, scrubbing at the skirting boards, uprooting the plates and bowls and baking trays to detox the insides of cupboards, using homemade cleaning fluids that made the whole house smell of vinegar. When she had finished, she would draw up lists of home improvements for my father to do when he staggered in from work – tasks he ignored or passed on to me. I shrugged them off. As my peers threw themselves into rumours and parties and each other, I threw myself more and more into my collection. From simply tinkering with the breaking apart and reconstituting of objects, my explorations started to gain direction. I borrowed books from the school library and spent my lunchtimes scouring the internet. I became obsessed with the ways things worked, building and rebuilding machines that fit together as precisely as the days I built them in. In this way, I made certain my routine stayed rigid, so there would be no room in it for anyone else. It was easier, I told myself. I didn't want friends anyway. I used my well-honed skills of maintenance and systematic research to look for a way to move out.

Sometimes on long nights, it is so easy to imagine my father still in the blue and yellow kitchen, surrounded by receipts for animal feed and tractor parts, and my mother fretting at him, the whole village shut tight and warm in their own little dramas in their own little rooms.

*

The ground here is rock-strewn and tussocky. My shadow stretches across it like a fractured version of myself, and I have to tread slowly to avoid ankle-grabbing dips and burrows. I've been walking under trees for most of the day, the sun's position obscured by branches and new leaves so that I only have a vague notion of where I am and in which direction I am walking. I am following a path which occasionally thins and peters out, only to emerge again a few metres later. It might not be a path at all. I follow it all the same.

To my left is a low wall, barely more than a pile of stones and so thick with moss that in places it almost disappears. As I walk, I come across another wall, and another, this one taller, the next one more intact. The path solidifies, then widens into a dirt road.

I stop in the middle of a small village, a half-standing collection of stones. In the last of the afternoon light, it looks golden and soft, the kind of sequestered beauty that has no right to exist any more.

The ruins here are old, abandoned centuries before the War made ghost towns so commonplace. None of the buildings have roofs, their windows open cavities with shrubs and ivy creeping through them. In one building, a bird's nest sits in a crook of stone. In another, a tree is rooted in the compact earth of a hearth. All of it is draped in moss or sprouting ferns.

The most complete house is a low bungalow on the edge of the village – a rectangular structure with just one window and a prickly bush part-blocking the doorway. I squeeze inside and am in a green world. The floor in here is mossy, but dry. I am as closed off from wildlife as I am likely to be tonight.

Later, with the drawstring of my sleeping bag pulled tight, I wonder what made the people of this village move away. I had forgotten there were people who uprooted themselves for reasons other than Sickness and War, people who did not move simply because a government told them they had to. People like me.

I try to picture those people loading the last of their possessions onto carts or horses, taking one final look around their bare rooms – how unsettling a place looks when stripped of all its furniture. I try to work out at what point a building stops being a home. Is it at this moment, when all private things are taken away and it reverts to its blank impersonal state? Or is it when you walk down the road laden with all your possessions, and the house at your back? Or is it always a home, even through its many stages of decay?

I think about my mother sitting in the kitchen, flicking through a magazine and licking her fingers to turn the pages. Of the places I have lived, that is the only one I have called home.

Maybe there is no such thing, only walls and a roof, a place secure enough to allow sleep. But how can I keep going if there is nowhere I am going to? How can I grow again without any roots? I close my eyes on the soft earth, and try not to imagine that I'm in my bedroom in my parents' house.

When I leave the next morning, I follow the dirt road out of the village. It quickly disintegrates into an overgrown track. Then a narrow path, fringed with vegetation. Then nothing.

*

As I hunker against a hedge at the roadside, hinging the lid from a tin of cubed vegetables, I realise how little I used to think about food. Eating was a task to be accomplished while I focused my attention on other things. The vitality of it was always lost. Now, as the watery carrots slide down my throat, I try to remember the taste of other food. Nothing elaborate – just the soft white and salt of a ham sandwich, the tang of fresh pineapple, or the chunky joints of beef my mother sometimes roasted on Sundays, filling the whole house with their thick, fatty smell. I try, but the memories slip away, leaving my mouth dry and tasting overwhelmingly of my own stale breath.

*

My mother used to bake gingerbread men for Christmas – little golden-brown figures that broke softly. Once, when I was young, she let me help, and I laid out my own irregular shapes on the tray. I made her leave mine in the oven longest, so they baked hard and dark, and broke with a snap. I liked their unforgiving crunch, the way they attracted my mother's frowns. I think of this and wonder if I was meant to be the last. Then I remember there is no such thing as fate, because there is nobody in control.

I was nine or ten – that awkward age of feeling too big for everything, but independence still a long way off. It must have been the summer holidays, because I was sitting in the high grass in the field behind the house, letting the sun burn the back of my neck. I remember wearing a sun cap. There was a shadow on my face and a band of sweat trapped between the fabric and my scalp. If I sat up, I could see into my back garden – the vegetable patch and the canes snaked with runner beans. I could see the washing, limp and sagging from the line, and my mother standing at the kitchen window. But if I hunched, I could let the grass rise above me until I felt as though I was invisible. The blades were sharp against my bare calves, and insects gathered faster than I could brush them away. But it was worth it for the quiet, for the sense of isolation, and for my discovery.

My discovery was a mouse. At least, I thought it was a mouse, but it was difficult to be certain. It was all bones, stripped bare, but still in the position it had died in, curled and complete and perfect. The tiny skull. A ribcage more like fishbones. Tail bones stacked end to end like elongated verte-brae, but in miniature.

I traced its shape, letting my fingertip hover just above it, fearful in case my touch might be too strong and I might break it. For a long time I looked at it, trying to absorb its complex structure, to understand the mechanics of its biology. I was so engrossed in this exquisite arrangement of bones, I didn't hear the other children until it was too late.

'Hey! Monster!'

Something small and dry hit my arm and fell into the grass

beside me. I looked up. Three boys were standing a few metres away, up to their knees in the grass and laughing. Callum Jenkins, Liam Harper, and a lanky boy I didn't know.

'Freak.' Callum Jenkins bent to scoop up a handful of dry sheep muck and lobbed it in my direction. It showered dustily around me and I covered the mouse skeleton with my hand.

The boy I didn't know laughed. It was high and grating, and seemed too loud in the still summer day.

'What you wearing that cap for?' asked Callum Jenkins. 'Hiding your stupid hair?'

Because it's sunny, you idiot.

I thought about leaving. I remember being so sorely tempted to get up, to give them the finger and stride away down the field towards home. I wanted to shut the door on them. But then I would have had to leave the mouse, and with the grass this overgrown, I knew I would never find it again.

'Is she bald?' asked the boy I didn't know.

Callum Jenkins lobbed another round of sheep muck. 'Basically.'

'Nah,' said Liam Harper, 'she's just a freak.'

I tried to ignore them. I focused on my mouse, how its tail curled back in on itself so its body formed an almost perfect oval, except for the head, which stuck forward as if it had wanted to get one last glimpse of the world, or as if it had been looking for a rescuer. The boys' laughter was loud and spiralling. I tried to tune out their jeers, but they bored into me, deeper and deeper into my brain, and I could not shut them out.

The mouse, I thought, *the mouse, the mouse, the mouse . . .*

My hands shook. I could see, where my right hand extended over the beautiful skeleton, a tremor that travelled through my wrists, back along my arm and into my chest, till my whole body was shaking and I couldn't make it stop.

And then, in the midst of it all, my mother.

She strode up the field, tramping down the grass in her wellies, her long skirt catching in her wake. She looked out of place here, in what I thought of as my domain, as if someone had taken an ornament from the mantelpiece and placed it on top of a mountain. But her face was pulled tight with a fierceness I had never seen before, and for the first time there was something broad and unwieldy about her. As she flattened the grass, I thought of a lorry veering across a motorway, crashing through the central reservation and levelling the traffic on the other side.

The boys saw her coming and made to scarper, but my mother was an unstoppable torrent, and she would not relinquish them so easily.

'Oh no you don't. Liam Harper and Callum Jenkins, you get back here right now.'

From my hollow I watched them turn, all their gleeful bigness gone, till they were only three pitiful boys, squirming under my mother's glare.

'And you,' she said to the third boy, 'I don't know you.'

The boy turned red and stuffed his hands deeper in his pockets. He shuffled.

'Well?'

'He's my cousin,' Liam Harper said, not looking my mother in the eye.

She folded her arms across her chest, her shoulders heaving. 'Well, let me make this very clear to the three of you. If I ever catch you being mean to my daughter again, I'm going to grab each of you by the ear, and I'm going to twist it till you can't even hear yourselves crying – is that understood?'

The boys looked at their feet. I sat with my head barely over the grass, watching my mother's face – the power and anger I had never seen in it before, the way it flared up when she said 'my daughter'. My *daughter*. Like *my* collection, or the way I had thought earlier about *my* mouse, as a thing to be cherished and protected.

'I said, is that understood?'

'Yes.'

'Yes.'

'You're not allowed to hurt us . . .'

My mother blazed like a rocket flare. 'Talk back to me again, Callum, and I'll make sure nobody in the shop sells you sweets for a year, you little shit.'

My mother's swearing thrilled through me. It was as though someone had opened a treasure chest, and for a second I got to glimpse the glittering jewel inside.

'Now,' she said, 'I'm going to go inside and phone your mothers. I think they'd like to know what you've been getting up to, don't you? And I think it'd be a good idea if you were home and ready to explain yourselves by the time they've hung up.'

The boys teetered, fidgeting.

'Go on!'

And suddenly they were gone, back across the field towards the stile and the lane, fleeing to escape the boundaries of my mother's rage.

My mother was still there, larger than herself, and suddenly all mine. She turned towards me and something in her shifted. The rage diminished. She was not any smaller in that big field, but she was somehow softer, stiller, so that for the first time I could remember I wondered what it would feel like to hug her, the way other children hugged their parents when they were picked up from school. Instead I sat and watched her walking towards me.

An arm's reach away, she crouched, bringing her eyes to my level. 'Are you OK?'

I shrugged.

I was fine. I was better than fine.

I said nothing.

'What were you doing out here anyway?'

I pulled away my hand to show her my mouse, but I must have knocked it in all the distraction, because its tail bones no longer aligned and it was no longer quite as beautiful.

My mother made a choked sound and stood up, pushing herself back from it.

'It's my mouse,' I said. I tried to nudge the bones back into place with my little finger, to recreate that undisturbed oval.

'Don't touch it!'

I looked up. My mother looked as though she wanted to snatch the words back into her mouth. Instead, she glanced in the direction of the stile and the retreating boys, then frowned back at me. And there she was again. My mother, petite and disapproving, exactly as I expected her to be.

'I've left the dishes in the sink.' She turned to leave, then half turned back to me. 'I'm just in the kitchen. If you need me.'

She hovered a moment, as though there was more to be said, but neither of us could think of anything. So I watched her walk away, an ungainly shuffle as she tried to stop her skirt from catching in the grass. I watched her go through the back gate and in the door, till I could see her again through the kitchen window, standing at the sink.

I sat there for the rest of the afternoon, till my legs itched from the grass and the bug life, and a rash had broken out along my calf. I coaxed the mouse skeleton painstakingly back into shape. And I watched my fierce and startling mother pottering around the kitchen.

*

My parents died in the Sickness. My mother first, my father twelve days later. He always was a little bit hopeless without her.

I didn't visit. At the time, the Sickness hadn't yet reached where I was living, and I wouldn't be the one to help it spread. Instead, I moved out of the city, rented a ramshackle house that was really more of a shed at the edge of an out-of-the-way village. Told myself it was right. My parents would want me to isolate myself.

I read their emails – frequent at first, full of optimism and denial, then growing briefer and more sporadic. I didn't reply.

Two weeks after the final one, I had an email from a neighbour telling me they were dead. Her own son had caught the Sickness too, she said. It had emptied the village, everyone already dead or dying, or doomed by proximity.

I closed the window on one of the last emails I ever received. Two weeks later, the servers crashed, sending what little infrastructure remained skittering like a deck of cards. In its place, information became a rare bird. The Safe Centres and military hubs shared news via what was left of the internet, leaving everybody else to root out dusty wind-up radios and spend fruitless nights searching for something to tune in to. By that time, I had got the job at the Seed Vault. Two years later, everyone was dead.

*

I am close now. Even with the fields overgrown or rotting and walls and buildings turned to rubble, I can still recognise bits of the place, like a familiar picture seen through wavy glass.

I pull myself to the top of the hill behind my parents' house. My calves are tight from the climb and under my layers I can feel my T-shirt sticking to my back. The sky is the same ambiguous grey it has been for days, the air cold and thirsty. In the distance, the familiar mountain range blurs into the clouds.

The drystone walls that divide the fields are mostly intact, grey mossy ribbons segmenting the landscape the way they have for hundreds of years. Here and there a section has crumbled. I remember seeing them like this at the end of winter: lengths of wall reduced to a tumbled pile of stone, where the water had got in and frozen.

Sometimes at the local summer fair, there would be a waller demonstrating his trade. He would set up his markers in the middle of a field, two pairs of wooden posts, each with a string running between them. Then he would build the wall up, starting with the big solid rocks at the bottom, using the string as a guide to keep the wall from bulging. He would turn the rocks in his rough hands, checking their size and edges, selecting just the right one for the space it had to occupy. He would leave the flat round ones for the top, standing them up on their sides to crown the wall, like a parade of soldiers puffing out their chests.

I used to love the fair. It was an annual tradition – one of the few my family had, alongside afternoon tea for my mother's birthday and church on Christmas Day. One morning in August, my mother would assemble a picnic, pack my father and me towards the car, and we would drive the busy road to the fair.

It was held in a big field on the edge of town. It was not a city fair, the kind with ferris wheels and dodgems and candy-floss. Ours was a country fair, an agricultural fair. It was the time of year when everyone – even the non-farm people in their spit-clean wellies – gathered to remember the area's past and to celebrate what remained of its industry.

There were no fairground rides, just a bouncy castle that came every year with a man from the next town – but it was only something to occupy the children while the real business of the day took place. This was the exhibition and judging of animals. Mostly that meant dogs and sheep, but sometimes also a coveted prize bull.

After he had parked up in the neighbouring field, my father would head straight for the judging ring, where he would sit for most of the day, making notes on the quality of the animals and the judges' decisions. He understood the slight distinctions of dogs and of livestock, the stance and colour and distribution of weight that made one animal more worthy of accolades than another. As for me, I would look at the ring of stubbly old men and quivering terriers, and think they all looked the same, animals and owners alike.

My mother, like me, had no interest in livestock. She would make her way to the marquee, where flower displays and vegetables and sponges had undergone their own eagle-eyed judging process. If my mother had won a prize, which only happened two or three times that I can remember, my father and I would be dragged to the tent to admire her achievement in loud, carrying voices. Otherwise, she would spend around an hour studying the exhibits, before bustling across to the tea tent, where she would inevitably find a group of women she knew.

With a parting gift of five pounds in my pocket, I was left free to wander. I rarely spent the money – even when I was small, I had no interest in the bouncy castle or the face-painting. Instead I would watch the drystone waller giving his demonstrations. His name was Ted. Over the years, as the world grew more complicated and the War circled ever nearer, Ted was an unerring constant. I suppose he became a friend of sorts.

'Morning, Monster,' he would say when I arrived by his plot, 'you're here early.' He said this every year, and every year it was true.

I would watch him set up and lay the first few stones, then I would wander off to check the other exhibits: the chugging vintage tractors, the man who could carve animals out of tree trunks, and the stick-dressing competition, where old men exhibited their carved walking sticks and shepherds' crooks. Every now and then, I would circle back around to check on Ted and his progress with the wall. Sometimes he would even let me put one of the crowning stones on the top.

I wonder what happened to Ted. I wonder whether he built any of these walls above the village. I take off my backpack and clamber across one, dislodging a couple of stones as I do. They tumble loudly as everything shifts under me. I consider putting them back, but what would be the point? There is no livestock left to segregate, no claims to be made on arbitrary squares of land. Just bigness, spreading out in all directions. If I had time, I could demolish every single one of these walls. It would make no difference to anything.

*

My parents' house sits squat and grey at the bottom of the hill. The whole village looks as I remember it. For all I know, my parents could be in the house still, waiting for somebody to burn or bury them. A lot of Sickness victims were left like that, everyone around them too afraid or too ill to do what needed to be done. For a moment, I almost turn back – but then I see the charred circle of earth at the edge of the village, and all the hair follicles on my head prickle.

I pull my pack higher on my shoulders. I stride down the hill.

When I reach the little road that runs through the village, the signs of neglect push themselves forward like boisterous children. Unmown grass along the verges. A broken window at a neighbour's house. Untended flower beds that were once kept so prim and proper.

The gate to my parents' garden is stiff on its hinges. I consider oiling it, just to feel the rightness of it opening smoothly under my hand, but that would be stupid. I'm not planning on staying.

The front door opens more easily. I had expected it to be locked, but of course there was nobody to lock it.

Inside, the hallway is dark and grey, and there is a smell of damp. It rests at the back of my throat and festers.

I check the downstairs first. It's strange, walking through these old rooms, exactly the way I remember them, down to my mother's china ornaments on the mantelpiece and my father's cluttered papers. Like I'm observing my childhood through someone else's eyes.

I search the kitchen, but the cupboards are empty, raided by our neighbours once my parents were dead, the way it was everywhere once quarantine was enforced. I check the secret cupboard at the back of my father's desk, the one that only opens when you pop a slat of wood from its notch. As a child, I thought this was a hiding place worthy of an adventure novel; as an adult it just looks obvious. I pop out the piece of wood and the cupboard creaks open.

Inside are two envelopes, one big, one small.

The big one contains documents: the deed to the house, birth certificates, and my parents' wills. I cast them aside and open the smaller envelope.

Stuffed inside it is more money than I've ever held in my life. There must be six or seven thousand pounds in twenty-pound notes, crammed inside this little envelope.

I run my thumb across their edges. They make a soft burring sound as I flip through them. My parents' rainy-day fund. I never knew they kept so much cash in the house.

I have an urge to take it with me. Even now, this amount of money inspires a kind of awe. I can't seem to put it down. It sits in my hand as I hover between staying and leaving, crouched on the patterned carpet in front of my father's old desk. It's a kind of power, tying me to this spot. The things this money can buy . . .

Could buy.

I look at the fat wad of notes in my hand and force myself to see a stack of useless coloured paper. I stuff both enve-lopes back in the secret cupboard. Out of habit, I close it up again.

I start upstairs, the musty smell still latched onto the walls of my throat. Even though I'm climbing, there's a feeling of going deeper into the house.

I check the bathroom and the spare bedroom. Nothing but

a few dead moths on the windowsill. When I can put it off no longer, I open the door to my parents' bedroom.

There's a lump in the bed.

I cover my eyes with my hand and force myself to count to ten. I feel foolish, like a child playing hide-and-seek with nobody to search for. I open my eyes.

Nothing. Just the bundled duvet and a couple of pillows. I take deep breaths and scan the room. Nothing to show that this was the room my parents sickened and grew weak and died in. Nothing but a smell of damp and empty house.

I step back along the landing into my old bedroom.

The walls are still the same garish green I chose when I was twelve because I knew it would upset my mother's muted tastes. On top of the chest of drawers is a wooden automaton of a man riding a bicycle, which Harry Symmonds gave me for my birthday and which I used to like to take apart and put back together again.

The unmade bed is piled with cardboard boxes: all the books and tools and instruction manuals I wouldn't let my parents throw away after I moved out. The brown parcel tape is cracked and flaking. On one of them there's a half-dead fly buzzing on its back.

I catch sight of myself in the mirror beside my bedroom door. I look thin. Where before my face was a globe lit by the sun, now it is all squares and triangles, where all the weeks of walking and not enough to eat have carved me into the narrowest version of myself. My limbs are too long for my reflection – tough and gangly like the branches of an old tree, so that my movements look forced and unreliable. The dusty film across the mirror makes my face dead and grey. It is the face of a woman in her forties, not one in her late twenties.

I reach under the bed, into the dust and carpet fluff, and pull out the shoe box.

I sit with it unopened in my lap, holding all its memories of childhood and weekends, of the pestering of raindrops on the window, of long hours building complex circuits like race-tracks, of Harry Symmonds hovering, desperate to touch. I hold these past days close to me, too afraid to open the box and let them out.

I do not know how long I sit like that, in the room where I grew into my adult self, not even daring to open a tatty fucking shoe box. I only remember about time and lateness when the wind picks up in the trees in the back garden.

I do not want to spend the night in my dead parents' house. Through all the days of walking here, home sparked within me like something electric, drawing me on. Now it is an emptiness, a house without a purpose. My parents are gone. I do not need to be here any more. I pick up the shoe box and shoulder my pack, and leave before it gets dark. I oil the gate on my way out.

*

I am halfway down the road when I hear them behind me: a low growl and a padding of paws on the tarmac. It takes a moment to place the sound, but when I do it sinks into me as if I had always expected to hear it. As if it had been waiting for me to dare to come home. If I had been the sort of person who placed some kind of value on proximity to other people, who gravitated towards family in their hour of need, if I had been the sort of person who cared, then this village is where I would have died. I should have known it would not let me leave so easily.

There are three of them, old farm dogs slinking low across the ground.

Farm dogs are always tough, bred for work on the unforgiving fells, but these three are something more. Shaped out of need and a fierce holding-on, they are more wolf than dog now. Like me, these three are survivors.

They prowl towards me in formation, eyes fixed, growls rumbling deep in their throats. The leader pulls back his lip in a snarl and the others follow him. I resist the urge to run, to let them give chase. I imagine those wet yellow teeth in my leg. I clutch the shoe box to my chest and plant my feet on the tarmac, claiming my territory.

I bare my own teeth.

The dogs keep coming.

I start to growl, a deep feral humming at the back of my throat. For a second, they pause, and I growl louder.

The leader steps out with one hesitant paw, and I lurch forward, spare arm whirling, a sudden explosion of movement and noise: 'Fuck off, you bastard little shits, fuck off!'

There's barking – the noise is everywhere. The dogs split and scatter and I try to keep my eyes on the leader, on his jaw snapping at my calves. I try to kick out but he's a quick dancer, and suddenly there's no noise, just a kind of wind tunnel in my head and one thought – *Be bold, be bold, be bold* . . . So I yell, 'I *am* bold!' and as I yell there's a pain in my left calf like a nail gun and a sudden weight, and a bitch with her teeth stuck through my trousers, and everything spins. My scream cuts the air and I smash the shoe box on her head with my whole body-weight behind it.

The bitch lets go. I can still feel the tooth-grip, but she cowers and slinks and she is on me and not on me, beaten and not beaten. The other mutts continue to growl and snap and I kick out. There's a sick crack as my foot connects with the leader's snout. He whimpers and backs away, making small noises like a broken child.

The others stop snapping. They look to their wounded leader. Everything hangs in the air. Then they follow him, low to the road, and away, away.

I'm breathing hard. My back and underarms are soaked with sweat, my T-shirt stuck to my skin. I become aware of my heart, the undimmable batter of it. I become aware of my veins and capillaries, the blood's flood-rush through them. I become aware of every part of me that is alive – and then I become aware of what is broken.

I put my hand to the wound and it comes away wet with my own blood and the dog's saliva. I take a step. The injured leg shakes, sends spasms rippling up through the rest of me, then gives. My body crumples and I hit the tarmac.

I do not know how long I lie there. Five seconds. Maybe ten. It feels longer.

I let the hurt run through me, testing this new pain, chalking it up alongside the blisters and the sores from my backpack straps and the deep cramps in my stomach and thighs. I stare at the million grits surfacing the road, and I build my injured leg into the rest of me.

Slowly, thinking through every movement, I stand. I test the weight of myself. The leg shakes a moment, then is still. I take two deep breaths and look around. The dogs are gone. I check the shoe box. The corners are scuffed and battered, and along one side where it hit the bitch's skull there is a cave I have to push back into place. The brown tape I once shut it with is barely holding, but the elastic bands are still intact. It isn't broken. Nothing is lost.

I step out. I force myself to continue as though nothing happened, as though the dog pack is still watching, as though my whole body isn't pounding. Hugging the shoe box to my chest, I follow the road. It rises steeply out of the village, its broad curves cutting across the fell where once I used to search for bones, or for tufts of wool caught on the stiff brown reeds. The wind through them makes a sound like a river in flood, and the sky has turned a thunderous lead. When I turn to look back, there is only the grey village and a thin strip of light between clouds and horizon.

At the top of the hill, the road forks. To the west, it dips into the next valley, where the military once guarded a hydro-electric plant, before it was bombed with the dispersing Sickness that spread and killed my parents. I cannot go there, just as I cannot stay here, with the village so keen to grab me in its jaws and add me to its horde of dead.

But I have to go somewhere. I have to find shelter far enough away that I can rest.

I head east, away from the dogs and the village, away from the sliver of light at the edge of everything, and into the vast dark sky.

*

The evening comes cold and blue. In the musty interior of an empty barn, I root in my bag for bandages. I ease off my boots and trousers.

My leg is a bluish white. There's a raised purple circle on the side of my calf, and around it, a collection of deep red puncture marks, crusty and already secreting that clear liquid that means they're healing. The skin is unnaturally shiny, filmed with a dried reddish smear. I use the smallest amount of water possible to clean it. When I wrap the bandages around, it stings.

I eat two digestive biscuits then climb into my sleeping bag in the flatbed of an abandoned truck. In the drive to reach my parents' house, I forgot to look for food. My rations are thin.

I try to think about my parents, try to remember the way they filled the house. I try to picture my father taking off his glasses to rub tired eyes, or my mother perched on the edge of the sofa rubbing cream into her hands. I try to picture their faces, smiling or cross or indifferent – but every time I try, my mind goes blank. I wonder if I should have brought a photo with me from the house, but it is too late now.

For a long time, I lie awake with my leg throbbing, listening to my stomach complaining.

*

I wake to a crushing dark and a rich hot pain in my leg like a welding torch. My face in contact with the air is cold, but the heat from my leg pushes through me till it fills my head and I think my skull is going to break apart. I lean over the side of the truck and vomit up the meagre contents of my stomach. It comes up thin and stinking.

I roll away and try to sleep again.

Dawn comes shyly. I get up as soon as it is light enough to see.

My leg is infected. The flesh is purple and huge, and the bite-marks themselves have turned deep red, ringed with yellow. Something thick and white oozes from them. With my last dribble of water, I wash them gently with the tips of two fingers, and the pain shoots up to my head and I have to force myself not to be sick again. I think of all the cuts and grazes I have given myself over the years, how liberally I rubbed in antiseptic. I eat another digestive biscuit and pack my things back into my bag. Somewhere, waiting for me to discover it, there is food. I tell myself there must be food.

*

I walk for three days. I try not to count them, but they tally themselves up on the wall of my brain and I cannot help myself. I measure distances in days now, each one shakier and smaller than the last. I am three days away from the abandoned truck, four days from the room my parents died in. Four days away from the dog pack. Surely that is enough?

I walk along narrow country lanes, their unkempt verges nodding towards one another and almost meeting in the middle. I skirt the edge of a blasted town, a charred maze of half-toppled walls and unnecessary possessions. A few hours later, I start to climb. The rise is steady at first, then gradually steeper, till I'm hauling myself up the slope and my pack is a dead weight trying to tug me back down. I do not know where I am going any more, but as I climb, the air becomes purer, brisker. I suppose this is a sort of ascension.

I fill my bottles whenever I find water: tannin-dark streams chattering downhill, a rain barrel, the clear top half of a silted animal trough. Once, when my reserves are low, I manage to squeeze a few precious drops from the moss clinging to an old wall. The drops are cloudy and bitter-tasting, and I am not sure if the effort is worth it. I toe the scattered green clumps into a pile then continue walking.

I can feel my steps growing scanter as my body grows lighter. I find no food, except the flat tan discs of mushrooms growing from the black bark of a tree. I stare at them for a long time.

I break a segment off one. The inside is white and fresh and smells of earth, and I touch my cracked lips to it. But I know nothing about which fungi might be safe to eat, so I drop it. For good measure, I kick them. They offer no resistance

61

to my boots, so I kick the mushrooms over and over, till big flakes of their flesh litter the grass. Then I turn my back on them.

*

I am not sure in which direction I have been walking. I am not sure if I have been walking in just one direction, or in many. My stomach has stopped making noises. Now it is only a pain like a clenched fist, and a ceaseless searching.

*

Night is approaching. I can feel it coming on the way animals can sense a storm.

I've walked too far again today. My stomach is light with lack of food. Somehow, my pack feels heavier.

My pace has slowed to a funeral march along the rocky path. The pain in my leg is sharper. The throbbing is up to my thigh now, and what I need is medicine. My water bottles are both empty. My throat is dry and my tongue feels too big for my mouth. Already I am finding it hard to swallow.

The grass and heather are thick on either side and the moorland stretches away into nothingness in all directions. The sky up here is endless – a great grey dome, too pale for rain, too impenetrable for sun. Somewhere beyond it all, night is falling. As the grey dome darkens, the sky feels as though it's contracting, squeezing everything beneath it into a tighter, blacker space, till even the air feels thick and heavy. Still the only sounds are my laboured footsteps, my own irregular breathing.

The straps of my backpack feel as if they're branding my shoulders. My feet grow and swell till they are too heavy to lift. I sit down in the middle of the path. There is nowhere to go. I take off my boots and dig extra socks out of my pack. In this treeless landscape, there is no chance of a fire. I climb into my sleeping bag and try to sleep.

My stomach grumbles. It is two days since I ran out of food, and the few houses I have found since then have been empty. I keep telling myself there must be something soon.

The hollow feeling deepens. It spreads up into my ribcage.

I curl myself as small as I can. I press my fists into my stomach to trick myself into feeling full. After what feels like a long time, I start to drift.

*

I wake in the dark. A faint glow where the moon is hidden behind a thick layer of cloud. Otherwise, only blackness, the moor stretching away unseen.

My body is heavy and cold. My toes ache with it. My bones are made of ice. I will never be warm again. Still my leg burns.

I feel for my pack beside me on the path. My fingers are so numb that I can barely unzip it, but I force myself to get up. As quickly as my clumsy hands will allow, I dress in all my layers and climb back into my sleeping bag. The cold is still inside me, not quite tamed. I wrap my arms around my chest and tuck my hands under my armpits. Somewhere close, a fox screams. I strain my eyes but there's nothing – only the dark. The fox screams again. I lie awake and listen.

*

I drift between fog and oblivion. I open my eyes to uncertain white, then close them again. In this small circle of existence, I sleep. It is all there is.

*

My mother in my student flat, the War already on home soil – on all soil, everywhere. The three Warhammer geeks I live with have already scuttled home. I spread myself through their empty rooms. I am enormous. I am bigger than the city.

My mother saying: 'Come home – it isn't safe – come home—'

Her face is blotchy, no make-up, turned up towards me like a leaf desperate for sun – and running with tears. But here in this city I can be somebody, so I say no.

My mother saying: 'Who do you have here?' My mother saying: 'You have nobody – come home—'

And I say, 'Myself—'

'Please—'

I say, 'I have myself.'

*

I am chasing something. Someone. The lane leads to my parents' village. It's night and my bag is heavy – I call out to it wait – come back—

I round the bend but there's no one, just a dog – a snarling dog with long teats, its hackles raised, mouth dripping. It lunges, its hot breath and rough tongue on my face—

And its mouth is a hand – my mother's hand, her palm on my forehead. She is singing.

I'm too old to be sung to.

She brushes the hair from my face.

'Wait—'

I reach out but she's gone.

*

I never understood the idea of total absence. I thought there must always be something. The alternative was too big to comprehend.

Now there is nothing. It is vast.

I sleep. I wake. I sleep.

*

I wake and the fog is gone. In its place is weak sunlight, an empty sky, and sprawling moorland covered in sharp brown grass. My body aches and my stomach heaves. The cold is still there, lodged deep inside me, but I am still here, too.

The path stretches on further than I can see. In the distance, like a bright shell washed up and left behind by the retreating fog, is a white spot in the landscape. It is too far to tell if it is a building.

I try to sit up. Everything tilts and I grab out to steady myself. My hand comes away wet. The fog has left each spike of grass covered in minute droplets. They coat the ground so thinly that the world looks out of focus.

I run my hand across it and again, dampness. A single pearl of water running down the centre of my palm. I lick it off, and it tastes of salt and earth and my own skin. I do this again and again, drop by minuscule drop. It is almost nothing. Perhaps it is enough.

I wriggle out of my sleeping bag and stand.

The movement sends a wave of nausea crashing through me. I retch up bile and spit it into the grass. My tongue is bitter. My throat burns with acid and thirst. My lips are cracked and the inside of my mouth feels cavernous and rasping. My head throbs with dehydration and I have to clench my teeth and breathe through my nostrils to stop myself vomiting again. In the face of this new pain, my leg has given way to a sapping ache and a vicious itching. My trousers are hard where the scab has broken wetly and then dried and broken again. I cannot bring myself to look. I force myself not to scratch.

Over the space of what must be an hour, I pack away my

sleeping bag. I look at my backpack for several minutes before heaving it onto my shoulders. As soon as it's in place, the straps rub and my knees threaten to buckle. I drag myself away.

The world spins. Every few steps, I stop and concentrate on breathing. I count my breaths until I can walk the next uneven steps, and then the next.

I do not know how long it takes to reach it: a soot-smeared wall, which is all that remains of a cottage. I imagine its occupants contracting the Sickness, dying inside and everyone too afraid to remove the bodies to burn them on an outside pyre. Easier just to stand outside the door and light a match.

Bits of rubble stick up like blackened teeth. A mish-mash of objects in what must once have been a homely yard. An iron boot-scraper. A flowerpot filled with earth. A jumble of perished wellies. An old stone sink, a few inches of stagnant water in the bottom.

The water is brown and thick-looking. A few dead leaves are suspended in its murk. I scoop them out and my hand comes away smelling of plant rot. I clench my teeth again. I do not know what this water will do to me, if it will make me vomit until there is nothing of me left, if it will dry me out completely so all my organs stop functioning and I am lost. I also do not know when I will next find water.

I dip a bottle into the sludge. The sediment swirls against my hand as it glugs into the open neck.

I take a deep breath, then lift the bottle to my lips, trying not to smell the rancid rot I am drinking. I force my constricted throat open, drink in trickles, ignore the sour taste filling the raw cavern of my mouth.

There is a high ringing in my ears and I can no longer hear my heartbeat. The itch in my leg is a dull constant.

At the edge of the moorland, I drag myself, metre by metre, to the top of a hill. My leg still shakes at every other step, but the hill is a vantage point. There's a stitch in my side and the climbing tugs and pulls at my muscles. It reminds me I am still here, that I am still human. I sit on top of the hill, regaining my breath, with the landscape unfolded below me. The world rises and falls around me, always keeping me at its centre. I need to understand my place in the world, even now, even if this is where my days run out.

In the distance is a city, a pre-War metropolis bristling with abandonment, a dark river winding through its centre. Beyond it, like a grey brushstroke, is the North Sea. Slumped here on this hilltop, I consider all the possibilities a city like that might hold: shops and warehouses, tool sheds, homes to scour for secret stores of food or medicines. Anything that might be useful. And on the edge of it all something I am too tired to understand nudges into the depths of my brain. A faint electric glow – machinery surviving even where life has failed.

The potential of it all swells and builds inside me, battling back at the aches and nauseating hunger. All that fortune, all those things, all mine, whenever I choose to claim them. It is as if I have stumbled on my own personal market where no money is demanded, where the only price is being alone.

From up here, I cannot tell how complete the city might be – how heavily it was bombed in the War, at what point its population was eviscerated by the Sickness, or whether anyone from here was evacuated to the Safe Centres to make it as far as the Last Fall. A city like this is an unknown element. Who knows what might be hiding in the shut-in buildings, what bombs were dropped here and are lying unexploded and full of dispersing Sickness, waiting for the touch of a boot to set their mechanisms working? And who knows how many dog packs fiercely guard the narrow streets? Animals, like people, are drawn to cities – to the stuff and mess of them, to the hiding places and the mounds of waste. I try not to think it, but I know they will also be drawn to the bodies that must be down there somewhere, too – laid out in beds or slumped on sofas, or perhaps trapped beneath exploded walls and waiting for the rubble to shift. I wonder how long ago this city's people died. Despite myself, I wonder how much remains.

Left in the open air, a human body can break down to only a skeleton in as little as two years. In the ground, it can take as many as twelve. I remember researching these details as a child, filled with fearful curiosity as I looked for facts to write on little white cards for my museum. I never expected to be thinking about it like this, so many years later, overlooking a museum the size of a city. It feels like childhood, and a fear of falling asleep.

At night there is always a feeling of being watched – a feeling like an eye in the dark. As a child I would sit in bed with my back against the cold plaster, running the torchlight across the familiar objects of my room. Now, that eye is a bright blue. Now, when the darkness closes in around me, I like to curl in on myself and keep close to the fire or lie wrapped in my sleeping bag. The city, with its black streets and hidden alleyways, would be the worst place for feeling watched. In the city there would be no solid edge to put my back against, no protective wall that might not also be a hiding place for something else. The city has become a place for daylight, and daylight only.

I scour the landscape, the unfamiliar vastness of it. Away from the city, at the bottom of the next valley, there is a grey smudge of buildings. A farmhouse, perhaps also a barn. A safer place to sleep, but can I make it there in my current condition? And if the buildings are empty, will I have the strength to make it to the city on an empty stomach tomorrow? In the city, there is bound to be food. There is also bound to be danger.

With the sweat cooling on my back, I look between the two. Safety or possibility? City or farm?

I cannot stay here. I haul myself up from the rock and thread my arms back through the shoulder straps of my pack. The sun is low in the sky and my shadow stretches away in front of me.

The sun has already gone behind the hills and there are shivers beginning to build inside me. The cobbled yard is quiet, an anticipatory hush like a library or a church, the only disturbance a murmuring that sounds like running water. I know it's fanciful and stupid, but it feels as though the farm has been waiting for me – or maybe I have been waiting for it.

I mutter my silent prayer, though I do not believe in anyone who could hear it. *Please no bodies. Please no death.* Tonight I need to concentrate only on living, on being alive.

I open the door.

Here is an inventory of what the farmhouse contains:

A kitchen with faded yellow walls and a laminate floor.

A big wood-burning stove on a stone hearth.

A table missing a leg.

A red electric cooker.

A faulty clock, ticking at irregular intervals.

Scrubbed wooden cupboards, filled with crockery and iron-ware pans.

Some foodstuff, mostly inedible – black and mushy vegetables, their juices seeping onto the shelf below. A hard mouldy lump that might once have been a heel of bread. An open pack of crackers.

But there are treasures I can salvage: a bag of rice, two tins of kidney beans, half a box of Cup-a-Soup, stock cubes, vinegar and a bottle of red wine. For a while I sit and cradle them against me.

A living room that smells of decay. Two armchairs. A shelf of *Reader's Digests*.

An old-style larder, with cold stone slabs for preserving food. The larder is empty.

Stairs. Up them, a bathroom with an avocado suite. A wilted spider plant. Six dead woodlice in the bath.

Across the hall, two bedrooms: a double and a twin. No clothes in the drawers or wardrobes. The beds are all unmade. In the airing cupboard, folded blankets and flowery bedding, the kind my mother used to keep as spares in her own airing cupboard, 'Just in case.'

I heave one of the single mattresses downstairs to the kitchen. It takes more strength than I think I have left to tug it into place. I go back up to fetch a single set of bedding. It smells of the must inside the cupboard, but underneath that, locked into the cotton's weave, is a smell of washing powder, and of breezy days drying on the line. For a moment I am at my parents' house helping my mother fold the bed linen, and I press the sheets close around my face.

I light the fire with one of the books and the drawers from the kitchen table, and make up a bed beside it. Once I am confident the fire will not go out, I take one of the heavy iron pans from the cupboard and go outside. In the last light of the day I clamber over the fence and discover a small stream to the side of the house. I set the water to boil on top of the wood-burner and finally let myself look at my leg.

The itch has been screaming louder with every step. The urge to scratch is so strong that if I gave in to it, I can picture myself clawing away whole chunks of flesh, tearing myself to pieces. I sit on the edge of the mattress, tug off my boots and start to peel away the grime-soaked fabric of my trousers.

The individual toothmarks are gone. In their place, where the skin was raised and infected, is a red wet wound like a shallow dish. At the centre of it, an infestation of wriggling grey maggots.

I cry out and brush them away – my hands are wild and it's agony as I brush and batter at my legs, tumbling them all to the floorboards where they flounder and squirm. My leg smarts from my fingers and the cold air, and I force myself to take deep breaths.

I look closer. The tissue is a soft pink, like the inside of a lip, and all that remains of the infection is a small grey and yellow swelling. I touch it and my whole leg throbs. My finger smells of dead animals.

I look at the maggots still writhing by my feet. Maybe it's being in a farmhouse, and the faint smell of land and lanolin that still pervades the place, but there's something . . . something I read or heard once, perhaps from one of the old farmers who brought their accounts to my father. Something about maggots and sheep. Something about a cure.

I shut my eyes and clench my hands. I pinch a few between my thumb and forefinger and deposit them back on the sore part of my leg.

Forcing myself not to look at them, at their miniature mouths burrowing into the dead flesh of my calf, I cut a strip from the bed sheet and bandage them in. I pull up my trousers and throw the remaining maggots on the fire, where they hiss briefly with escaping air. I try to push the unbearable itching to a separate corner of my brain. I tell myself I am a survivor.

I am a survivor.

Once the water has started to boil, I cook some of the rice and one lot of kidney beans in their can. I eat. I drink the boiled rice water. The farmhouse curls around me, still and protective, like a reward for choosing safety over the city. Already I can feel my body returning to itself, restored by food and heat and four solid walls. I am going to live.

For the first time in months, I lie on a mattress. It is softer than I could ever have imagined. I tuck myself into my flowery duvet, and sleep swirls at my edges like a persistent current. All my days and weeks of walking are stored inside my body. They drag it down, and I am swept away.

*

I wake the next morning in near silence, the only sound the broken kitchen clock. Soon the light will lift the lid on the sky and all the noises of morning will begin. Birds will chitter and call. When they flit from branch to branch their wings will flutter and disturb the leaves. Twigs will break and fall to the soft earth, where insects and small mammals commute under the leaf mould. All these things have a sound. With the death of human noises, I have become good at hearing these other quieter things. The day is a noisy place, so long as I listen.

For now, though, it is dark and still. I slide myself out of my makeshift bed, taking care to keep the warmth of the night folded under the duvet, in case I need to get back in.

The laminate is cold under my feet. I stuff on my socks and boots, and stoke and blow on last night's fire until it has reignited itself. Once there is a solid orange blaze, I take the pan and head outside to collect water.

For a few minutes I do nothing but stand on the back step, metal pan in hand, looking out at the paling yard. I think of old family photos, the kind found buried in the drawers of dead grandparents or distant aunts: a man, a woman, sometimes with a child balanced on the hip, standing at the door to a house, a look of pride. A name nobody can read scrawled on the back, and sometimes not even that. Sometimes their only identity is that look, that pride in ownership, in containment: this is me, this is where I live, where I make my life.

I stand on the back step and watch the dark horizon distinguishing itself from the sky.

I used to wake up early in the past, too. It made me feel

as though the day belonged to me, because I had been there at its beginning. In its early vulnerability, before the business of society took hold, the day had shown itself to me. Back then, of course, the business of a day began with dustbin men and the first heavy-eyed office workers. Now, it begins with light.

I do not know how long I stand there, watching the day come into being. How many days have I seen begin? Each one nudging me imperceptibly here. Standing in the doorway of an old farm on the outskirts of a city. Alone.

I do not mind the isolation. As a child, my favourite moments were always spent alone. Only alone could I shut out all the noise, make my mind go still enough to explore, to experiment with circuits and motors and cogs, to create. It was what I craved, I told myself, to be always on my own. I would become an inventor, left alone in a lab or workshop to develop my brilliant ideas, to bring my new creations into being. The logical complexities of objects, set apart from human inconsistency.

Of course it would take time. Unlike most of my classmates, I always knew that I could not just leave school, put on a white coat, stick some coloured pens in my breast pocket and call myself an inventor. I knew that was not how creation worked.

So I practised. At weekends and in the holidays, in the early mornings before school and in the evenings once my homework was complete, I learned. I taught myself mechanics, electronics, computing. I learned to fix and repurpose. After school and self-learning had taught me all they could, I went to college. I worked outside of class.

When the War broke out, I was doing odd jobs part-time on the university campus. The 'odd-job man-woman', they called me. I called them other things. I kept to myself, expanding my expertise, always striving for the experience and the isolation that would allow me to invent.

Now there is nothing to create, and nobody to create it for. There is only survival, a continuous plateau of existence, and an endless rising and falling of days. Thinking now about that childhood dream – the inventor locked away with her own creative genius – I wonder whether I ever believed it.

As the sunlight edges across the sky, the secrecy of this day starts to slip away from me. The morning opens itself up like a flower. The quiet dark becomes a cobblestoned yard with empty dog sheds, a crumbling barn. They come into view like an assertion of all the day's possessions. An old wooden washtub planted with weedy flowers. An early fly, buzzing, landing on the corner of the doorbell. The dark band of trees that fringes the stream. Fields. Walls. Fences. A rusty metal gate. At the day's edges, a dull spread of hills.

This is me. This is where I am going to make my life.

I climb the fence at the corner of the field and pick my way down the bank towards the stream. The water runs cold across my hand as I dip the pan in and out of the current.

Tomorrow I will explore a few miles upstream to see if the water can be drunk without boiling. The next day I will make the hike to the city to see what I can scavenge. After that I will construct a wood store and haul and chop logs for the kitchen fire. Then, if I am still alive, I will dig the fields and find something to plant them with.

An image of the Seed Vault flashes across my mind, but I push it quickly away. Erik would laugh if he could see this new desire. Or he would despair that it has come too late. Or he would do nothing.

As I cross the yard back towards the farmhouse, slowly, so as not to spill any of this precious water, there's a muted scratching from the intact end of the barn. At first I think it must be rats, but then I hear it again: scrabbling claws, followed by a weak, high keening.

I stop myself. Hope is a killer. It puffs you up like a balloon, then turns away as reality jabs like a needle. Hope is no help to a survivor.

I put down the pan and ease open the upper half of the barn door. Inside is dark and fetid. Shafts of grey dissect the lower end where the beams and roof have caved. A pale spot on the ground where a gap leads out into the yard. I let my eyes adjust to the murky light, holding my breath against the smell. Still it makes my eyes water. I shift and my foot clangs against a rusted tin of turpentine. I hold myself there, waiting.

One by one, they swim up out of the gloom: four chickens, thin and ragged, bits of skin raw where their feathers have been pecked or scratched or worn away. Perched on a ledge, making that desperate keening I heard from the yard, is the cockerel.

I shut the door. I walk back across the yard to where I left the pan. I kneel down beside it and press my face into the dank cobblestones.

*

I fetch an extra pan of water from the stream. In the clear space in front of the fire, I peel off my trousers. Already the wound is cleaner. I start to rinse the maggots from my leg.

The first touch of the water stings, but along with the maggots, it washes away all the days of thirst and pain, the possibility of not surviving, the nothingness that threatened to pull me in. I pour cup after cup of water over my calf, until all the maggots are bobbing and squirming in the bowl underneath it. Then I take the turpentine from the yard and bash at the rusted screwcap with a stone, till the metal gives and I can get at the sharp-smelling liquid inside. I tip some onto a fresh wad of bed sheet and dab it on the clean wound. It stings like fire and I grind my teeth to keep from crying out.

I bandage it with another torn-off bit of sheet, and silently thank my mother for her makeshift remedies. Then, since there is nobody around to hear, I thank her out loud, too.

A city is a vast unmanageable thing. Once, they were mutable, changing and transforming with every person passing through. Their architecture was born out of layers of history and decisions made long ago.

Now, the city is still and dead. It sits placid in the landscape like a washed-up jellyfish. It takes me more than two hours, or what I think must be more than two hours, to walk from the first gated, big-gardened houses to what feels like the centre: a wide paved area with broken shops and sporadic trees. I keep expecting to see people. There are no people, but I keep expecting them. The back of my neck prickles and I spend the morning looking over my shoulder, as if the streets have eyes and are watching me, and I think again about the animals that must be prowling here somewhere. Even empty, the city is a place for keeping my head down.

I come to the wide river I saw from the hill. It is a dull grey, reflecting the sky. A sharp breeze ruffles the water, biting at my uncovered head as I cross a curving white metal bridge towards an enormous building, lumpy and silver, like a gigantic mirrored grub. Outside it, shreds of concert posters lift and flap.

My mother brought me here to see an orchestra once. I was very young, and she was desperate to channel my meticulousness into something she understood – like music. I remember the lights. There were hundreds of them, embedded in the ceilings and hanging from rigs, all changing together or in sequence, rising and dimming, flowing from colour to colour so it was as if the lights themselves were the orchestra, and the music was only incidental. And I remember us getting lost on the long drive home, and my mother blaming my father even though he wasn't with us – or perhaps because he wasn't with us.

I had forgotten that occasion. It is as though I had left the memory here, beside the river, reflected in the building's mirrored surface, waiting patiently for me to come back and collect it. It is strange how a particular place can unlock a particular memory.

Something rustles in an overgrown hedge and I square myself, but there is only me and the rats, the muddy river, and miles of unmined buildings.

There are tags and slogans scrawled on the walls, built up on top of each other like layers of clothing. The bottom ones, partly hidden, are spray-can pictures, the kind that used to draw tourists and bloggers the world over. The kind of riotous colour that probably meant something to somebody once upon a time.

On top of that are the asinine declarations, the washed-up statements of everyday life. Phone numbers, initials, hearts. Some half scrubbed off, most of them just ignored.

The newest marks are the most urgent, the most deeply felt, the roughest, the ones painstakingly stencilled. These are the words that came from the depths of people, forged in the desperation of the War and the Sickness. These are the final futile pleas before the Last Fall.

In black sprayed-on letters running the length of a restaurant wall, someone has stencilled SAY NO TO NUKES, followed by a phallic bomb in a circle with a line through it. Underneath it in green paint, someone else has daubed the call: Go Vegan. I like this – a last attempt to better a dying world.

At the bottom of the wall, someone with a black marker pen has simply scribbled: heroine.

Here and there, a street ends in a crater, or in a wide expanse of rubble – legacies of the bombing that marked the escalating War. Mostly, though, the city is intact. Sickness, then. I have already climbed a dozen roadblocks, sectioning off infected areas for quarantine. Some of these roadblocks were clearly official – heavy concrete barricades pasted with reflective strips, barbed wire coiling across their tops. The rest are makeshift, thrown together by panicked civilians using cars and furniture and broken window glass.

I keep thinking about one section, near the edge of the city. The streets are broader, the houses bigger without being ostentatious. There are overgrown gardens and driveways with rusting cars. And pasted on lampposts and in the windows of empty shops, faded evacuation posters, offering a way out.

I keep imagining those people, surrounded by a city of Sickness, quarantined in their suburban houses, not for other people's good but for their own. I can picture their disbelieving joy when the posters went up, their determination as they packed suitcases and prepared for evacuation to the Safe Centres, where there would be clean air and plenty of food. I can picture their hope on arriving, their loved ones in tow – before it all collapsed. Before the resources thinned and the Safe Centres went to war with one another, with themselves. Before the remnants of humanity were burning, and all the while, me: huddled in the Seed Vault, beneath rock and snow and ice, surviving.

*

Even from the outside, the clinic is a marvel of engineering – not one of the old constructions, clanking and groaning and striving to fulfil its purpose, but a huge cylinder of concrete and toughened glass. It is the ideological cousin of the Seed Vault, a life-support machine made to outlast human stupidity, to look beyond catastrophe to the survival of the human race. On the evening I first saw it from the top of the hill, it rooted in me and shone like a distant pinprick of hope. While I rested at the farm, the idea of it kindled in my mind: that when all the other buildings are dark tombs and megaliths, when the scavenging dogs growl and snap on the edge of their territories, there is still this, a hub of power and perseverance, shining as a monument to the human urge to endure. I cannot stop myself from hoping.

In the daylight, the clinic looks haughty and unnatural.

At each compass point, a turbine stands sentry. Racks of solar panels surround the building like planetary rings, the strange outlines of clouds reflected in their depths. I remember hearing about these so-called clinics in the early days of the Sickness. I remember how they would act as an ark to carry what was left of humanity into the future, and how hardly any ever made it to completion before the world gave up on the future, retreating to the newer Safe Centres to huddle together and attempt to just survive the present.

Inside, the corridor is dark, leading deep into the building as if descending into a bunker. For a moment I am in the Seed Vault and I have to put out a hand to steady myself. My fingers brush against something: a black and silver switch. I press it and the corridor gutters into light. I switch it off, then on again. I do this four more times, and each time I picture the switch snapping the circuit shut, sending electrons humming through the wires. I had forgotten the sheer marvel of pressing a button in one place and seeing light come into existence in another.

Somewhere during this miracle, I become aware of a sound, something deep and constant, impossible to shake. It's a while before I recognise the hum of electricity, the mechanical pulse I must have lived with for most of my life, which now seems as alien as the building itself.

I am quick with my search. I find stores of redundant medical supplies, fridges filled with insulin and vaccinations, rooms kept cold for things people once believed were worthy of preservation. I find a half-used tube of antiseptic that feels like a vow, like a voice saying *Never again*, and I stop to treat and rebandage my leg, although already the bite seems to be healing.

Other than that, there is nothing to take time over. There are no stores of protein, processed and packaged for optimum endurance, no cartons of food waiting for a lonely survivor to need them. Instead there are empty boxes, a few discarded wrappers, a smashed table and overturned stack of chairs: all the detritus of the looting, of the people who came and emptied the place before heading back out into the city. The death throes of humanity, drawn here like blundering moths to a flame, leaving nothing for me.

That evening, sitting by the kitchen fire in a house that already feels like a home, I cannot shake the feeling of the clinic, its smell of newness, its determined existence even when all its stores are either useless or empty. I picture the lights guttering on, the only unnatural glow in this vast dark world, like an unseen adversary, mocking me with its senseless persistence. *Look*, it catcalls, *you're not the only one who can endure. You're not the only one to survive. Which of us will last the longest, Monster?*

And I want to run at it, through the burst streets and split tower blocks, through the packs of dogs, straight at that arrogant construction. To break down the turbines and smash the solar panels, to revel in the clatter of busted metal as the lights black out and everything preserved there grows warm and sour. To stand sweating and cold in the darkness and say, *See? I'm the one who will last the longest.*

But then I remember the building itself, the structural beauty of it. I remember how minimal it is. Like the Seed Vault, it revels in its clinical functionality. Nothing decorative. Nothing wasted, until the looters interfered. Like me, the designer of the clinic understood that survival is a matter of necessity, not of joy.

I try to imagine him – I make him male because of the dogged self-assurance necessary to engineer a structure such as this, something so completely autonomous and certain of its own success. And because of Erik. Because of his absolute faith in perseverance, and because of how little it took for that perseverance to fail. I picture them blending, these two undoubting men, until they are one person, until everything the clinic stands for is in some way broken.

I suppose that, too, is the price of survival: a hope so false it burns and dies like a firework.

*

I do not know where to start. I make a mental list of what I need. Food. Matches. Clothes. Fresh batteries for my torch if I can find them. Tools.

For a second I think about all the paraphernalia I used to throw away, all the tools and commodities I have so casually expunged from my life, now buried somewhere on a rubbish heap, their usefulness prematurely discarded. I think about all the so-called rubbish this city must have once created. If I could find it . . .

I stop myself. A horde like that would not be unclaimed. It would be occupied by scavenging dogs, by savage gulls, by rats carrying all kinds of diseases. And besides, I would not know where to begin to look for it.

I will have to settle for more traditional outlets. A hardware shop. A supermarket.

Most of the shops are empty. Many have their fronts smashed in. Some are missing their signs. Not for the first time, I find my fingers twitching towards my pocket: a base instinct of longing for a phone, for information.

I will have to do this the old-fashioned way. Not even the old-fashioned way, but the prehistoric way. I have become a hunter-gatherer.

I find seven shops. In one, four broken shelving units. In another, a stack of bubble-wrapped toilet seats. Nothing I can use. Nothing that might save me.

It is a strange idea, being saved. When I picked up broken appliances as a child, I thought I was saving them, fixing them up to give them a new lease of life. I would mend them, even repurpose them, and the best would earn a place in my collection.

What have I been saved for? I cannot fix myself. At school, teachers would urge us to go to college or university or join the army so we could 'reinvent ourselves'. I cannot invent myself as anything but what I am, waking, eating, shitting, sleeping. I do not know what being saved means any more, or what the reward might be for achieving it.

I move further out, towards the periphery of the city, where the chaos is thinner and the infrastructure more whole.

It is on the western edge that I find it. A retail park. A whole complex dedicated to the buying and selling of things. Of course, most of the buildings are boarded and shuttered, abandoned long before the rest of the city was evacuated, when the War and then the Sickness made international trade next to impossible.

The fullest, most normal-looking is a pet shop. Browsing the shelves stocked with retractable leads and hamster cages, I can almost believe that a bored shop assistant will saunter over to ask what I am looking for. Clearly most of this stock became extraneous once the Sickness set in for good, when people were quarantined and had to eat their pets to stay alive.

I am about to leave when I spot a large crate filled with foil packets of bird seed. Something to feed to the scratty chickens roosting in the barn. I cannot carry a whole one, so I decant some into a carrier bag, tie it off and cram it in my backpack. I put in four tins of dog food and a bag of dog biscuits. The biscuits are over a year out of date, but they will do in case I can find nothing else to eat tonight.

Next to the pet shop is a computer store, packed with defunct technology. On the other side is an empty sports outlet. Across the car park is an outdoors shop, the kind of place that once sold recreational camping and hiking as part of the dream that everyone could be an explorer at the end of a working week.

I tell myself not to hope.

It is dark inside the shop. I fish in the pocket of my rucksack for my torch. It wavers as I switch it on, and everything inside me clenches in a desperate plea for fresh batteries. *Let it be like the pet shop. Let it be full.*

As I flash the torch beam around the room, my eyes become accustomed, and I take stock.

A bare display unit.

The ripped shell of a tent.

Leaflets advertising loyalty cards.

A bashed-in till.

I move further in, flash my torch over any shelf that might harbour something I could use, but there is nothing. The shop is bare and useless. Around every shelf and hanging rack I think, this is where it must be. But no. Only emptiness and a conspicuous scurrying from whatever rodent life has taken up residence just beyond my torch-light.

Perhaps if I only go further, deeper, then at some point I will strike lucky. Surely, eventually, there must be something.

But then the wall is looming, dusty and grey, pockmarked with clothes hooks. I follow it along. In the back corner of the shop is a door, shut with a combination lock. I press my hand against the lock and it bleeps wearily. Still some battery left. I try a couple of combinations, but none of them work. No matter. Basic combination locks like this are easy to get past.

I fumble to the front of the shop and unstick one of the loyalty cards from its leaflet. Back by the door, I slide it down the edge of the lock, turning the handle until I hear a click. The door opens.

Through it is a metal staircase leading down into a basement. I descend to the sound of more scurrying claws. At the bottom I find another door, also locked. I trick my way through it with the card, and push it open.

When I was small, I stole a book about Ancient Egypt from school. There were coloured drawings of Egyptians farming the land on either side of the Nile and of slaves building pyramids, and on the cover was an embossed picture of Tutankhamun's death mask, which shone gold and showed up the fingerprints of every child who had read it. My favourite picture in the book was a sepia photograph. It showed Howard Carter and Lord Carnarvon standing in the entrance to Tutankhamun's burial chamber in 1922, looking a little bit overwhelmed by the enormous treasure trove they had just uncovered.

I open a locked door in the basement of an abandoned outdoors shop on the western edge of a dead city, and I find Tutankhamun's tomb.

I stand for a moment in the torchlight and allow myself just to look.

There are piles of plastic-packaged clothes, and boxes of torches, batteries, bottles, a water filter, sleeping bags, camping lanterns, firelighters . . .

I change into new clothes and boots and leave my old ones bundled in a corner. I swap the batteries in my torch, and pack my backpack with as much as I can carry. It is full and heavy, and I will be tired by the time I get back to the farm, but I know I will sleep well tonight.

*

In the days to come, I raid the back rooms of all the super-
markets I can find, but they are mostly empty. I even try several
cafés, most of which closed during the War when people
stopped spending money. As I expected, they are all bare. I
take a few packets of oats and grains from houses in the suburbs
– the ones with closed doors and unbroken windows, which
have not already been ransacked. In one I find a tub of salt.
In another, a sealed jar of flour with weevils crawling through
it, which I can sift clean back at the farm.

At first I consider making the long trek across the city to
look for food in the sea, but that would require fishing tackle
or crab pots, or combing the beach for cockles, and I know
nothing about any of it – and if I close my eyes I can still feel
the pitch and swell of the waves, the undertow dragging at
my feet. I can picture myself pushed under, scraping along the
rough sand, flailing and gasping for air. Better to stick to
scavenging.

So I explore the city until I find a garden centre, dark and
sprawling next to the remains of a looted supermarket. I wrench
the door open.

Inside, the air feels thick and moist. It clings to me with a
sense of possibility – even the smell makes me think of things
burgeoning, of compost and cultivated growth, and of my
mother in her gardening gloves, whispering to a tray of seed-
lings, wheedling them into the light. For a moment I feel a
pang of something for her, for her ability to make things
flourish. I shrug it off. I never wanted that – to be the sort of
person who poured hours into the painstaking nourishment
of an allotment, who hunched over a vegetable patch like my

mother and sometimes my father, gauging onions with a tape measure in the hope they might be fat enough to win a prize at the fair. There was no point to that, as far as I could tell. Not when the supermarket had onions bagged and ready to go.

Now, it is different. Now, I think of my mother's pristine rows of cabbages and potatoes and beans, picked clean of slugs and caterpillars every morning by her attentive hands, and I think about survival.

I wander between the shelves, ignoring the useless decorative items – the sundials and water features and bird baths. Like the pet shop, much of the garden centre is intact, displays brimming as though the shop shut for the night and just never reopened – but here and there, bare runs of shelving tell a different story.

The main central aisle is totally empty, apart from a dusty stack of half-price greetings cards. At the end of it, displayed in faded coloured packets across the back wall, are the seeds.

I run my hand across them and they swing gently on their hooks, like I am nothing more than a breeze. I have no idea if they will grow. How long do seeds last, protected by nothing but waxy paper? I think of the Seed Vault and its state-of-the-art technology keeping everything in stasis, how even that was not enough in the end. What chance do these seeds have, here in this corrugated shed? Erik would have known. Probably my mother would know, too. Perhaps any attempts at planting are useless. Still, I select an assortment of vegetable seeds from the racks.

I plant the seeds in plastic trays to urge them along. Every day I search for signs of growth, and every day the bare compost is a condemnation, until I want to hurl it at the wall. I try not to wonder how long I can survive on tinned food and dry goods. I try not to wonder how long these foods will remain edible. I tell myself to be patient, but there is less and less hope – until one day, poking through the black, spots of bright green appear like promises. I hold them up to my eye level and stare at the freshness, the real burgeoning life of them. They have succeeded. I have succeeded.

When the plants have grown bigger, I dig over a row of earth along one side of the field and transplant them. I check them every day for snails or aphids.

On my walk upstream from where the water runs past the house, I discover two apple trees. As long as the plants are not diseased, I will have fresh fruit and vegetables when the time is right. I build up the end of the barn and fatten the chickens, so they will start to lay again. With each success, I can feel my roots growing deeper. With each day, the world solidifies around me.

*

I have been at the farmhouse two weeks when I make my second big discovery in the city. It does not seem promising to begin with. I almost don't even go inside.

It is a corner shop, with a broken awning and boarded-up windows, the kind that used to sell newspapers and cigarettes and sweets. I only check it on the off-chance of finding a stray bar of chocolate or packet of crisps.

I turn the door knob. It's stiff, but stiffness is a good thing, because it means the dogs and foxes can't get in.

Inside is an old wooden floor, scratched almost white by decades of shoes. A central magazine stand and a counter at the far end. A row of cupboards on the near wall. There are a few empty packets on the shelves by the counter. Other than that, the shop is bare. It looks as though the place closed before the city's people died or moved away to the new centres.

At the back of the shop is a door leading into what was once the owner's house. As I open it, it sets a flurry of dust whirling, and I have to blink through it into the darkness. The windows in here are boarded up, too. I have taken to carrying a long metal bar with me on my trips to the city – something I found in the farmyard, and something that makes me feel safer, like I can protect myself. I use it to pry the boards from the windows, and the daylight comes streaming in.

I am in a small living space, carpeted, with a faux-leather sofa and the far wall stacked with high cupboards. Expecting more of the same emptiness I found in the shop, I check them. There are cans of soup, vegetables, hot-dog sausages. There are jars of jam and pickles and peanut butter. There are packets and packets of dried foods: cereals, biscuits, breadsticks, lentils. There is an enormous cardboard box full of chocolate bars.

On a full stomach, I can build more of a home at the farmhouse. I fix up the outside toilet so it is easy for me to clean out. I cobble together a new table, and pull the least mildewed of the armchairs into the kitchen so I can sit by the fire. I dig up more of the field behind the house, to prepare it for planting. I construct a log store. The shallow wound on my calf scabs thinly, then heals to a toughened patch of pink sheen. My hens begin to lay.

If I have to survive alone, then I will do it in my own world. Here, even if nowhere else, everything will work and seed and grow and bear fruit as it is supposed to.

*

I haven't bled in over a year. Maybe I will never bleed again. Sometimes I put my hand between my legs and feel the void there.

My mother used to call it 'the curse', when I skulked on the sofa once a month, a hot water bottle on my belly and a moan in my throat. My mother was like that – religious in small ways. She called it a curse and I, full of cramps and anger, believed her.

Of course, my mother was wrong as always. Bleeding wasn't a curse. It was a reminder of possibility, a bodily conviction of the future. Now there is nothing.

Sometimes I wonder if I can still call myself a woman, even though I no longer bleed. Then I wonder if I ever thought of myself as a woman even when I did. Then I remember that there are no women anyway, just as there are no men, so what does it matter? What does any of it matter?

I always stop wondering after that. Until the next time I remember my womb – like a shrivelled fruit – and start questioning all over again. My mind goes round like that, round and round, like a wheeling vulture, swooping in and out, closer then away.

This thought comes most often when I am looking at the moon. I talk to the moon – especially the full moon – as if the shining silver disc is a woman's face, just as people used to say it was a man's. The kind of face with smile lines and a double chin, that might belong to a favourite aunt, if I ever had one.

Maybe linguists were right. Maybe women are connected

to the moon, like 'month', like 'menstruate' – a menstrual bond, each circling around and back around to our own womanness: a pale round face; a memory of blood between the legs.

Or maybe linguists were right in other ways, connecting me to the moon. Luna . . . lunar . . . lunatic. Maybe I am finally turning mad. Or maybe I'm just lonely.

*

I sit by the kitchen fire with one leg tucked under the other in the easy chair and my shoe box on my lap. The drying elastic band is the only thing securing the lid. I do not need to open it. I hold it just for the weight.

I close my eyes, and the world contracts to dusty cardboard against my hands, the chair's lumpy upholstery at my back, heat from the fire, the irregular tick of the broken clock.

*

I never did fit into boxes, back when there were boxes people could be sorted into. I did not have friends, apart from Harry Symmonds, and he did not fit into their neat little boxes either.

'She'll settle,' my mother used to say, reassuring herself as much as the gathered friends. 'She'll settle down when she's older.'

I had no interest in settling. Settling is what sediment does when it falls to the bottom of a sea or lake, right before it compresses for several million years and turns into a fossil. I did not understand why that was something anyone would want.

But still people tried to group and categorise me, the way I analysed, sorted and categorised them. Some of the categories they put me in were kind, or perhaps just optimistic: strong-willed, clever, confident, individual. Some, like 'weird' and 'antisocial', were less so. I was never sure where my mother's 'uncontrollable' was supposed to fit.

As I got older, there were more categories, more boxes to be squeezed into or have built up around me. More shapes I would not fit. Speculation skittered through the school with a sound like dead leaves: who might be what, who might want to do what, and who with. I took a step back from it all. The idea of human touch still repulsed me, that horrid intimacy of another person's flesh encroaching on mine – how could anybody *desire* that?

During my first week at college, I made friends with a girl called Nick. Nick was loud and clever, and laughed whenever I said something cutting. She landed in my new life and made herself comfortable, sprawling across my living-room sofa till

105

she looked more at home in my flat than I did. At first I enjoyed it, the bright and unassuming presence of another person, one who said what she thought and had no hidden agendas. Surprisingly, I found it easy.

A few weeks into this unexpected friendship, we went to an Italian restaurant – the kind of place with candle wax dripping down wine bottles and old film posters stuck to the walls. We ate pasta and drank cheap beer. We talked – or rather, Nick talked and I kept up a sarcastic commentary. It was only at the end of the meal, when Nick insisted on paying the full bill, that I realised this was meant to be a date, and that she had had a hidden agenda after all. I made some excuse and left. I stopped answering my phone. A couple of weeks later, Nick stopped calling.

I continued to be Monster, setting myself apart from the illogical complexities that came along with other people. Whenever anyone approached again, I felt the fear and uncertainty grip me, and I veered away. My instinct was always to say no. I did not need them. I told myself repeatedly I did not want them. I was enough, all by myself.

I was not 'asexual'. I had found the word in a glossary at the back of a science book at school. It said an asexual person was free from sexual desires. I remember 'free from', as if the sexual desires my peers had fallen into were somehow a trap. An asexual person, the book said, may still have a functional, caring relationship with their partner, but without sexual desire. That is how I knew I was not asexual. It was not desire that I was free from, but caring.

The empty maths room, after the bell had gone and the school day was over. I was bent over the orange exercise book with its crosshatching of squares, the spike of a pair of compasses stabbed into its centre as I measured out an equilateral triangle.

I remember the lesson because I remember the beauty of it, constructing such a perfect form from only arcs and lines and a few simple tools.

Which is why I was still there, completing this section of the question book after the rest of the class had packed up its mediocre attempts and left.

A movement behind me. I had thought I was alone.

'You OK?' Naomi Dodds, half sitting, half leaning against the windowsill, fake designer bag slung over one shoulder with practised casual perfection. Naomi Dodds: highlighted hair and an arch look, wearing lip gloss and heavy foundation like they were a symbol of her rank. I did not think I had ever seen her on her own before.

'Fine.' I was not thinking about the strangeness of this, of her being there, of her even speaking to me. My head was still filled with triangles. I got up and started packing away my things.

She walked over – *glided*, somehow – and tried to help me. I wanted to tell her to stop, but she was the type of person I tended to avoid, so I just let her get on with it.

'Only . . .' she carried on, with a flick of her hair that caught my cheek, 'only I thought you maybe weren't, you know? I thought, maybe, you'd heard what Sam Harper said about you, and, you know, I thought you might have taken it the wrong way?'

Exactly as Naomi Dodds intended, my curiosity was piqued. 'What did Sam Harper say about me?'

She was separating my pencil from the compasses, looking down at the table and the crater I had gouged out with safety scissors the term before. She was close enough that her perfume caught in my throat.

'He said you were like a boy, how you pick fights all the time.'

'Oh,' I said. Is that all, I thought.

'I think that's all he meant though,' she said, 'about being like a boy, I mean. Just about picking fights. I don't think he meant in other ways. Not – you know – sex.'

'Oh,' I said again, and then, because I had nothing else to say, 'right.'

'It's all right,' she said, looking at me now, wide-eyed under her big fake eyelashes.

What was all right? Her eyeliner was slightly thicker on her left eye than on her right and it irked me. Why do it if she couldn't do it right?

'It's all right.' Her voice was cloying, like tinned pears. 'It's OK to be different.'

I treated her to my best sardonic smile. Of course it was OK to be different.

'It's OK,' she whispered again.

She leaned in.

She pushed her mouth at me.

Her lips were too warm and moist. They were too close and then they were pressing on mine. They were fat and sticky with lip gloss. They were mushrooms in plastic packaging.

I jerked back.

'It's OK,' she said yet again, as though this was some great truth and I was supposed to divine some hidden meaning from it, 'I won't tell anyone.'

She leaned in again, her face flat and false at close quarters.

I stepped back into the desk. 'I'm not a lezzer.'

She frowned and dark ravines appeared in the foundation. She whispered, 'Oh, come *on*.'

'Come on what?'

'Come on!' She raised a plucked and pencilled eyebrow. 'Course you are. No way are you straight.'

'Fuck off.'

She scoured me with that arch look.

'I don't fancy you,' I frowned. 'I don't even like you.'

I packed the rest of my things into my bag. I headed for the door, but Naomi Dodds was there first. She grabbed my face, squeezing. She put her own face up close and I flinched but there was no danger of her kissing me this time. Her eyes were burning. She hissed, 'Tell anyone about this and I'll cut you.'

Then she was gone, out of the classroom door and into the last trickle of people meandering home.

*

Once a year, my mother would announce it was a day to paint the windows. She would pass the job to my father and my father would pass the job to me. In this way, our family was a waterfall. My mother hurled her tasks and opinions down our small domestic hierarchy. They pooled in me and hollowed me out, and my father was a smooth rock face who offered no resistance. I grew, hidden and deep, until I was bigger than either of them imagined. People always marvel at waterfalls, and nobody pays enough attention to the chasm underneath.

Today I am painting the windows at the farm. I slap the paint across the frames with a thick brush, letting it fleck the glass and spatter the surrounding stone. Every time this happens, I think about my mother's neatness and paint all the more haphazardly.

The air is still and thick. As the sun rises higher, I take off my jumper and throw it across the gate, where it hangs heavy like a side of meat. I keep painting. I am tempted to leave the windows of the rooms I never use, but rotten wood means draughts in any part of the house, and I was never one to leave a job half done.

By midday, the sun is blazing and the window frames are ready for a second coat. I unbutton the bottom of my shirt and tie it up around my middle. For a moment I consider taking it off entirely, working bare-chested and letting the sun spread across my uncovered back – but as soon as I think it I can feel eyes on me and my skin prickles. I wrap the fabric tighter across my chest.

Sometimes, I wonder who the eyes belong to. My mother

maybe, although these eyes are silent and my mother was never one to look without commenting. Maybe my father, or Erik. More likely there is a fox or stray dog prowling, which my subconscious has picked up on. I wear my cotton shirt like armour. When it comes to isolating myself from whatever might be lurking, state of mind is what matters, and for that fabric is as good a defence as steel.

*

What I know is this: survival is not about being stronger than other people. It is about ignoring other people altogether.

Longyearbyen, Svalbard, on the cusp of winter. I stood on the edge of the harbour, wrapped in oilskins, laden with everything I could rescue from the base. Food, blankets, clothes. Even some of Erik's equipment, though most of the stuff in the labs was redundant by then. In front of me were the boats. The bigger ones called to me, beckoning with their safety of iron and steel. If I had to go out onto the vastness of the sea, I thought, I should make myself larger than I already was.

A breeze whipped up small waves and there was a metal clang from somewhere on the water. I could not have handled one of those boats on my own.

So I turned to the smaller boats. The cold sun rose higher as I stood there, sizing them up, easy prey at the edge of the land and sea. Thank god there were no polar bears any more.

In the end, I chose the largest boat I thought I could handle. It was not very big, but it had a sail – a token gesture for tourists, just for running tours around the peninsula. Still, I thought it could come in handy. I loaded my bags of provisions. I scoured the harbour for stashed jerry cans of fuel, then loaded them onto my little boat as well. I wondered, had it not been for the fuel shortage, would people have taken care to squirrel away this much? Would there have been less?

The boat was small. The boat was possibly too small. I thought this a thousand times in the days to come.

I forced myself to cast off.

The Vikings did this, I reminded myself, as the gap between

boat and dock widened. The Vikings did this in their wooden rowing boats – or so Erik told me. They did this without engines or maps, with only a raven to guide them.

I chugged my little boat from the harbour, past the buoys and wave-energy converters bobbing on the surface, out to the open sea, towards home.

*

In those endless days that followed, I learned about the sea. The sea is not a physical thing. It does not exist through force and dimension, through gravity and thrust and resistance. Knowing the mechanics of how a vessel stays afloat, or how the engine propels it forward – these are not enough. The sea is a creature of the mind. It is a leviathan lurking, in perpetual motion, an essay in the impossible.

The sea took all my physics and mathematics and threw them back in my face with the spray. It howled and stung and hissed and slapped. It gloried in my smallness, crashing and swelling with a raucous belly-laugh, like a fat woman bursting out of clothes too tight for her.

I fought her. I cursed and spat. I turned my mind into steel, something sharp and metallic, that could slice through water without rusting. I barely slept. I ate only what was to hand, fighting the waves, existing in the leanest way possible, eating and shitting and pissing where I stood. I stopped being human. I became a machine – less than a machine, a parasite clinging to its host. I barely thought, only operated. I kept on moving forward. I kept afloat.

Sometimes when I am digging the field or preparing food, I think about history, about all the people who have ever lived. The kings and queens and emperors, the peasants and farmers, scientists and priests, the prehistoric women, the Neanderthals – all that evolution, the weight of history and DNA and adaption, all coming down to me. When I dip the bucket for water and the stream tugs at my hand, I remember where the stream is headed. I remember the weight of the sea, the vile, heaving mass of it, buffeting my little boat, desperate to pull me under, and I wonder why I kept fighting it. Why I still keep fighting.

*

The city has moods. On some days it treats me like a friend, lays out smooth paths to welcome me and offers up an interior of gifts. Some days it is an obliging stranger: *Here, Monster – try this turning. Take whatever you like.*

Today, the city is cantankerous and cold. The morning has yielded nothing but empty office buildings and a spool of ribbon that I will tie to a pole, and which may or may not work to keep the crows off the field. Somehow, I cannot bring myself to make a scarecrow with a human form.

The road is a barrage of obstacles and it takes hours just to clamber the mile from the city centre. On the chassis of an overturned bus, with a view of concrete and tarmac and shattered glass, I sit and eat two boiled eggs.

Afterwards, I trudge back towards the parts of the city I know. As the familiar front of the corner shop edges into view, I am already picturing filling my bag from its stocked cupboards. I am already yearning for the farmhouse, the bright flame of the kitchen cooker, the safety and solitude of the easy chair.

The shop door is ajar.

I left it closed. I definitely left it closed tight, the way I always do.

But here I am in the middle of this empty city, and the heavy shop door is ajar.

*

A door – this door – opens when the latch pulls back, away from the strike plate in the frame. The latch is connected to the spindle, so, to achieve this, the spindle must be turned. The spindle is locked into the back of the door knob, which requires a hand to turn it – which in turn requires an opposable thumb and a rotating wrist.

Which in turns means some kind of ape. Which means a human.

*

The door is ajar.

In the gap is a sliver of dark, a sudden expansion of possibility. My skin feels tight, stretched, like all the hairs on my body are keening. I can hear my blood thudding through my ears.

I stretch my hand towards the half-open door and push.

Inside, the shop is mostly normal, jars and empty packets still littering the shelves. But there is one gaping cupboard door that was shut last time I left it. My hand is tight and hot around my metal bar, ready to strike out. I edge through to the back room.

There's a second when I think the room is empty, when my eyes see nothing but the gloom and lumpy furniture. Then a shift in the shadows – and I spot it.

A creature. A small, ragged creature, hunkering in the corner. It flexes forward into the light, all angle and bone, skinny body low to the carpet. Its skin is scratched and bruised, grey with rubble dust. It raises its pinched face . . .

This creature is a girl. A starved, scrawny human child.

She shouldn't exist. She can't. A girl who somehow survived the War and the Sickness and the Last Fall. A girl who endures.

We face each other in the grubby back room of the corner shop. The seconds spiral and build around us. Neither of us moves.

'Hello,' I say. My voice cracks.

She hisses and leaps back like a cat.

'It's OK,' I tell her, 'I won't hurt you.'

She hisses again, teeth bared, her little fingers curling into claws.

'Can you understand me?'

She lets out a desperate shriek – a guttural, feral noise, bursting with fear and warning.

All right, I think. All right. Let's find another way to do this.

I start to crouch, pulling myself down to her level. Her eyes never leave my face.

Slowly, very slowly, I put down the metal pipe. I hold my hands up to her to show they're empty, hoping she sees that this isn't a threat. I attempt a smile. The muscles in my cheeks creak and stretch where I haven't used them for months; I can feel it in my forehead and down my throat, like something unnatural. Maybe it doesn't even look like a smile. Maybe my face has forgotten how.

The girl's body starts to relax. She makes another wordless noise, a breathy one which sounds something like 'her'.

I turn my hands, palms up, and offer them towards her, an invitation to touch.

At first she flinches, but after minutes of squatting till my thigh muscles burn, she crawls out to meet me, hand outstretched. With bird-like hesitancy, her fingers touch mine. She runs her fingers over my cleaner, brighter skin. Her touch is light, agonisingly light. I want to grasp her hands. I want to grasp them tightly, to cling to the solid reassurance that she's there, she's real, I am not alone.

I am not alone.

I can hardly breathe for the simple beauty of another human face, the unexpected ecstasy of touch. I want to hug this little body to me till I break it, to know and know and know that I am not alone.

But I can't scare her away. So I use my free hand to point to myself. Monster, I am about to say – but what if she recognises the word and is afraid? Instead, I think of the most comforting and caring word I can. I point to myself and say, 'Mother.'

She looks to where my hand points to my chest, and then up at my mouth, like she's studying its workings.

I try again: 'Mother.'

Her lips flex and waver.

'Mother,' I say again.

She creases her forehead in concentration. 'Mubber . . .'

I smile at her. 'Mother.'

'Muvver.'

'Almost,' I tell her. 'Mother.'

'Muvver. Mothah.' She frowns. 'Mother.'

'Yes,' I smile again, looser and easier this time. 'Mother.'

She touches my chest, eyes on my face. 'Mother.'

I take her hands and slowly rise. The girl stands with me, eyes still on mine. I smile at her again, and she smiles back: a fresh, honest smile that splits her face and again makes me want to hug her too hard.

'Come with me,' I say, hoping my tone and gestures will convey the words she doesn't understand. I lead her over to the high cupboards. She follows me warily, but it is clear that she has decided – for the moment – to trust me.

Reaching up, my hand comes back with a tin of tomatoes. She watches as I puncture the top with the chisel I carry on my belt and hand it to her.

'You can drink it.' I puncture another one for myself and demonstrate, sucking the tomato juice through the hole.

The girl copies me, uncertain at first. Then the sugary tomato juice hits her tongue and her eyes blaze, and she gulps it down greedily. When she finishes, her top lip is tomato red and she is breathing excitedly. I give her the rest of my can to finish.

After both cans are gone, she grins at me, panting with the

excitement of so much goodness consumed so quickly. She spreads her hands across her belly and looks down.

I watch her and I fall a little bit in love with her.

She is older than I first thought. Her body is petite and angular, a starved tautness to her skin and an untamed wildness behind her eyes. But her chest curves smally, and there are sproutings of downy hair in her private places. I quickly look away, back to her face. I focus on her boundless joy at fullness and the taste of sugar – old and young together, so that trying to guess her age would be impossible. For a moment I wonder how she got like this, how she became such a blank slate, with no language, no way to communicate. I wonder what happened to her to turn her into this.

But that is not what matters. She is lost and alone in this big broken empty world. I can help her. I can teach her language, and I can teach her survival. I can fix her.

Now that I have found her, I cannot let her leave me. Now that I know I am not alone, I do not think I can be alone again. There could be others . . . The thought flashes into my mind and I feel it stick: if there is a girl, this girl, here, so close to where I've made my home, then maybe there could be others.

I watch her trying to suck any last vestiges of tomato juice from the cans – loud desperate slurps that leave her gasping and light-headed. I think of the blackened fields on the edges of towns, the emails from my dying parents, the houses left like living museums by sick or fleeing occupants. I think of the emptiness I have walked through to get here, and I remember how the smell of burning hung around the base for thirty-eight days. *Whoever pays the greatest price gets to survive the longest . . .*

There are no others. There can't be. There is only me, and now her.

'Come with me,' I say again, packing more cans into my backpack. As I leave the shop, I look back at her, smiling. She follows, one small hand still spread across her full belly.

We walk all the way back to the farmhouse. I keep thinking she will stop and refuse to walk further, or will turn back towards the city to be somewhere she knows, but she doesn't. She stays with me, all the way home.

When we reach the farm, one of the chickens is still scratting in the yard. The girl stops to watch it. The chicken pauses, one claw held tentatively above the ground, its head cocked to one side. It lets out a hollow, curious cluck, and the girl shrieks with laughter. The chicken squawks and flaps away back to the barn.

I take the girl into the house. The embers in the kitchen fire are still glowing, so I add kindling and prod the fire into life. The girl sucks in her breath and moves closer.

I point: 'Fire.'

She looks at me, and I point again. 'Fire.'

I say it three more times before she joins in.

'Fire,' she says eventually.

'Yes.'

'Fire,' she says, pointing, and then, 'Mother.'

And when I nod and smile, she grins her enormous face-splitting grin.

*

Night arrives unexpectedly. I have been so focused on the girl – on her watchful eyes, the way the room seems much smaller around her, as though I have forgotten what it is like to exist in a space with another person – that I have not yet closed down for the night the way I usually do. By the time I go out into the yard, the chickens are already roosting in the barn, and all I need to do is shut the door.

The girl stands behind me, skinny in one of my oversized T-shirts, her eyes wide and staring as she takes in the empty yard at night, the still, blue dark of it.

I usher her back into the house. I leave the washing water for tonight.

I lead the girl upstairs. At the top I hesitate, deciding – but I need to keep my own private space somewhere in the house, so I lead her into the smaller bedroom. It is dark in here, and cold after the warmth of the fire, and the girl wraps her arms around herself and eyes me doubtfully. I switch on my torch and the room is filled with a dusty yellow light.

As I take spare sheets from the airing cupboard and make up the bed, the girl pads after me. She watches me stuffing the pillows into their cases, her face blank and unresponsive. As soon as I am done, she climbs in, curling into a ball and tucking the blankets under herself, pulling them up around her neck as though settling herself into a nest. She smiles at me again – that soft smile with nothing held back – and her eyes flutter closed.

In my own bed, I lie awake, letting my eyes adjust to the night the way I used to as a child, trying to spot shapes in the dark and enjoying the way everything becomes unfamiliar, like sounds heard underwater. I think about the girl and her sudden appearance in my life, like a gift from the city, how everything has shifted with her arrival.

In the quiet, there is a creak and the clicking of a latch. I listen. Feet on the stairs – so quiet I almost miss them, as if she is an imagined noise conjured from the silence by listening too hard. Then the door opening at the bottom of the stairs. Quiet.

Perhaps she is running away, sneaking out into the night while she thinks I am asleep, to leave me alone again and always wondering. For a moment I grip the sheets and cannot move. Then the downstairs door clicks shut and I hear those ghost-quiet feet on the stairs. Another pause in which I lie there, breathless, waiting – until my bedroom door is open, and there she is: the shadowy outline of a girl, her eyes faint spots of some unknown reflected light.

'Mother.'

The name takes me by surprise. 'Go back to bed.'

Still the girl stands there, staring.

I get up and half push, half encourage her back into the other room, back into her nest of blankets.

As I leave, she watches, her eyes still those two faint silver reflections.

I shut the doors and clamber back into my own bed, seeking out the scant patch of body-warmth left in the sheets – but almost before I have closed my eyes, the girl is there again, standing and watching from my doorway.

'Go back to your own room.'

She doesn't understand. Of course she doesn't, but I am hopeful that something in my tone might help her see what I want. Instead, she walks over and tries to climb in under the covers beside me.

I push her away. 'Get out.'

She is still for a moment, then tries again, her cold limbs burrowing under the blanket.

I get out of bed and she stops, watching, waiting. I take my pillow and all my covers and pull her back through to the other room.

'This is your bed,' I point, and I can hear the bite in my own voice. 'I'll sleep here. But only for tonight.'

As I arrange my bedding on the floor, the girl finally seems to understand. She gets back into bed and curls up with her face turned towards me.

'Mother,' she says, and her voice is almost not a voice but a breath.

I think of my own nights at home in my bedroom in my parents' house, in the small cocoon of my single bed. I try not to, but they are carried towards me in the silvery reflection of the girl's eyes. I think of my mother's eyes in the dark, and the night I first learned about death and the unavoidable terror of it. Refusing to go to sleep in case I didn't wake up. Pulling the covers closer to my small body, my own protective nest. My mother curved around me on the bed, the duvet a fat barrier between us, her voice washing over me, like a whisper, like a breath.

I had forgotten that, till now.

The floor is hard and cold and the dry smell of dust is everywhere, but I do not care as long as I can sleep. The girl lies awake, watching me.

*

I have decided to call her Monster.

I want her to be a survivor, and so my name will survive with her. It is the talisman I have carried with me, jostling for space with my water bottles and socks and scraps of food, proving its usefulness, keeping me distant and keeping me alive. It will be a talisman for both of us, now. The girl will learn to endure.

I will teach her to work the soil and collect food and equipment from the city. I will teach her how to grow vegetables and care for the chickens. She will feed them and collect the eggs, and sometimes we will leave a few eggs to hatch into chicks. I will teach her language, so that she can understand me and the world.

I do not know how she has survived until now. I do not know how I have survived either, come to think of it. I have just kept going. I have paid the right price. I have continued to live. Now, we will survive together. I will be her Mother, and she will be my Monster.

*

I take Monster back into the city to look for clothes. She walks behind me as I name things for her: wall, road, building, tree. She copies me in her sharp voice. Twice she stops to touch the thing she's just named, laying her hands on it as if naming is a kind of blessing. Then she jogs to catch up.

We go straight for the outdoors shop with the hidden basement. In the stairwell, Monster stays close to me, and when a rat scuttles somewhere in the dark, she jumps.

As I shine the torch over the boxed and packaged stock, I watch her face, expecting the same joyous awe she gave the chickens or the tinned tomatoes. Instead she just looks. A hairline crease appears between her eyebrows.

'Here.' I unearth a T-shirt from a box of children's clothes and hold it up for size.

She takes it and stares at me.

Resting the torch on a stack of boot boxes, I help her into the T-shirt. It hangs loosely from her skinny frame, but, as my mother would have said, there's plenty of room for growth.

Gradually, over the next half hour or so, I manage to dress her. I find her a waterproof, a fleece and a pair of sturdy boots, then I pack some spare clothes into my backpack. When I look back at her, she's hugging her arms in the thick fleecy jumper, smiling down at her new apparel.

We emerge, blinking, into the watery light of the retail park. Monster swings her arms and legs, watching the patterns they make. Along the road out of the city, she skips every few steps, and each time she does this she smiles at me.

We've almost reached the suburbs when we spot them: four

dogs, three smaller ones and an Alsatian, their faces buried in something slumped across the road – a fox, perhaps, or another dog. As we watch, one of the smaller dogs tears a leg from the carcass.

I take another step. The Alsatian looks up and growls, and I fling my arm in front of Monster. All four dogs are growling now, and although three of them are just what my mother would call 'yappy dogs', we're still outnumbered, and we've just seen that their jaws are strong enough to tear flesh. I start to retreat, and that's when Monster moves. Pushing me aside, she runs at the dogs, her arms whirling and a brash wordless yell flailing from her mouth. I shout at her to stop, but she can't hear or doesn't hear or doesn't understand, just runs at the growling dogs whose teeth are bared to attack her – and they scatter, leaving their kill in the middle of the road. They lurk at a few metres' distance, low to the ground, as Monster bends, picks up the torn-off leg and walks calmly back towards me. The dogs slink back to their meal.

By the time she reaches me, Monster is smiling and skipping again. I want to smack her for her stupidity.

'What the hell do you think you were doing?' I don't care that she can't understand – my heart is forcing all the blood to my skin so I'm hot and shaking, and I speak just to get the words out. 'You could have been bitten – you could have been killed!'

Monster simply watches as I try to calm my breathing.

I close my eyes, then open them again. 'Those wolves could have ripped you apart.'

She blinks, looks away from me to the red lump of meat in her hand. She lifts it to her mouth.

'Stop it!' I snatch it away. There's a smear of blood on her lip. 'You can't eat that – it hasn't been cooked.'

Monster frowns, her eyes darting from my face to the bloody animal leg I'm still clutching.

'Don't go near the dogs,' I tell her, 'and don't eat raw meat. It's bad for you.'

We stand in the street staring at one another, and I think of dogs not breaking eye-contact, asserting their superiority over the pack. Then Monster looks back down at the meat I'm holding.

I turn away from the four dogs scrapping over the remains of their meal, and lead Monster out of the city, back towards the farm. Once or twice I look behind to check she's following. Her expression is placid. Flat. She watches her own arms, swinging them again in her vibrant new clothes, and she watches me.

*

I cook the meat in a pan on the stove, with salt rubbed into it. To mark the occasion, I open a jar of beetroot.

Monster eats slowly. I watch her sitting on her cushion by the fire, turning each bite through her mouth, seeking out every last morsel of flavour.

*

Monster is remembering how to speak – or perhaps she is learning from scratch. I cannot find any vestiges of language in her. Not for the first time, I wonder how she managed to reach such an age without it.

So we start with everyday objects: chair, pan, water, chicken, bed, hammer, nails, saw, wood, spade. She follows me around the farm, naming the things she sees like she's cataloguing them. I teach her how to fetch water from the stream and how to plant vegetables in the field, and her vocabulary expands to verbs: pour, boil, dig, sow, work.

She learns quickly, as if she wants to drink in the whole scope of this little farmyard world, as if she could consume it the way she consumed the cans of tomatoes. She is all appetite. She fills her little body with food and words and information till I think it can't hold any more, but somehow it always does.

At first, I try to catch some sign of memory surfacing from the depths of her, but there is nothing. I do not know if she is even aware of her own lost time, though I do not understand how she cannot be. In the evenings, when she sits on the cushion by the fire, she watches the flames as though their movement and this flickering moment are all there is – as though the farm and the city and me are the boundaries of her existence, and always have been.

So I help her fill in all the spaces of this limited world, give her words for everything within it. I need to teach her until I cannot tell where I end and where Monster begins.

What she loves most are the chickens. Frequently they manage to tear her from her task, and she stops to watch their methodical pecking at the cobbles – so occupied in their own little worlds, and yet always ready to be terrified by something outside of them. I teach her the word 'scratting' and she sings it over and over, 'Scratting scratting scratting scratting', gleefully dancing the word around the yard as the chickens tilt towards the safety of the barn.

So I teach her calm and stillness, how to hold quiet inside her the way the chickens carry their eggs. I show her how to collect those eggs and bring them safely into the house for cooking.

Before long, she makes it her role to watch the eggs in the pan, and to shout as soon as the water starts to bubble. In her own limited way, she asks me what it's called.

'Boiling.'

She shakes her head. 'The noise.' Then she tuts her tongue against the back of her teeth to imitate the eggs bumping up against the sides of the pan.

I try to think whether I ever knew a word for this noise. I cannot think why anyone would bother naming it, but I do not know how to explain this to Monster, so I just say, 'Ticking.'

She tuts her tongue a few times on the back of her teeth, then says, 'Tickerting.'

I'm about to correct her, but then I think, what does it matter? There's only the two of us, and Monster doesn't know the difference.

'Right,' I say, 'tickerting.'

Smiling her makeshift smile, she turns and watches the eggs boil.

*

Monster is her own fresh start. She is like a bare patch of earth, ready for me to map her new landscape onto. Perhaps she is also my fresh start.

I take her to fetch water from the stream behind the house. She dips her small hand in, then snatches it back from the cold. Slowly, bracing herself against it, she tries again. She lets her hand go limp, so that the current tugs at it and her fingers waver like water weeds, then she watches, fascinated, moving her hand through the water to see where its pull is strongest.

I wonder what happened to her to transform her into this strange and empty vessel, completely unaware of her own forgetting. I think about all the things that I have seen, and which I still have to remember.

*

The scientists and researchers left Longyearbyen when the Sickness hit, hurrying back to find their loved ones. The locals left because of worry: worry over food shortages, worry over the Sickness, worry that the vault would be attacked. Erik stayed because he believed in the work. I stayed because I had nowhere else to go.

By the time the Last Fall started, there were just the two of us left. Me and Erik: the only two people on the vast Arctic island, and the rest of the world tucked up in the new Safe Centres, hundreds of miles away. At the time I thought that was the loneliest I would ever feel.

During the long northern nights, Erik would show me photos of his home and his wife. Always the same eleven photos, every time. There were nights when I let this wash over me like the lights of the aurora outside. There were nights when I wanted to rip them from his hands and tear them into shreds.

Mostly, we just existed.

When it eventually happens it's early evening, already dark, and we're sitting in the yellow glow of the main control room. Erik's re-reading some old tome about the permafrost; I'm tinkering with the computer system. Since the web crashed, there is only the network used by the Safe Centres and the military, so I've set up our machine to patch into this and store news bulletins for when we're out at the vault or on the Ski-Doos. Erik doesn't understand the need – he's been yawning all evening to remind me – but I like the idea of the machine as a collector, gathering and hoarding information the way I used to gather screws and nails and plugs.

He's just tossed the book aside when they flash up on the screen: two pulsating green lights on a flight trajectory for the town.

'Erik?'

He looks over.

The dots are too small for aircraft, moving too quickly for drones. 'Missiles . . .'

Erik's reply sputters and dies in his throat.

'We have to evacuate.'

'Missiles . . . Did you say – *missiles?*' It's as if his brain has become a slug, squelching through information an inch at a time.

I spin myself away from the monitor, my mind already racing through survival strategies. 'We'll hide in the vault.'

'The vault?'

'Yes, fuck's sake, the vault. Now, Erik – go!'

He jerks up at my shout and then we're both cramming things into bags and stuffing our limbs into all the thermal layers we can find, and I'm shouting about keys and grabbing the stove and all the time those little flashing dots are getting closer on the screen, and we still need to make it out of there and all the way up the hillside to the vault, which suddenly feels so far away.

We hurl ourselves outside with clunking bags of provisions which I later realise were never going to be enough – but for now it's a whirl and a panic as we lurch at the Ski-Doos, and I'm balancing two cans of Calor gas between my knees which is a bad idea, but what choice do I have?

We're flying up the hillside on the Ski-Doos, snow spitting in our faces, and neither of us took time to grab goggles, so Erik breaks out in front and I'm caught in the fierce tail of his driving and it stings, it really fucking stings, but I keep thinking about those two green dots rushing closer, and who knows if they're short-range or nukes or packed with a dispersing sickness or what – and we've both lived through the War, we know the kind of devastation these things can unleash – but we're close now, so close to the vault, which is after all the safest place on the planet, maybe the only safe place, and we can make it. We can so nearly make it.

The vehicles skid to a halt in another flurry of ice and snow and Erik's already at the door fumbling through his jacket for his key. For a second I think he's lost it and this is it, but then the door's open and we're in, a tumble of arms and legs and food and thermals and rolling gas cans. I reach up and slam the door shut and the strip lights flicker out.

For a few seconds we lie in the dark, letting the adrenaline course through us. I can feel Erik's ragged breath burning the back of my hand.

Then the ground rumbles, and rumbles again, and it's time to move.

I stand and slap the wall for the emergency lighting panel. The corridor stutters into view: a hundred metres of corrugated tunnel leading deep into the side of the mountain.

'Now what?' Erik is still on the ground, surrounded by the spilt contents of the bags, a blank look on his face – like he's made it this far and can't see where to go next.

Helplessness has always disgusted me. I turn away, retrieve one of the delivery trolleys, and start loading our things onto it. It looks too small, this collection of supplies.

Erik finally stands, shrugging his skewed jacket back into place. He lifts one of the gas canisters. 'What did you bring these for?'

'Heat.' I take it from him and lay it back in the trolley.

'But,' he falters, 'but – we can't *use* them. We can't have heat in the vault.'

'You want to avoid a missile just to freeze to death?'

'But the *seeds* . . .'

The seeds. Erik and his precious seeds that will one day save the planet.

If I was someone else, a kinder person, I might pity him. I might try to soothe him, tell him in a gentle voice that everything will be all right, that the planet and the natural world will find a way to endure. But I'm not.

'I don't give a fuck about your seeds,' I tell him, 'or your precious Sofia, or her baby. I don't care, Erik – I never fucking have.'

I stand there, breathing hard, waiting for him to throw something back at me, to call me a heartless bitch – god, I even want him to hit me, it would serve me right.

But he doesn't. He just looks at me, one glove hanging pathetically from his hand, his mouth half open as though it might let words fall out.

I turn away. I start to push the trolley down the long, narrow tunnel, into the vault.

Five and a half weeks later, Erik is dead. The days are tallied on the concrete wall of the vault, thirty-eight of them scratched with a bent iron nail in five-bar gates. Thirty-eight days. It turns out that thirty-eight days is how long it takes the last vestiges of the human race to snuff themselves out of existence.

The seeds are all dying or sprouting in the warmed-up vault, a brocade of green that will wither once the Arctic air gets in.

I let the Arctic air in. After thirty-eight days of scraps of food and pissing in a corner, I can't stay underground any longer. The mountain is a vast throat and if I don't let it cough me back up I'll be swallowed.

Erik's body is where I left it, wedged in a delivery trolley by the door, now the coldest part of the vault. His left hand

137

juts out into the corridor, frozen blue, his fingers curled in an upwards-pointing death grip, like tree roots waiting to trip me or grab hold. For a long time I don't think I can pass it.

I break through the snowdrift into the Arctic glare.

The world looks the same, just as vast, just as icebound. Greyer. A thin layer of ash filmed across the snow.

Then I see that half of the distant town is blackened and burned, and the ground around the buildings is snow-free and charred.

The air tingles. For a second I think it might be radioactive, every molecule I breathe poisoning and mutating my cells, but I don't think it can be – and even if it is I don't care. I would rather be out here dying slowly than back in there with that curling hand pulling me out of my mind.

I Ski-Doo back to base. Most of the living quarters have been reduced to rubble, but the control centre is mercifully still standing. The missiles definitely weren't nuclear, then. That much is good to know.

I left my key pass inside, but I know the intimate mechanisms of these doors and it only takes a few minutes to work them open.

I search the systems for the latest downloaded news – nothing for thirty-seven days. The final reports show what is left of humanity clustered in the so-called Safe Centres in a few tight pockets of the globe, clamouring for access to drugs to combat the unstoppable Sickness, hurling blame at each other for its outbreak. A desperate struggle for resources, then the resurgence of the War, one Last Fall, and the final silence.

This is where my story starts. Me, sitting by a window on an island locked in ice, the only human left.

I say my story starts here because endings are always a kind of beginning. I say it also because before I was alone there was no story, because I was not interesting enough to have one. Things happened. I worked, I bought food, I fixed objects that were broken. I was just like everybody else.

Now, there is only me and Monster, and Monster is a part of my tale. Now, the whole world is my story.

*

The seasons close down around us. During the days, we explore the city. I teach Monster the safety of open spaces. I teach her to be afraid of the dogs. I show her how to distinguish the looted buildings from the ones that might yield supplies, how to make a mental map of our route so she can always navigate her way back to the farm. In the evenings, I teach her how to stoke the fire, how to use book pages to make the embers catch and avoid wasting precious matches. We sit in the kitchen, me in the easy chair, her on a cushion by the hearth, and I teach her new words. However many words I give her, there is always room in her for more. The winter is deep and dark and empty, so we fill it with an endless supply of language and learning.

*

We build ourselves a new pattern, a routine that ebbs and flows with the contracting and lengthening of the days. As winter gives way to spring, we take less and less from the city. We plant and reap and preserve. Gradually, like stocking a larder, I help her to understand the small sphere of her existence, and she grows quick and wiry under my care.

*

I teach Monster about possession. 'Something is either mine,' I tell her, pointing to myself, 'or it's yours.'

We're walking past the big houses on the edge of the city, the houses that belong to no one. Monster swings off one of the gates. 'And what is mine?'

'This.' I touch her skinny forearm. 'This is yours. It belongs to you.'

She looks pityingly at me, as though I am the one struggling with the mechanism of language. 'The arm doesn't belong to me. It is me. Look,' she says, waving her arm.

Later she points to a skyscraper, magnificent against the vacant sky: 'Is that mine?'

'No.'

'Then it's yours?'

'No,' I explain. 'It doesn't belong to anybody.'

She's quiet for a long time after that, kicking rubble along the pavement, head bowed as if this broken stretch of concrete could occupy the rest of her life. Much later, when I think she's forgotten all about it, she asks, 'If it isn't yours, why isn't it mine?' And I don't know how to answer.

*

Sometimes, I think about how people died. Not just any people, but the people I knew, people who were trapped on the fringes of my life like refugees.

Here is what I think happened to Harry Symmonds:

After school, he went to university to become what he'd always dreamed of becoming, a scientist of sorts. He studied engines and planes, how to make them fly faster, quieter, less detectable. Once free from the confines of the village where he grew up, once apart from the children who had ridiculed him, he found himself liked. *Befriended.*

He was quiet and stoic, a good listener. Smart, often top in the class. He was liked by his tutors.

Gradually, he attracted the attentions of girls, who assumed that behind his silence and thick-rimmed, newly fashionable glasses there lay mystery and intrigue. Flattered, and having no precedent to fall back on, he started to date the first girl who suggested it to him, leaving the others to retreat into their short-lived jealousy.

When the War came, Harry Symmonds was posted to an airbase, where he could best use his extensive knowledge of aeronautics. The girl, unwilling to question what she no doubt saw as his bravery and patriotic duty, put up no objections, and they relocated to the military.

For a few years, he was a quiet war hero. He built and engineered aircraft that would be fit to fight the good fight, because in those early years, people still pretended that the side they fought on was good. When praised he would smile a small smile to himself and look sideways at the floor. When something went wrong – an aircraft failed or was hacked or a fleet was shot down – he would take off his glasses, polish them on the bottom of his shirt, then place them back over his tired eyes and start working again.

Harry Symmonds died in the War. That is what I think.

I think that he was too compliant, and that I taught him that – too afraid of minor conflict to avoid the bigger War. I think he died when a bomb fell on the military base where he lived with the first girl to ever ask him out, and that was that. He died quickly, not from chlorine gas or a dispersing sickness, but a normal explosive. The kind that hit the ground and burst it apart, and Harry Symmonds along with it. I think Harry Symmonds was lucky this way, in his quick death, surrounded by his beloved planes.

*

And sometimes I think about the bodies, slumped behind the wheels of rusting cars or tucked into beds. I try not to, but they lurk just below the surface, waiting for my mind to drop its guard.

Sometimes in these moments, I think about my own death, and all the times it brushed against me then turned away. I look across at Monster when we're eating or shelling peas or chopping potatoes, and the thought of our death passes like a shadow across the room. Will it come rushing in a dark part of the city, or will it creep up on us like a mist? I think about our death and wonder, will I recognise it when it comes?

*

I decide that Monster needs to become more civilised. I start to be stricter about the daily rituals of washing, of cleaning her teeth, of using a knife and fork. When she objects to my washing her hair, I slap her leg and upend the jug of water over her. When she tries to dig straight into her meal with her hands, I take away the food until she complies. Sometimes, I think I see something flicker just behind her eyes, like some hidden part of her that wants to battle my attempts to tame her. But when I look again, it's always gone.

She starts to learn, till she accepts these things, as if she's forgotten a time before they were ever a part of her life. Over the months, I see the animal in her drop away, until we're out in the field on the first truly hot day of the year. We're working barefoot to save our shoes, constructing pyramids from willow twists so we can grow beans, and we have to keep stopping to wipe our brows. I watch Monster reach up to tie the top, and there's such intelligence and practical judgement in her face that I realise I've finally managed to chase out all the feral parts of her. What I'm left with is a gangly human child.

I cut the end of the twine with a knife. 'Thank you.'

She turns to pick up another willow twist. 'You're welcome, Mother.'

*

The farm becomes an island in a drowned world. The pattern of survival is everything.

We wake early. I rekindle the fire from the night before, while Monster goes to the stream and coaxes the chickens from their eggs. I heat oats and water on the stove, and after breakfast we walk into the city to see what we can salvage, or we stay and work on the farm. We plant seeds in trays taken from the garden centre, or we dig the plugs and seed potatoes into the field. We hoe out the weeds and pick off any slugs or caterpillars that have managed to get too close. When the time is right, we reap our crops. We dry and salt and pickle whatever we can. In the evenings, we take stock of our supplies and scratch together a meal. I teach Monster how to make and mend and sew, or we sit quietly, each engrossed in our separate chores. After I have tucked Monster into bed in the small back room, I sit by the fire and do nothing. Surviving is an endless task, but in these moments, I let the last dregs of the day settle into place around me, and the effort seems worth almost everything.

*

I'm pegging washing in the yard when there's a cry from the outhouse – a noise of terror and despair, the kind that exists beyond language, the kind born from the deeper parts of the brain.

Monster.

I drop the bed sheets and run to her, flinging back the door.

The girl sits half-naked, pale legs stark in the gloom, horror etched across her face. She looks at me as if I'm her last hope for salvation.

'Mother . . .' she whispers, and the word comes from that same deep, fearful, instinctive place. 'Help me.'

She looks down at her knickers. Cradled in the gusset is a dark gash of blood.

I stare at it for a long time. This mark of adulthood. The curse. As if womanness, the moon, the whole universe has chosen to back her over me. As if it has chosen her as the future, and I am just a remnant of the past.

'Mother?' Monster's small voice makes me look back to her face. 'Am I going to die?'

Yes, I want to say, yes, you're going to die, and there's nothing I can do to stop it.

I crouch to her level. 'No,' I tell her, 'it's natural to bleed.'

'But why?'

'It means you've become a woman. Here,' I pull an old handkerchief from my apron and fashion it into a makeshift pad, 'put this in your knickers to soak up the blood. We'll find you some proper pads in the city.'

I stay with her as she cleans herself up and gets dressed again.

148

She asks, 'Do you bleed?'

'Tuck your shirt in.'

'But do you?'

'Tuck your shirt in so you don't catch cold.'

I try to focus on her little fingers pushing the fabric into the waistband of her trousers, but her fingers aren't so little any more. Her hands are nearly as ungainly as my own. When did I let her grow so much, and how did I miss it happening?

And again I want to snap at her, this curious child, all big eyes and innocence, this not-quite-child-any-more. I take a deep breath. 'Get dressed and you can finish hanging out the bedding.'

'OK, Mother,' she nods, and she gives me her special crooked smile.

That night, when Monster is in bed and there is only me and the kitchen fire, I think about solitude. I sink into the dusty cushions of the easy chair and feel the upholstery give under my weight. The chair folds its arms around me and the firelight folds its arms around the chair and the room folds its arms around the light. Outside there is only wilderness and dark. It stretches away from me like the roots of an insidious plant, sucking in the warmth till the only comfort is here, in this tiny room, in this easy chair. This is what I mean by solitude. This is what I mean by beautiful: me, and the whole world howling around me. Exactly where you would expect to find a Monster.

Sometimes I wonder if, in giving Monster my name, I have given away something else. I rub my thumb across my knuckles, trying to gauge whether my body always felt this loose. The skin there is still rough. My thumb is still calloused. If I have softened at all, it is not in my hands.

I close my eyes and try to picture myself before Monster. I

reach for the muscle memory of walking, of hauling myself across a relentless landscape. I try to remember where it sits in my feet, how it spreads across the joints. But I cannot bring back the feeling.

Perhaps this is it. Perhaps after so many months working the farm, I have finally settled, like the dust, into this easy chair by the kitchen fire.

I drag myself up and start to pace the kitchen. As soon as I am on my feet the old motion returns, that circular rhythm of stepping out, of always moving on. It rekindles like the last embers of a dying fire, tentatively at first, then louder and fiercer until I'm blazing and my body is desperate with the idea of a journey. I pace quicker, breathe sharper. I could leave now, set out while Monster is still sleeping. I could stir myself up, become that woman again. I could set out to conquer the world, if conquering only means arrival. My fingers twitch towards the door handle.

I stop myself. Decisions made at night are tricksters, elusive and fickle, slippery as fish. I force myself to sit, to let the firelit room cradle me in its solitude, and I push all thoughts of wandering to the back of my mind. I hold them in the depths of my brain and count my breaths. I feel how the rhythm of walking fills my muscles, and I let it sit there. I wonder if simply knowing is enough.

As the fire diminishes, I watch it flicker then smoulder. I count my breaths.

I remember once at school – I was maybe fourteen – coming back to my locker at breaktime and seeing it open. They were only cheap locks; you could pick them open with an uncurled paper clip. It was easy if you wiggled it the right way and listened for the click. It was me who taught the others how to do it.

I came back from a history lesson and found my locker open, my pens and textbooks scattered across the floor. My classmates stood about in small clusters, watching me without looking, the way you might guard against a dangerous animal. That was how I thought of myself in those days.

Nobody was taking credit for the vandalism. I bent to pick up my protractor, and someone pushed into me hard so I fell, splayed on the shiny blue floor that smelled of dirty mop heads.

There was a chorus of laughter and I scrambled to get up.

I was hot. My face was red. I could feel it glowing and prickling.

One of the Harper brothers threw my dictionary at me. I caught it square in my chest, a hard thud of knowledge, and I staggered back into a group of girls. Kelly Armstrong. Dawn Simpson. Natalie Rayner.

Naomi Dodds.

They grabbed my arms and shoulders. One of them had a hand on my back. I could feel the gleeful mockery in the pushing and probing of their fingers.

'Ooh,' Natalie Rayner crooned, 'bet she's loving this.'

Dawn Simpson: 'She'll be frothing in her knickers.'

Natalie Rayner again: 'Bet she stinks of fish.'

Another high shout of laughter as I struggled to get away.

'What's the matter?' asked Naomi Dodds, beige-plastered face up against mine. 'Don't you want me any more?'

She pushed and I was away from her – trapped in the ring of onlookers, but at least I was away, away—

'Changed your mind, have you?' asked Naomi Dodds, her eyes hard. 'Dyke?'

'I'm not—' I stammered, my words caught in my mouth like buzzing flies. 'I don't—'

'Dyke,' she said again. She said it softly, with a little laugh, a perfectly orchestrated toss of her hair to hide the steel in

151

her eyes. 'Dyke,' like it was a throwaway comment, meant to be heard once and then forgotten – but it was a word that built and rose, passed like an electric current around the watching circle until it became a chant, a war dance: dyke, dyke, dyke, dyke, dyke, dyke. And Naomi Dodds in the middle of it, a satisfied glint in her eye, enshrining her own inculpability.

They're dead now. All of them. The Harper brothers. Naomi Dodds. Kelly Armstrong. Natalie Rayner. Dawn Simpson. Some quickly, hit by bombs or killed in the fighting. Most of them probably caught the Sickness or died in the starvation that followed it. One or two may have made it as far as the Last Fall. There will never be a way of knowing for certain.

I hope Naomi Dodds died of the Sickness. I hope she caught one of the early strains, the kind that burgeoned slowly, that let her live in false hope of a cure while she hacked and coughed and grew crooked like an old woman. I hope it hurt her, that Sickness. And when, close to the end, she vomited up her insides, I hope they came out white and gelatinous, like undercooked eggs, and I hope she saw that this was all that she had inside her, and I hope in her dying moments that she hated herself for it.

*

Monster is gone.

*

I go to wake her one morning and her bed is empty and her shoes and backpack are missing from beside the door.

I dash out of the house, my boots only half on my feet. 'Monster! Monster!'

Her name echoes back at me from the barn wall.

'Monster!'

I venture out along the lane, but she's nowhere in sight. I scan the horizon, hoping to see her small silhouette. I check the field and the stream. I open the barn door, hoping to find her huddled with her beloved chickens, but their eyes just glint shrewdly out of the gloom.

For a while I can only stand in the yard, staring at nothing, until the cold creeps inside my jacket and I can't deny it any longer.

Monster is gone.

Monster has left me.

I go back inside to see to the fire. I tell myself it doesn't matter, I was alone before, I can be alone again. As I prepare the porridge, I try to wrap myself in my aloneness as if it's a fine fur and I can revel in it. Refuge – isn't that the word? A breaking apart from the noise of other people? Monster disappearing has given me back my refuge, the refuge I felt on that first morning at the farm, when I stood in the doorway and watched the sun coming up over everything that was now mine.

Monster can stay away or Monster can return. It doesn't matter either way. I say it in my head, and then again out loud: 'It doesn't matter either way.' What's important is the farm, this refuge of stone and soil and stability which I must tend and nurture. Monster no longer matters. She does not matter.

I scoop my half of the porridge into my bowl and decide not to think about her.

Still, all day I listen to small noises.

I start to build the chicken shed I've been planning, to free up the barn for storing food in the winter – although since the War, and especially since the Last Fall, the seasons have been unreliable, bleeding into one another like an abstract painting.

I measure and saw the planks we collected from the building yard at the edge of the city, and which Monster and I wheeled back along the lane on an industrial trolley. As I take each one down from the pile, I remember Monster's frown, the serious concentration on her face as she struggled to make the trolley steer straight, how I wanted to laugh because it seemed so ridiculous that even here, at the end of everything, we got the trolley with the wonky wheel.

In the quiet spaces between saw-strokes, I hear footsteps, the cries of a small voice. Every time this happens, I turn to look, and every time the yard is empty. Only the chickens, pecking between the cobbles. Once, the sound of boots scuffing along tarmac makes me run to the edge of the yard and squint down the lane, but Monster isn't there.

Darkness comes. I bank up the fire and go to bed. For hours I lie awake, listening to the faint gurgle of the stream, the rustle and call of night creatures.

When I sleep, I sleep in fits and starts.

*

The rule of three lurks at the back of my mind as if it could pull me under. Three months without company. During the day, I tell myself that I lasted for three months and more before I discovered Monster. I can do it again. I'm a survivor, I was made for being alone.

But at night, when the work is done and there is only the fire to talk to, I think too much about her. Sometimes I think I see her in the flames, her sharp face and bony limbs like kindling. I see her diminutive body curled up at the edge of a road, or broken from a fall, or caught by wild dogs, or drowned.

It isn't until the fourth night that I realise I've started to think of Monster as dead. The thought has crept up on me slowly, like a tide cutting me off from the shore – until suddenly I look around and realise the land is gone, and I am being pulled out by the current.

I lie in bed shivering. I take the extra blankets from Monster's room, which smell of her, and I pile them on top of me. But still I can't stop shivering.

I shake. At one point in the early hours, I half think that with all this shaking, I ought to be rattling, and I wonder why I can't hear anything, until I realise there's nothing inside me to make a noise. So I just shiver – except I must sleep at some point because I dream. They are narrow dreams, deep as wells. I fall into them and batter against the sides until they spill me back out into more shivering and a wakeful dark.

*

I dream of London at rush hour.

I'm standing outside a station in winter, in the sparsity of leafless trees, bundled in the kind of stylish wrap-around coat I have never owned. It's still not properly light, the way December can go for days and still the grey edge of darkness will never leave the sky.

Suited commuters stream across the square from the station, a dark river breaking onto the pavement. I try to walk over, to join them in their ceaseless flow, but I can't get through – there are iron railings, and my coat gets caught on gateposts and branches and in the chains of a parked bike. The harder I struggle, the further I am from the river of commuters, and the faster the river flows, until they're gone, trickled away into coffee shops and offices.

I'm alone in the not-quite light. The silence that fills the square is deafening. It rebounds off the tower blocks and through my head, and I'm screaming and screaming till I'm awake.

I wake and for a moment the big room in the farmhouse is Euston Square, with a grey morning leaking in and an awful deafening silence. Then a bird starts to twitter in the creeper outside my window, and there is the scratchy feel of woollen blankets and the smell of Monster, and I remember.

*

I get up before it's properly light, before the dreams can pull me under again, and I make my way downstairs. Through the kitchen doors I can see the flicker of warm light where the fire must have reignited in the night, as if it could be aware of the turmoil in my dreams and has lit itself up in sympathy, although I know this thought is probably the madness taking root.

I open the door. Squatting in front of the fire is Monster.

I have to grip the handle to steady myself. I force myself to take two deep breaths, and the words blunder out of me like a train: 'Where were you?'

Monster turns to look at me. The toes of her socks are wet and there's dirt all up her right side as though she's been lying in it. Her hair is a tangle of knots and bits of leaf.

'I went for a walk.' Her voice is hoarse from nights spent out in the cold.

'A walk?' A *fucking walk?*

Something passes across her face, but she shrugs to cover it. 'I wanted to see a mountain,' she says, and the way she says mountain makes it sound like something holy, as if her walk was a pilgrimage. 'Properly. Up close.'

'A mountain!' Before I know it I'm rushing at her, because this girl, this little bird-like sack of skin and bone, this is the reason I've barely slept, why I've spent the past days teetering on the edge of madness, and I want to throttle her or crush her or crack her head against the metal stove – but then I think of Erik and the way he talked, with that same reverence, so I don't. Instead I grab her and hold her to me, fold my arms around her angular body so tight she wriggles, but still I hold on.

I hold her like that for a long time, until the fire starts to dim and Monster breaks away to add another log.

I adjust my jumper and take my place in the armchair. 'Never do that again.'

And Monster hesitates as she looks at me, but she says 'OK', and I force myself to forget about it.

We cannot leave each other, Monster and me. We are one unit now, like bonded atoms, each incomplete without the other.

We have our rhythm and our roles, a rhythm of planting and growth and harvest, a rhythm of cooking and eating and washing, of waking and sleeping. Our world runs on rhythm, the way the whole world must have done before clocks and factories and twenty-four-hour opening, before the flurry and frenzy of the digital age and globalisation and flights across the dateline. Before the War and the Sickness blasted the last remnants of our rhythm away.

The world feels at home in its rhythm, as though it's glad to get back to it: everything measured, from the rapid beat of a vole's minuscule heart to the orbital path of the Earth.

We wake, we work the ground, we collect what we can from the city, we eat, we talk, I teach Monster a little, we wash, we go to bed. This is how we make it through the days, existing in time with one another like the two hands on a clock face. Part us and the rhythm would break. I could not go back to how I was before she came, not now I have eaten and worked and lived beside her, not since we became part of one another's rhythm. There are some things you can never go back from.

*

We find ourselves outside a shop. One of those glass-fronted places that existed on high streets across the country, with gaudy posters in its windows to lure in passers-by. Except that the entire front of this shop has been shattered. A steel girder hangs from the broken upper floor, and strands of coloured wiring reach into the space below like tentacles. Glass fragments carpet the inside of the shop, glinting.

Shattering is good. Shattered glass means bombs, whereas bigger shards would mean looting and nothing left inside worth stealing.

'Is it safe?' asks Monster, her eyes on the tilting steel girder.

'Yes,' I tell her. The back of my neck prickles, but I ignore it. 'It's safe.'

We step over the threshold.

Inside the shop is bare, stripped of most of its stock. Only the magazine stands are still full, their once-glossy covers sun-bleached and curling with damp.

'Look around,' I tell Monster. 'I'll check the back.'

Monster pulls her pack up onto her shoulders like a bearing of responsibility. She starts scouring the remains of the shop floor.

I cannot shake the feeling of being watched. Even though I know there cannot be any other people out there, still there are always wild dogs and rats and the feeling of something lurking. I smash the CCTV camera with my iron bar, and the noise of shattering glass is loud in the empty room. Still the feeling does not go away. I did not really expect it to. I catch sight of one of the magazine covers, a young man with gelled-up hair and a daytime-television smile, and eyes the same brilliant blue as Erik's.

At the back of the shop is a pair of dusty swing doors padlocked with a chain. It takes me a minute or two to dismantle it.

There is another reason I always take the back rooms of shops and let Monster search the fronts; the danger is only secondary. What comes first is the intimate satisfaction of a locked door, the beauty of picking it. There are some things that I need to be alone for, even now – to savour the achievement, this opening up of space, without the presence of another person.

During the early nineteenth century, there existed such things as unbreakable locks, unyielding to hair pins and pick guns and torsion wrenches and all the other tools of the trade. They were the complex constructions of Joseph Bramah and Jeremiah Chubb, advertised as unbeatable, perfect security, gauntlets thrown down to the thieves and lock-pickers of the world.

Plenty took up the challenge, from respectable gentlemen right down to convicted criminals – but the only man to succeed was neither thief nor safe-cracker. He was A.C. Hobbs, an American locksmith, creator of secure locks of his own. Hobbs was not the enemy. He was the competition.

I always liked this story, the puffed-up pride of the two English lock-makers, resting on their laurels for thirty years with their so-called unbeatable locks, only to be beaten by one of their own. Which was inevitable, of course. To understand a thing on such an intimate level, you have to experience that act of creation for yourself. To break a lock, you have to know how it is brought into being.

The back room of the shop is grey and smells of damp. Even the carpet has been removed. There is only a thick layer of plaster dust on the bare floor, and two dead mice in a nest.

On the off-chance, I take a closer look. Sometimes animals squirrel things away.

Nothing.

I turn back towards the door and it's there again, that awareness of space at my back, the feeling of something coming through it. Inexplicably, I think of Monster, how she came back to me across the void. Monster went out into the world and found it wanting, and so she returned to me.

'Monster?'

No reply.

I retreat to the main shop. Monster is not there. For the briefest of moments I am tumbling, driven down by my own weight. My voice comes half-strangled. 'Monster!'

'Mother?' She emerges from behind a shelving unit, face glowing and eyes shining, and I have to stop myself from grabbing her.

I swallow my deep breaths. 'There you are.'

'Did you find anything?'

Still breathing hard, I shake my head. I am about to suggest we move on to the next shop when I notice Monster has something – a slip of paper – clutched in her left hand.

I nod towards it. 'What did you find?'

Her hand twitches, as though she might hide her discovery. Then a smile starts to creep across her face, up her cheeks and into her eyes, till she's biting her lip to stop all her excitement spilling out. With a trembling hand, she offers me what she's found.

It is a scrap from a magazine, glossy, the kind of paper that always made me think of wasted time. I take it from her, turn it over so I can see the picture on the other side. A naked woman. A splay-legged, fake-breasted, orange-tanned woman, seductively eyeing the camera. A hardness in the woman's eyes.

'Isn't she beautiful?' says Monster, her puppy-dog eyes

desperate for my reaction. 'Look at her, Mother – don't you think she's beautiful?'

I look at her. I look at them both, the fake woman touching herself, the eager girl before me. 'No, I think it's disgusting.'

Monster's face collapses. 'But—'

'It's filth,' I tell her, and I screw up the picture in my fist.

Monster lets off an untamed cry, like she has momentarily forgotten about words. For a second I think she might try to grab the picture from between my clenched fingers – I see the unfolding battle in her eyes, the fight between obedience and desire. I force all my will-power towards her as if it could scoop her up and reel her back in and that way I could keep her close.

Then her eyes harden. She sets her shoulders and says, 'Sorry.'

I watch her for any signs of wavering, but her face is blank. 'OK,' I say, and throw the scrumpled picture into a pile of broken glass. 'Now let's go.'

I turn away and leave the shop, and after a couple of stubborn seconds I hear Monster begin to follow. I remember the farm dogs outside my parents' house a lifetime ago, and force myself to walk without looking back. Monster is with me. Monster is still here. Monster has not left.

I lead her away from the blown-out shop, back towards parts of the city we already know. Here, with no new discoveries to make, there is nothing to tear Monster away. I hear her pattering behind me.

The wind picks up. Dead leaves and old papers whirl across the road. They whip at our ankles. To the south of the city, storm clouds are banking. We will be quick with our collections today.

The urge for haste follows us home, like the rain, which breaks only seconds after we make it back through the farmhouse door.

All through dinner I can barely keep my mind from leaking away. My face feels heavy and hot, my head dropping onto my chest. My skin itches. There's something like a shadow shifting at the back of my eyes. I've felt sharp and jumpy all day, but when Monster says she wants an early night, I barely hear her. She has to say it again, and even then I'm sluggish to rise.

I heat the washing water on the fire and carry it up the stairs for her, Monster climbing in front of me with the torch. I stay while she gets ready.

Once she's in bed, I tuck the blankets around her shoulders and under her chin, so she's bundled and warm for the night. I move on autopilot. Through the fog in my brain, I notice the length of her under the covers, how much she's grown from the feral stick-child I found in the shop.

I kiss the top of her head. 'Night, Monster.'

'Night, Mother.'

Her eyes are closed before I shut the door, and I'm back to that old feeling of being alone in the house, a one-woman world, like I'm rattling.

I can feel that shadow trailing me. All the way down the stairs I can feel it at the nape of my neck. I dash down the last few steps. When I reach the kitchen, I slam the door and press myself against it, breathing hard. The little kitchen flickers warmly back at me.

Stupid. I sit back in my armchair by the fire. My fingers are fidgety; they won't settle to anything. I try forcing them to sew, or to fix up the broken trowel handle, but then my hands go limp and the fidget shifts to my eyes, flitting between the doors.

I go through to the storage room. I take out my shoe box full of bits and pieces and bring it back to the kitchen fire.

This is what I have always done in moments like this. When my hands twitch and flutter like insects, when my body raises questions I don't know how to answer, it is always my collection that saves me.

For the first time since I left home, I pull away the tired elastic band. It snaps. The battered cardboard lid falls away, and I am back in my teenage bedroom, feeling angular and out of place, re-enacting my own confinement. It is as though all the days I have channelled into these assorted objects are stacked inside the box alongside them.

I lay out the pieces one by one, in neat rows segregated by purpose, type and condition. Correctly wired plugs kept apart from the ones without fuses. Circuit boards distinct from defunct batteries. Separate categories for chisels and tapers and reels of wire. Their little shadows dance in the firelight. When I pass my hands across them, I soak up their shapes through my fingertips.

I lean against the legs of the easy chair and close my eyes. This is how objects are understood: through touch. Colour and the way an object looks in the light, these come later, like the paint used to decorate a tired house. To understand how an object is made, you have to put these things aside. To understand the truth of it, you have to look at it with your eyes closed.

I let my fingers wander. I explore the shapes and textures of my collection. I learn the precise mechanics of their bodies.

I think of a cloud bank tracing the tops of trees, the way it is both separate to the forest and a part of it. I imagine my hand is a rolling cloud bank, and I'm pushing my fingers through the branches. I am separate from these objects and yet a part of them. I think of myself brushing through soft pine needles to learn about the spaces in between. If I look down, there's a darkening corridor and a brown carpet running the length of the forest floor.

And I'm falling, falling out of the cloud bank and down

through the tangle of trees, down towards that brown-carpeted corridor . . .

I'm in the tunnel now.

I'm running down the tunnel in the Seed Vault.

My footsteps spark and resound off the concrete, off all the corrugated metal, and it's smaller than I remember, tighter, like a ridged trachea squeezing me down into a lung without enough air.

And now I'm in the vault, packed into the cubby-hole I built from plastic boxes to keep out the worst of the cold, and there's only the dim glow of the emergency exit sign, and opposite me, Erik.

Both of us standing, now, in the metal and concrete vault room, me and Erik, drawn and gaunt in the half-light. My whole body's fluttering and burning, though the first time this happened – when it really happened – I was cold. I was so cold my feet felt like iron bars and then they felt like nothing at all.

Which is why we're standing, Erik and me, standing and stamping the blood back into our frozen feet.

And Erik stops.

And me – the me in the dream, the me who knows where this is leading, what happens next – that me wants to scream at him to keep going, to keep moving, to bully him back into action. But I don't – I can't control him. I'm trapped in the dream me, and there's nothing the dream me can do or say to change what happens next.

He stops. His arms flop to his sides and his face collapses. His eyes are streaming and he looks at me again. He whispers, 'Is she dead?'

In the crucible of the vault it sounds like a hurricane.

'Sofia and the baby – are they dead?'

And I tell him yes and I keep stamping.

He's crying now and I want him to stop, I need him to stop – me then and me now, the real me and the dream me, we both need him to stop, because what is the fucking point?

'They're gone,' he sobs. 'They're gone they're gone they're gone they're gone—'

And just as he did the first time, he reaches out to touch me. He lifts a metal-cold arm to touch me because he's grieving and isn't that what grieving people do, and apart from our collapse into the tunnel while fleeing the missiles he hasn't touched another person in months, and because he isn't a survivor he needs that reminder of what it is to be human.

And because he's broken and can't be fixed and I hate him, I spit at his face, 'Get off!'

But because he's driven by need and can't help himself, he puts his raw hand on my cheek.

His skin is clammy and plastic and I pull back. And because his hand is the hand of my father who died alone within days of my mother, and because for a second he's snivelling Harry Symmonds, and because weakness disgusts me, I shove him away.

In the dream version, he crumples the moment my hands push into his body.

He doesn't fall, too unsteady with grief even to hold his own weight upright. He doesn't stumble back into the concrete wall of the vault and hit his head and let it crack the life from him. He doesn't leak blood across the floor like a split carton. His eyes don't turn to stone.

In the dream version, none of that needs to happen. In the dream, he's gone the second I touch him.

I wake and I'm hot.

For a second Erik is there, sprawled on the scrubbed laminate floor, those blank eyes – then I blink and he's gone.

But the shadow's still here – the shadow that's been with me all day, circling the front of my brain. My legs itch in the heat of the kitchen fire. There's a spasm in my thigh and a feeling of depth in my stomach. My body is tensed like wire, like I could twang and set the whole world shaking. The air tastes thin and metallic.

I think of Monster, how she is a thing unto herself and yet all mine, how she has become a part of me like a daughter and so her touch does not repulse me, how I have teased out and discarded all the feral parts of her – how even when they surface, like today with that filthy magazine, I can turn her away from them. I try to think of her as an extension of me, like an extra limb, a calm part of my body. And I try to picture that calmness flowing from her back into me.

I think of Monster like this and I become a little less storm-tossed.

I breathe in. I breathe out.

I hold my body less stiffly.

I sit like this for a few moments, trying to keep my mind from falling apart. I imagine what would happen if I let it. I imagine all its miniature cogs and springs spilling across the laminate floor.

I breathe in.

I breathe out.

In the quiet, there's a small, held-back moan from the room above, as if Monster is having a nightmare. It bumps up against my stillness and sets all the taut parts of me quivering again.

Another moan. *Dear god, Monster, stop. Dear god, leave my precious peace alone.*

But Monster is the rock I have anchored my little boat to. Where she goes, I go, and anyway, we all want to be woken from our nightmares.

The shadow hurries with me back up the stairs, and I'm

breathing fast and my legs are itching again. I slam back the door – and it's Erik, contorted and broken on the bed—

And then it's Monster – my Monster, disobedient, naked and sprawling, that picture stuck to her thigh. My Monster, my refuge. My words are all jangle and fury and my hand is a wild bird smacking her face.

And I'm out of the room with the picture in my hand and I'm down the stairs and stuffing it onto the kitchen fire and the flames take it and it's gone – and I do all this quickly so I can't think about Monster's face, hiding herself from me in the dark, about her desire, how I smacked her and I saw her face redden and how the ribbon that ran between us snapped.

My knees give way and I rock backwards and forwards by the fire as the world contracts around me.

PART TWO

MONSTER

'You taught me language, and my profit on't
Is, I know how to curse.'

The Tempest, William Shakespeare

My name is Monster.

I am small and bony like a blackbird. My feet turn in when I walk and there is nearly always dust in my knuckles. My hair is thick and dark. When I sweat it sticks down the back of my neck and I can feel it clinging there.

Mother says I am like water.

You can't grab hold of water. It has nothing to grip onto. It goes where it wants to, like a thought, except that thoughts can run uphill and water can't.

There's nothing true about water. It fills the shape of whatever bowl or cup or tin you put it in. I think what Mother means when she says that I am like water is that I am good at filling the shape I am supposed to fill. What I mean is, Mother cups her hands and I lay myself in them and she thinks that is the shape I am. And I do try to be that shape, the way Mother wants me to be. I try, but I am not very good at it.

Mother thinks all my words belong to her. I know this, because when she tells me a word, she does it like she's giving me something precious and new. But sometimes the words she gives me are more like things that used to be mine already, so really all Mother is doing is giving them back.

She thinks I don't remember any people but her, either. She thinks I get confused by the pictures of people we find in the City, but I know they are pictures of people who are now all dead. I know that the woman in the shiny picture is also dead, that she died when all the other people died. And I know that now there is only me and Mother.

But I know that there were other people before. I've seen them in the buildings where the wolf-dogs haven't got at them. And I remember a woman.

I don't know who she is. She's not Mother, so she must be one of the dead people, but I know that she was more than just a dead person. I remember holding her hand, and how her hand felt warm and happy in mine. And I remember that she was beautiful. Not beautiful like the shiny woman in the picture, but soft like a petal, with big eyes and a small pink smile.

Mother is not beautiful, not like the shiny woman or like the soft woman. Mother is sharp and spiky like me. We are two not-beautiful people trying to keep ourselves alive in a tumbledown farmhouse on the edge of the City. But maybe that is beautiful as well.

The soft woman did not try to keep herself alive. She wasn't hard and certain like Mother.

I only remember her once. I mean, I only remember one moment of her.

It was on the edge of a city. Not the City where I go now with Mother to find things we can't get at our farmhouse. A different city. It was next to a river, and the river had a bridge over it. The bridge was high above the river, so that when you stood on the bridge it was always windy, and the river looked hard and small at the bottom.

I remember standing on that bridge with the soft woman. I must have been very small because I had to look almost straight up to see into her face.

She sat me on the railing so that my feet hung over the space, and held onto me so that I wouldn't fall. Her hand on my back was warm and strong, but it was also shaking. I remember not liking that her hand was shaking. And I remember when I looked down I could see my feet with round blue shoes on, and below them this little fierce grey river.

The soft woman climbed up to sit next to me on the edge of the railing, and she held my hand. Both of us looked down at our feet dangling above the river.

Then she looked at me, and her face was the softest and warmest it had been. And sad. When I think of her now, I know she was sad. But I knew that being next to me made her less sad, the same way that being next to her made me feel warmer. And I knew that she was going to fall off the edge of that high bridge, that she wanted to fall, and that she wanted me to keep holding her hand, and to fall with her. And I wanted to. I wanted to stay next to this warm soft woman even when we were falling from the bridge.

But then her hand in mine was shaking. Her warm hand turned cold and slippery. She shook and shook and now she didn't feel like the soft woman any more, she felt like a person I didn't know, and she took a deep breath before she jumped and I let go.

I let go.

I remember her falling, how it took a long time for her to fall but also not very long at all. I remember she made a sound as she fell, like a wolf-dog sound, but sadder. Sometimes when I dream about her, I wake up still hearing that sound, and for a moment I forget how to speak.

I haven't told Mother about the soft woman. If I told her

it would mean sharing the soft woman, and at the moment she is all mine. I clutch her to my chest, wear her hidden under my shirt like the picture of the shiny woman.

Mother doesn't know about her, either.

Mother says the picture is dirty, that the woman is dirty too. But I think it's clean. When I first held the shiny woman in my hands, her skin was as bright as the cooker flame. What I mean is, she shone so brightly I could see all the dust in my knuckles and the dirt and chicken mess under my nails. For the first time I understood what Mother means when she tells me I'm a filthy child, and for the first time I wanted to be clean.

We are the same and not the same, the shiny woman and me.

She's lying on her back, propped up on a pillow so that she looks straight at me out of the picture. It's so clever the way she does that – as if she can really see me. Like she's so close I could touch her, and when I do, the paper is smooth and warm, the way her skin looks like it ought to feel.

All the way home from the City, I keep her hidden. She waits under my shirt while I boil the potatoes and Mother cooks two cans on the fire.

I can feel her lying there. In the heat of the kitchen, the paper is warm and sticky against my body. I want to touch that sweaty, itchy patch of skin, but Mother might realise and make me take her back to the City. Or maybe she will shout and pull at my hair, and make me burn her on the kitchen fire, the way we burn book pages to make it light. I do not want to make Mother shout at me.

I can make a picture in my head of the shiny woman surrounded by flames, her long clean legs glowing like the copper pan while her big eyes keep looking out. I think it would be a little bit beautiful to see her burning like that, but she's more beautiful kept like this, on shiny paper – like the vegetables that Mother keeps fresh and new by pickling them in jars so that we have sweet and good things when it's cold. I think the woman is a sweet and good thing too. I mean, I think she is something I want to keep for as long as I can, which means I can't let Mother discover her.

As soon as dinner is done, I run upstairs and hide her in the dust under my mattress. I think about her as we wash and dry the dishes, glowing in that room full of grime and dirt. I tell Mother I want to go to bed early.

When I'm alone, after Mother has emptied the wash-water and tucked up my blankets, I take the shiny woman out again. She is so bright that even with just the moon for light I can see her clearly. Those big eyes look at me. They are the colour of tea when Mother lets me put the milk powder in it, and I think if I fall into them they will be warm and milky and I will come apart in them like a sugar cube.

I take off my nightclothes and prop myself up on the pillows. I spread my legs apart like hers with the knees bent up.

Even though I'm not wearing anything, all the firm bits of my body are hot. I put the picture on the top bit of my leg so I can see her, and she sticks to my skin.

I want to copy her, this beautiful woman. I want to see all the ways we are the same.

I try to flatten out my hair on the pillow, but while hers glows red like it's made of a sunrise, mine is tough and knotted and I can only split it into three damp clumps.

The woman watches me. I think that even if she was real and not just a picture, she would watch me like that. Not blinking, not calling me a silly girl, not telling me to be quicker or to give up trying to be beautiful. She would just watch, swirling me round in those tea-coloured eyes.

One of her hands is on her chest, her pointing finger resting on the red-pink bump there. Her chest is soft and round. I make a bowl of my hand around my own chest. It fits neatly into the space, like my hand is supposed to curl around it. Maybe that's what hands are made for, for filling. It is my own little curve – smaller, but warm and beautiful like the woman's. So far, we are the same.

I think Mother is the same, too. Sometimes when she washes or changes into her nightclothes, I see the curves of her chest. I don't know if they would fill her hands or not. Maybe she doesn't know either – Mother doesn't understand how things are beautiful. She doesn't understand this shiny woman with her hot, glowing skin, or how I need to keep her.

I rest my pointing finger on the red-pink bump of my own chest. The touch of it feels like a shiver, like when the corner of the blanket touches against my skin too lightly, so lightly I almost can't feel it. It feels like that on the red-pink bump of my chest, and it sends that shivering feeling right through my whole body, so I can feel it even in the hard bottoms of my feet.

The woman's other hand is touching between her legs. Her skin there is red and swollen, and makes me think of old tomatoes.

I wonder if my skin there is the same colour. I've never looked at it. Mother always says that part of the body is dirty because it's where the toilet bits come from. Maybe that's why Mother called the picture dirty, because the woman is touching those toilet parts with her hands and no paper.

I touch my own toilet parts to see what they feel like. I expect it to feel like ordinary skin, but it's slippy and warm, like egg yolk. I move my hand around and my whole body tightens. It feels as if everything's being pulled inwards, like there's a string that runs right up inside my body and it's getting tighter and tighter until it will pull me inside out – and I want it to. I want to turn in and out of myself.

I move my hand again, both hands, and it's like someone has put their finger on the string, like the shiny woman has plucked the string that runs inside the length of my body and it's shaking, the way the tight string on the gate latch trembles and makes music when I pluck it.

And I can't stop my voice sounding. My voice is making quiet noises and the shiny woman is watching me with her warm brown eyes, and I'm watching her and I think I really am falling apart in them, or that maybe I have gone and put her on the fire and I'm on it with her and I don't care – I don't care—

There's a bang as the door smacks the bedroom wall, and Mother's boy-cat screech – *'What are you doing!'*

'Mother . . .' It's like she didn't exist. Like in that room and the whole of everywhere was only me and the shiny woman – until suddenly there was Mother. Loud, hard, unbeautiful Mother.

'You bitch!' she screams, and it isn't a word I know, so I think of the closest thing I can and make a picture of it in my head.

You bitch, I think. *You bridge.*

Mother's word becomes a high place on the edge of a city, and the feeling of hanging over an empty space.

'Mother—'

She grabs the shiny woman from my leg and her hand makes a loud crack against my face. 'You fucking bitch!'

You fucking bridge.

Her eyes are like a fire, but not like the beautiful woman, not that kind of bright-flame burning. Mother's eyes burn like a hot metal pan, like they could blacken and blister my skin.

I'm falling and not falling. I'm sitting on the railing and watching myself hit the thin river below.

You bridge.

The room feels cold, as if Mother took all the warmth out with her and with the picture of the shiny woman. I tuck myself back into the blanket and think about bridges, how they are what separate people and how there's no way for them to get back to each other.

I nearly run out into the dark to find her. I want to grab her hand and hold it tight, as tight as I can, and say please not to let go, and I won't let go either, not this time. I'm not a bridge. I won't let go of Mother.

But my nightclothes are lost somewhere at the bottom of the blanket, and without the shiny woman looking at me, I don't feel beautiful any more.

I want to remember what it felt like to be beautiful. I want to be looked at like I'm beautiful again. But Mother has probably thrown the shiny woman on the fire and I didn't even get to see her go, so maybe Mother is a bridge as well. Maybe we are both bridges, pulling each other away from everything else.

I find my nightclothes and put them on. In the dark, I shuffle down the stairs into the kitchen.

Mother is sitting by the fire, hugging her arms. Her face looks like empty rucksacks, like she's sad and there's nothing left inside her to make her happy again. I can't see what's happened to the shiny woman.

'Mother?' My voice sounds small and far away, and I think of the thin river at the bottom of the gully.

She looks up. Her eyes are empty, too.

'Mother? Are you going to leave me?'

As soon as I say this, I see something in those deep rucksack eyes, like she's about to reach over and grab my hand so we can always fall or not fall together. But she doesn't. She just says, 'No, Monster. I'm not going to leave you.'

'Not ever?'

'No. Not ever.'

'Promise?'

That makes her smile, like I've reminded her that she's my Mother and I'm her Monster, and she says, 'I promise.'

And I know then that it's going to be all right, because even though we're both bridges, I won't separate us because I know I don't want to be alone, and Mother won't separate us because she said 'I promise' and that means you have to do it. That promise sits inside me like the kitchen fire, like the fire that we feed coal and dry wood, and that we never let go out.

Mother says our days are all the same. 'We wake up, we survive, we go to sleep. End of.'

She doesn't tell me what it's the end of, and I don't tell her that she's wrong.

Some days are City days and some days are farm days. Some days are bright and happy. Some days are warm on the inside. Some days are too full, like when the chickens try to squeeze through a little gap and there are too many wings and feathers and all of them scratch at each other. Sometimes the days are like the egg Mother showed me how to prick with a needle, so that the middle leaked out and there was only the empty shell.

More and more, the days are short and cold and full of bad weather. We spend every moment we can bringing in whatever vegetables are ready from the field, or collecting food from the City. Sometimes, on City days, I stop at the top of the hill behind the farm. It's the closest we ever come to the top of the mountain, but I don't tell Mother this, either. I just tell her I like the way the farm looks different from up here, the way I can see moss on the roof and how the tiles get smaller the closer they get to the top.

But I also like to look towards the edges of the world, and try to make pictures of the things on the other side of it. If I screw my eyes up really small, I sometimes think I can see through the gap between the ground and the sky. And sometimes I even think I can see the other city through it, with its high bridge and little river, but that's just a picture in my head.

I wonder if Mother knows what's really there. Probably not.

She says she knows there are no more people who are not dead people, but she can't know for certain what there's not, only what there is – and sometimes she doesn't even know that. When we search for things in the City, she never knows what's there until we find it.

When I look hard at the edge of the world, I can make a picture of another farm somewhere, with another Mother making clicking noises with her teeth, while she waits at the top of the hill for another Monster.

*

One of the walls around the vegetable field is tumbling down. As we build it back up, Mother tells me that my name means 'Survivor'. I like that my name means survivor. I like that I am someone who can keep going, who can plant and reap and scavenge and not become one of the dead people.

I stop to rub my hands together because even with my gloves on they're still cold. 'What does Mother mean?'

She bends over to pick up another stone. 'Creator.' She tells me she is called this because she created me.

'What about the other people? The dead ones. Do they have names?'

Mother concentrates on positioning the stone in our rebuilt wall. 'They used to.'

'What happened to them?' How can a person have a name and then not have a name?

'They died, Monster.'

I think about the soft woman and the shiny woman, how they used to have names that meant something, but now they are dead and so there is no one to remember what their names were or what they meant, except that they were soft or shiny. We finish building the wall without talking.

*

After all the work is done and the food is eaten and the bowls are washed, we sit by the fire, Mother in the comfy chair and me on the cushion on the floor. Mother doesn't talk. She works at something small with her hands. Sometimes I help her with these evening jobs, but tonight I just sit and listen to the quiet while she fixes her button back to her shirt.

It's a warm quiet, full of little noises. The fire rushing like a tree in the wind, Mother breathing in and out, the clock saying its one word over and over.

When I'm not thinking about the soft woman or trying to remember more about the bridge, I like to look for shapes in the fire. They're not real shapes, not made out of things you can touch, like wood or ash or the metal grate. I see them in the fire itself, after I've been looking for a long time. Tonight I see a person waving her long arms in the air, floating above a city full of pointed buildings. If I look hard enough, I can turn the buildings into more people, all with their arms and faces pointed up. When I look away, my eyes paint bright dots across the rest of the kitchen, like when the sun is too bright on the stream behind the house, and all the fish inside it flash. Mother doesn't know about the fish – she thinks the stream is only for water. She doesn't know about the people in the fire, either. She watches the needle going in and out of the button, and I keep what I know hidden inside me like a chicken's egg.

I wake up one morning to find everything broken.

As soon as I open my eyes I can tell something is wrong. There's frost under my nose on the edge of my blanket and the sky is bright and yellow, the colour of a bruise after the purple has faded.

I swing my legs out of the covers and stuff my feet in my shoes before they can touch the cold floorboards, then run to the window.

The field is gone. Where the rows of vegetables should be is just nothing. Thick blank nothing, as if someone has snuck into the farm during the night and cleared everything away. It's empty. It looks hard and cold, and it makes me think of the dead people, how there's nothing left but bone.

How will we survive now the farm is gone? What will we eat?

There's food in the City, but we can't survive on cans and crackers – or maybe we can. I don't know. I can't remember. But if we can't grow anything we will have to only eat small things, and I don't want to only eat small things.

I try to make a picture of the chickens like this, their soft feathers all covered and made hard like bone, but I can't do it. Maybe the chickens are dead like the farm. I remember them scratting in the yard, the way they would hold one yellow foot in the air like a limp hand, before spreading it flat on the cobbles. Maybe if I remember them hard enough they'll come back – although I know it doesn't really work like that. Once in the City I made a picture of shining chocolate bars stacked inside a shop we found. I pictured them until it was as if I could already smell them, but when we broke in the shop was empty and we left the City without finding any chocolate bars at all.

The City.

I put my hand against the cold wall to make myself steady. What if the City is gone as well?

I run downstairs to Mother, thinking I will find her with her head in her hands, or counting out what's left to see how much longer we will live for, or even worse, that she will have become one of the dead people during the night. A picture of Mother comes into my head, of her lying with her face against the kitchen floor and her arms and legs splayed out, the way I found a dead woman once in a house in the City, with one side of her face normal and the other side flat against the kitchen tiles, and I don't want to open the door.

I close my eyes and open them again, and the door is still in front of me, so I push it open and see Mother. Mother, sitting in the comfy chair with her hands over the fire to warm them as if this is just another morning, as if the farm isn't dead and the world hasn't ended and we aren't about to turn into dead people.

'Morning,' she says.

I listen and I can't hear the ending in her voice – but maybe she's trying to hide it from me so I won't be afraid. Maybe she thinks I haven't already seen what has happened.

'Shut the door,' she says, 'you'll let the cold in.'

Because I don't know what else to do, I shut the door and sit opposite Mother. I snuggle as close to the fire as I can without falling off my cushion.

Mother says nothing. I watch her carefully, the way the chickens used to watch when they couldn't decide whether to run away from something or not, and my breathing comes quicker when I think about the poor chickens being gone, but

Mother doesn't look any different to normal. Maybe the grey skin under her eyes is a bit darker, but that's all. Her face doesn't change as she sits and waits for the pot of water to boil.

For a while I don't say anything either, but I can feel it bubbling up inside me like the water pot, until suddenly it bursts out: 'Mother!'

She looks at me.

'Mother, the farm . . .'

'What about it?'

Everything collapses inside me, then, like a stone wall tumbling, as I realise that Mother doesn't know. She has no idea. I am the only one who knows the terrible thing that has happened, and now I have to break it to her. That's what Mother calls it when she has to say something bad: breaking it. I never knew why before, but now I understand, how the words can make a crack down the middle of an ordinary morning, then push the two edges of it apart until the crack is a river and there is no getting back across it to how things used to be. And now I have to break today.

I take a huge breath as though I'm going to shout it, but the words come out small and frightened. 'The farm's gone. Everything's dead.'

It's quiet for a moment, just the fire-crackle and the pot beginning to boil. Then Mother starts to laugh.

I've never seen Mother laugh before, not like this, not so hard that her eyes crease up and her breathing is short and difficult. It's as if she's trying to laugh away the bad news, like she could push all the emptiness out of her in those quick breaths, or like she could use them to breathe the farm back to life. I just sit there, watching, not knowing how to help, but the more worried I look, the more it makes Mother laugh. I start to feel warm. I shift away from the fire but it doesn't help. I feel hot and empty. It feels like all the thoughts I hold inside of me because Mother says they're silly, like they're all on the outside for Mother to see and laugh at, and all that's left inside of me is this uncomfortable heat that makes everything prickle.

Eventually, the laughing stops, and Mother manages to breathe normally again. 'Oh Monster,' she says, once she can speak.

I frown at the fire instead of looking her in the eye. 'What?'

'It's snow.'

So she tells me about snow. She tells me that this is what happens to water when it gets really cold, that all the raindrops turn white and cover everything like a big blanket, and how the field with the vegetables isn't gone, just hidden, and how when it gets warmer the snow will turn back to water, which will either run into the stream or sink into the soil to help the grass and trees and vegetables grow. Then she starts to tell me about a place she used to live a long time ago, where it was so cold that the snow could be higher than me, and where it covered the ground for months at a time.

I ask her what a month is.

Mother thinks for a moment, then tells me it's about thirty days, which I understand because that's how often I bleed, although I didn't know there was a word for it. *Month*. When I say it out loud, all at the front of my mouth, it sounds like blood, like the first day of bleeding when everything feels like it's tumbling out of me in heavy drops. *Month*.

I ask Mother to tell me more about where she lived, with all the snow. How did she keep warm? Was it frightening, not being able to see the ground for so long? Why did she leave?

But Mother just shakes her head and pours the boiling water into a cup. She picks out the teabag with her fingernails then squeezes it and dumps it in her own cup.

'Drink your tea,' she says, then turns away to finish the porridge.

I curl my hands around my cup to keep them warm, and think about snow. Mother might not want to talk about it, but it's all around us now, so she can't stop me finding out about it for myself. I curl my toes inside my trainers and try not to burn my tongue on my tea by being too impatient.

*

Snow is not like water. Snow keeps its edges when you tread through it. It makes a pattern of holes across the yard. Snow is solid like sheep's wool. Snow lets me sink through it like a stream. Snow is bright and grey at the same time, and has dark spots hidden in its bumps and dips. When I turn my head or flick my eyes to the side, the grey patches shift like sly animals. The snow is alive.

Mother stands in the doorway, watching me plunge my feet into the deep whiteness. I stamp faster and faster, spinning with my arms out like the bits of ribbon that blow from the posts around the field. I turn so fast it feels like I'm going to fall, but I don't, I keep spinning and stamping, always just ahead of losing my balance and my whole body collapsing in the snow.

A small sound from the doorway. A laugh. Not bright and sharp like my laugh, or too loud like when I didn't know about snow. Mother's laugh is like the belly clucks the chickens make, soft like feathers, kept inside herself.

I stop. Mother has her arms crossed, but her face is uncrossed. What I mean is, her face is all opened out like when I uncross my arms and Mother can see the softer parts on the insides of my wrists, and the front of my body isn't hidden and hunched over any more. What I mean is, Mother looks happy.

I smile at her. 'Come and try it.'

For a moment I think she will. She leans forward, just a bit, as if there's a breeze behind her and she can't help it, and her arms start to uncross. But then she shivers and looks over her shoulder as if there's a wolf-dog watching from inside the

192

house. A frown appears on her face like one of those grey patches on the snow, and she shakes her head.

'There's too much to do.' She turns inside, leaving me in the empty yard, which is too quiet with the chickens shut away in their shed. I don't feel like spinning any more.

Snow is cold. It sits heavy inside me like I've swallowed a handful of it. It's a heavy weight across the fields. Snow is wet, tugging on the bottoms of my trousers and on my coat cuffs. I can shout and shout at the snow, but I can't make it talk back to me.

I fold my arms around myself to keep in the warm, and go back inside after Mother.

Later, we bring in the wood for the fire. We bring in lots because Mother says we don't know how long the snow will last, and by the time we're finished I can't feel my fingers very well. After that, we still have to go out to feed the chickens and make sure they have water, but mostly we just stay inside.

*

The snow lasts for four days. We sit by the fire and don't talk much. Mother's face stays hidden again like crossed arms, and I don't know how to uncross it.

*

On day number five, the snow starts to disappear, so slowly that if I look right at it, I can't see it happening. The yard is full of the sound of dripping water.

By day number six, enough of it has gone for us to walk to the City.

When we get back, we check on the onions and broad beans growing in the field, but everything is the same as it was before the snow except maybe the stream, which is fuller and colder, and snaps at my hands when I go to fetch the water.

Mother has found nine sheep, though she says that they are really eight sheep and a ram.

A sheep is a soft fat animal that makes a lot of noise. It looks like it's wearing a thick, dirty white coat. Mother says that once upon a time, before the dead people were dead people, they used to cut off a sheep's coat and make rugs and jumpers and blankets with it, but we don't need to do that because we have the shops in the City, which are full of jumpers already.

Mother says she got up in the night because she couldn't sleep, and went for a walk to try to make herself tired. She says she was just following the stream upwards so she could find her way back, the way she taught me to always know where the farm is, and that she heard noises coming from inside something called a sheepfold, which she says is like a wall that folds around the sheep to keep them warm. She put the gate across so they couldn't get back out. She says she can't believe the sheep haven't been eaten by wolf-dogs, but I know this is just something she says, because she can see them so she has to believe it. I know this the same way I know she wasn't just walking to make herself tired, because normally Mother doesn't like to go out when it's night, and because her rucksack is full of all the things she needs to survive away from the farm.

I think about the mountain. I think about how cold it is to sleep outside even when the days are long and warm, and how much colder it must be now when the inside of my window sparkles every morning and the top of my blanket is white and hard from where my breath has turned to frost in the night. I think Mother would be bad at surviving away from the farm, because she is a creator and not a survivor. Which is maybe why she decided to come back.

I don't say anything. I just make two cups of tea and pretend not to watch as Mother hides her full rucksack behind the broken chair in the storage room, where she keeps the box of wires and bits of plastic she thinks I don't know about. She looks at me to check if I've seen her, but I look at the fire instead. I tell her I want to go looking for more animals, but she says there aren't any. She says it's only us and the sheep and the chickens, and that's it. But before she found the sheep it was only us and the chickens, and there are already birds and ground bugs and wolf-dogs and boy-cats and fish and foxes and the rats in the City, so probably there are more different kinds of animals somewhere, too, we just haven't found them yet.

Mother thinks the world is empty. It has the City and the farm and sometimes things we collect to help us survive, but apart from that it's like at the end of the day when the sun goes behind the hill and everything becomes dark greens and blues because all the other colours are gone. Mother thinks I am empty the same way.

Mother isn't very good at looking at things. I don't mean like when I screw my eyes up and all the things in front of me lose their shapes. What I mean is, Mother isn't very good at understanding the things she's looking at. Sometimes she doesn't understand so hard, I think she wants the world to be empty.

But the world isn't empty. This is something I know and Mother doesn't, that the world is full. There are all the worms that wriggle about in the vegetable field. There's the stream next to the farm, and wherever it brings its water from. There are buildings that go on for ever in the City, and all of them are full of something, even if it's only old chairs and boxes and things we can't use. There are all the different kinds of grass and flowers along the edges of the lane, which are sometimes there and sometimes not, but still the lane is never quite empty. There are the chickens carrying their eggs around inside them. And now there are the sheep.

I think about the top of the mountain. I think about how big the world was from up there, and how full. I hold its fullness close to me, the way I held the shiny woman when I didn't want Mother to find her.

Later, I help Mother bring the sheep to one of the fields a little bit closer to the farm. She says this is so we can keep an eye on them, which I know means being able to make sure they only do things that Mother wants them to do. We build a sort of lane from the sheep fold to the road using old gates and branches, and a long bit of fence we have to dig up and then plant again. It isn't very far from the sheep fold to the road, but it still takes us all morning as well as a little bit of the afternoon. Then Mother opens the gate and we chase them out of the sheep fold and into the lane. Mother walks behind them with her arms out, saying things like 'Hey hey hey, go go' to keep them moving. I have to run around the outside to the bottom of our new little lane to stop them going the wrong way down the road, and then my job is to get in the way of any that look like they might start running away in different directions, because they don't always want to go where we tell them to. When we get closer, I have to jump over the wall and run through the field so I can get to the gate and open it in time to let the sheep through.

Once they're in the new field, we close the gate and watch them looking around at their new home. Then they start to eat the grass as if they haven't even been on a journey.

They look so strange, standing there munching grass as if

we don't even exist, as if we're not standing right there watching them, that I start to laugh. One of the sheep looks up and laughs back at me, a long flat laugh which makes me laugh even harder. More of the sheep join in, until my laugh has opened up their laughter like opening a box, and we're all laughing, me and the sheep, and Mother just looks at us.

Mother says I have a laugh like breaking glass. I know what she means.

She smashed a window once with a brick so we could get at the treasure inside: a shiny coat and trousers that don't let the mud or water in, a rucksack like Mother's so I can help collect things on our trips to the City, and – most precious of all – my torch, which can make light in the darkness and show there are no wolf-dogs hiding in the shadows.

When Mother broke the window it made a bright, high noise, like the feeling when my torch breaks through the night.

I think it's a wonderful thing to have a laugh like breaking glass. It means that when I laugh, it's like breaking into a room full of treasures, it's like a whole possibility for better things, like light in the darkness.

Because of the sheep, we set off late for the City. The sun's already moving downwards in the sky, and at first I think Mother might decide to wait until tomorrow, but she doesn't. She says it's because there are things we need today, because we are getting too thin and that's a bad thing, but really I think the reason Mother wants to go now is because of all the things she takes out of her rucksack when she thinks I'm not looking, and because she decided to walk away from the farm and then she didn't, so now she has to do something else instead. I think Mother is like me in that way. She doesn't like to change her mind.

*

The City feels different at night. The streets and buildings all become as black as each other, and I keep thinking I can hear wolf-dogs growling from the doorways. I scurry to keep close to Mother.

She takes us to a part of the City I've never seen before, where the buildings are smaller and there's less glass to give our torchlight back to us. We go inside some of them, but we have to move slowly and even then we don't find anything. In one, I hear a noise like small animals running through a pile of dry leaves, and when I turn my torch to the ceiling, a dark cloud of birds flies at me and I have to duck. Mother says they're called bats and that they're dangerous. We leave before they can bite us.

Back out in the road, Mother is still for a long time. I know my breath is making little clouds, even if it's too dark to see them, and my fingers go so cold that I can't feel them holding my torch. I shine the light at Mother to see if I can tell what she's thinking.

She puts an arm across her eyes. 'Stop it.'

I turn the torch to the ground.

'This is stupid,' she says, then walks away down the road. I don't know what's stupid, but I don't think she means me, so I follow her.

We walk without speaking. Even though our torches have new batteries in them, the darkness still feels big behind me. I keep turning around to check what's there, but I never see anything. Mother doesn't stop, so I keep having to do skips to catch up with her.

I move my torch to my other hand and stuff the cold one in my pocket. 'Where are we going?'

Mother doesn't look around. 'Not far now.'

We walk past building after building, lots of them unbroken and maybe full of food, but we don't go inside. It's only when I think Mother must have forgotten about collecting that I notice it getting lighter. I frown up at the sky, but it can't be morning yet, and anyway the light isn't pink or white like the sun coming up. It's yellow, like the kitchen fire without the flickering.

We turn the corner. I stop in the middle of the road.

Instead of darkness, the building in front of us is like a whole shop full of torches pointing outwards into the night. I stare at the light so hard it starts to hurt my eyes. It makes me think of something, but I don't know what. 'Mother . . .'

'Come on.'

She walks right up to the building. It's so bright it makes the rest of the City seem even darker. I can feel it prickling, not just in one place like grass, but all around me, like something I don't know how to remember – like there are more wolf-dogs watching than I know how to count. I try to not look, but the building has eyes, too. I can feel them looking over me, the way Mother looks over vegetables to check if they're all right to eat, till all my hidden places are full of this bright yellow light and I think that if Mother looks round she'll see everything I've never told her, even the things I don't remember myself.

Mother looks back and says, 'Monster, come on,' and the way she says it sounds like when water boils too quickly and some of it gets out between the pan and the lid, like she's trying to get away from something.

I keep staring, and it's like Mother isn't even there, like it's just me and the lights, and the rest of the City around me is the soft woman, as if something that used to be just a picture in my head is now outside it and real.

*

The floor looks like someone has poured water over it.

Mother touches a box on the wall and the ceiling gets brighter, till I have to look away. I kick my feet against the shiny floor. They leave little black marks that make me think of the fish in the stream behind the farm.

'It's called a Clinic.'

I don't look at Mother. I make the sound of the word Clinic in my head, like making a picture but out of noise, with all its hard shapes cracking like an egg.

She says the Clinic was built by the dead people when they had the Sickness, and I think maybe that's why it's prickling, maybe this is what the Sickness feels like when it's all around you, except I know really it isn't. She says they built it for survivors, and I know that means me.

I switch off my torch, because we don't need it any more. 'Is the Sickness still here?'

'No,' Mother says. She takes a big breath, then says it again. 'No.'

The middle of the Clinic is the same as I remember it. It's so big and empty it's almost like being outside, except there are those little lights like torches in the walls, so everything is either white or covered in shadows, and above me where the ceiling should be is a big glass window. Through it, I can see the night.

I throw out my arms and tip my head back. I make a loud shout that sounds like the word 'way', but isn't, so that the walls and doors and ceiling-window throw the sound back to me.

'Monster!'

Mother moves inside the Clinic the way she moves in the clothes shop or the vegetable-growing building, like the place belongs to her because she's been here before. I don't tell her how really it belongs to me. I don't say anything. If Mother can keep things hidden, then so can I.

*

A room full of tall silver cupboards. Their insides are cold and shining like the walls.

Mother hands me plastic bottles smaller than my fist which she calls food supplements and which she says will make us fatter. I don't understand how such little bottles could make us fatter, but Mother is watching me so I pack them away in my bag.

*

There are so many things stored at the Clinic. More than I can remember. They are all things the dead people must have thought we would need to survive. I pick up a small pot of white circles that look a bit like seeds. For Sickness, Mother says.

'I thought it wasn't here any more.'

'That's a different Sickness.' Mother's voice is hard, and it hurts like the metal edge of the potato peeler. 'Made in a lab. They couldn't cure it.'

Lab. It makes me think of slab, like the stone shelf in the larder which is always cold, and I make a picture in my head of the dead people creating the Sickness on a cold stone shelf, only I don't know what the Sickness looks like so I make it a fog. And the light in the Clinic feels heavy, till I think I can't move, because there were dead people who were creators. Dead people who were like Mother.

But the Clinic isn't for the dead people. It's for survivors.

I make a picture in my head of Mother in the Clinic, and dead people who aren't dead people in the other rooms, and me hiding in the cold, cold room where the dead people won't look for me. Except I don't make the picture by trying. It just appears in my head and I can't make it go away again. And in the picture Mother doesn't look like Mother. She doesn't look like the soft woman or the shiny woman either, the way when the snow was melting it wasn't quite water and it wasn't quite snow. She is Mother and at the same time she isn't.

In the room in the picture, everything is grey and white and silver and blue, like even the colours are made of cold.

There's a table that goes all round the walls, which is where I'm hiding because the dead people are loud and hard and if they find me they'll hurt me, and in the middle of the floor are big white pots with blue lids on, like fat animals wearing bright blue hats. In the picture that isn't a picture, Mother doesn't see me. She cuts through a plastic string on one of the pots, and when she lifts up the lid, there's a white cloud like the pot's freezing breath, which drifts away and disappears. Mother puts on a pair of thick, rough gloves. She pulls four glass tubes out of the pot and puts them in a tray, and I know what she wants because for a moment she looks at me like she could be my creator and is sad that she isn't, and for a moment I want to let her be. But she can't because she isn't really Mother, only in my head.

And then I'm on my own in the picture and Mother is gone – and the dead people are louder now, and I'm shaking. Not on the outside, but on the inside. I think I'm the bird that got trapped in the string net covering the cabbages, when it struggled and shook and made everything else shake with it, till Mother let it out. So I curl up under the table in the cold room in the picture in my head, but the dead people are there and they grab me and I struggle and shake but their hands are hard and tight and covered with thick black hairs.

*

The light in the Clinic is so heavy, I think it's twisted around me like the string net, only the net is just part of the picture in my head and the light is real which is worse. I think about the hands, like I can still feel them grabbing me. They squeeze my arms and my sides and their squeezing feels like bruises.

I can feel my words getting smaller, going further away.

*

We walk away from the Clinic, back towards the normal parts of the City. I think about the sea and the soft woman on the bridge. I think about the mountain and how Mother hid her rucksack in the storage room after she found the sheep. I think about the Clinic and the cold room and how Mother's name means creator, and I think about what that room was for. There are so many things Mother doesn't know I know.

I watch her torch waving over the road and bits of building, like it's one of the night birds that sometimes fly around the farm, with their flat round faces like circles of torchlight and their huge wings that never make a sound, so that if I couldn't see them, I wouldn't even know they were there. I think Mother is sometimes like a night bird.

She steps over a tree root that's growing through the road, and I look up to see the tower with the hole in the wall.

We make our way to the building with all the vegetable-growing things in it, Mother flashing her torch from side to side to check for wolf-dogs. Once, we hear a low growling, but when Mother turns the light towards it, all we see is a tail running away.

To get there, we have to climb over a pile of cars that blocks the road. We've done it before, but it's more difficult at night. All the grips and footholds disappear in the dark, and even when Mother shines her torch for me, the light shines back off the metal, and I can't tell what's a shadow and what's a hole.

There's a dead person in one of these cars. I found it once, when I was looking too closely for a way to clamber over, just a pile of bones in one of the seats. In the dark, it takes me longer to place my hands and feet, in case I do it wrong and my foot slips through a hole and I kick the dead person.

I don't say this to Mother. Mother doesn't like to talk about the dead people, and I know what she would say. 'Dead people are dead, Monster. They can't hurt you.'

I know they can't hurt me. I just don't want to hear the clatter of all the bits of bone jumbling together. I wonder if this dead person had the Sickness, the one they created in the lab that sounds like slab, and that they couldn't make go away.

Once we're over the cars, we're almost there. I nearly run the last few steps to the building, but I don't because then Mother might laugh at me and say I was being silly. So we walk, still checking side to side for wolf-dogs, as if this is normal, to be here so late at night. As if we're not just here because it's the only way for Mother to stop herself leaving the farm.

When we get to the vegetable-growing building, Mother forces the doors apart with the flat bit of metal she keeps there. Then I help her push them closed again to stop anything following us inside.

I love the smell of the vegetable-growing building. It's like everything the Clinic isn't. It smells of earth and plants, and of the painted metal tools that have never been used. From here, we can collect more seeds to plant in the fields. We collect bean seeds and carrot seeds and radish seeds. I stand in front of the wall of packets, looking at the pictures of all the things they can grow into, and at the words underneath them. Mother thinks I don't know about words when they're pictures on things instead of said out loud. She doesn't see when I use book pages to catch the kitchen fire back at the farmhouse, how I touch the shapes of the words with my pointing finger before I put the pages to the embers, so it feels like they're mine even if I can't tell what they say.

Mother picks up a packet with yellow and purple flowers on it which she says are called pansies, and which she says I can plant in one of the big pots in the yard. They aren't for eating, she says, just for looking bright and colourful.

Whenever we plant seeds, I like to hold them in my hands before putting them in the soil, just so I can look at them – little dots that will somehow grow into food that will help to keep us alive. How can such a tiny thing carry so much bigness inside it? I don't understand how it works, but I love that it does.

I feel the hard bumps inside the packet of pansies. 'Are there men's seeds here, too?'

I say it without really knowing I am going to say it.

Mother looks at me the way she did when I came back from the mountain, like she's a bag full of vegetables that's suddenly torn, so everything tumbles out and she's left empty and drifting in the wind. She just looks at me and it's like she's forgotten how to speak.

I do not know how I know that men have seeds, the way carrots and pansies do. There are lots of things I don't remember learning, like the way I sometimes know words without Mother having to tell me. Sometimes, I wonder if maybe I know them the way the chickens know things without being told, like how to lay eggs or that it's safer inside the shed when it's dark. But then there is the soft woman on the bridge, and there is the Clinic with its cold room and pictures of dead people, and I realise some of the things I know must be things I was told when there were other people, before it was just me and Mother, which I don't remember and I don't really understand.

Mother is still looking at me like she's trying to see into

211

all the hidden places in my head, so I shrug and put the packet of pansies in my rucksack, and we get on with collecting things.

I think Mother maybe doesn't know very much about men's seeds, because all the men are now dead people, so probably she has forgotten. I wonder what else Mother has forgotten. Perhaps there are lots of things. Perhaps she doesn't really know much about the dead people, or the different kinds of Sickness, or about how vegetables grow under the ground, or about how she created me. Perhaps she only half-remembers.

I won't tell her. I think it must be frightening to suddenly find out that you don't know things you thought you knew, like everything pushes you away and there's nothing there to catch you. I think it must be like when I fall out of bed, like the moment between rolling over the edge of the mattress and hitting the floor, when you know you're falling but you can't quite grab the mattress to stop it happening. Or when you're clambering over the car pile and you feel your foot go through a hole, and there's nothing to hold on to to keep yourself up.

*

I'm bleeding again, but I knew it was coming. Mother makes me keep marks of how many days there are between them, so I know when to expect it.

Mother doesn't bleed. I know this because when you bleed you need pads or tampers and before I started bleeding we didn't have any in the house. Once, I saw her holding one of the new pads in its bright wrapper. She held it like it was something precious, something like an egg, and she stared at it for a long time.

I think it must be something very special to bleed. Maybe I am one of the only people in the world who has ever bled like this. Whenever we collect pads and tampers from the City, there are always plenty of them, so other people can't have needed to use them very much.

I don't like the stain the bleeding can make on my knickers and bed sheets, or the way it can sometimes feel as if the blood and mess is collapsing out of me. But sometimes I think maybe it is clean, all the red and dirty things passing from my body. It feels like when I've been to the City and I come back and scrape all the dirt and grime from my skin.

The light starts to last for longer. Sometimes I think Mother might try to leave again, but she never does, and I think maybe she has remembered her promise to me, or maybe she just doesn't want to be outside all the time on her own. During the days, we go to the City or mend bits of the farm, or check on the sheep. Mother says they must like our grass because they're getting fatter. She says it's a good job winters are warmer than they used to be, because otherwise the sheep would starve like some of the dead people, which makes me wonder how anybody ever stayed warm in those colder winters, because it's difficult enough now. She says next year we will have to make hay, which is like long grass that the sheep will like to eat.

In the evenings, we stay warm in the kitchen and I watch for shapes in the fire. Sometimes I just sit on my cushion and look at the clock.

The clock is my favourite thing at the farm, even more than the chickens. It's a shiny wooden box hanging on the wall, with a white circle like the moon and two pointy black sticks that go round and round. Inside a glass cupboard, a metal circle swings from side to side, except when it gets stuck and I have to ask Mother to set it going again. The wood of the box is all in beautiful shapes which I have to wipe the dust off with a yellow cloth, and on top of it are two little wooden people, a man and a woman. They have thin arms that look as if they might snap, and smiling wooden faces. I don't know how I know they are a man and a woman, because I don't remember Mother ever telling me, but maybe it's just one of the forgotten things, like before the soft woman and the bridge. Or maybe I just know it without having to remember, the way I know words sometimes.

One of the wooden people is wearing normal clothes, but the other is wearing a sheet around her waist which goes right down to the floor and makes her middle look too thin, so that sometimes I think her middle might snap, too. When I'm dusting them, I like to make a picture in my head of the two wooden people growing bigger until they're the same size as me, and then becoming real so they can move and I can teach them how to talk.

Mother says the clock is supposed to tell the time. Telling the time is what it's called when the clock keeps saying the same small word that sounds like an egg tickerting in the pan. Every time it says it, it's reminding us that time is still happening and we're still here. Mother says the time is wrong, but I think she can't understand what the clock is saying, because time either is or it isn't, so it can't be right or wrong.

*

The mornings are gold, now, like the swinging metal circle in the clock cupboard. Everywhere there's a smell of wet earth that makes the memory of the Clinic seem small, and I want to be out in the field all the time with my hands in the soil. When we walk into the City, there are bright yellow flowers growing at the side of the road. Mother lets me pick some to put in a jug of water in the kitchen, so that even on rainy days it looks bright and sunny inside.

On one of these gold mornings, we have a lamb. That's what Mother calls it. I come downstairs and Mother has it wrapped in a blanket with just the small face poking out. It looks across the kitchen at me and makes a little sound like it's laughing from inside its tummy and its mouth goes wide like a smile. It has round black eyes like pebbles from the stream.

'Where did it come from?'

'One of the sheep had a baby,' says Mother. 'It needed warming up a bit. Here, hold it while I do the breakfast.'

She puts it into my arms, this sheep-baby, and I cuddle it close. It feels heavy and warm, not like the chickens which scratch and fuss when I try to hold them, or like the sheep that run in all different directions, but solid and real, like the top of the mountain, the way it's just there instead of thinking about being somewhere else. Its face is white, cleaner than the sheep's wool, but there are bits of shiny pink something caught in its fluff like wet threads.

When it makes its small laughing noise I can feel its whole body shaking, so I wrap it closer in my arms and laugh with it. I put my nose to its skin and it smells of the sheep and metal and woollen jumpers.

Mother goes back to the porridge.

When she isn't looking, I dip my finger in the pan of water we are heating for tea, and try to give it to the lamb. It makes slipping noises as its mouth moves, and it wraps its tongue and hard gums around my finger as if it never wants to let me go. It makes me smile – I hadn't expected its suck to be so strong. It's like it's sucking all the early morning cold out of me and filling me with warm, like fire heat, or the heat that lives inside thick clothes. Maybe that's where jumper heat comes from, from the sheep and from lambs. I cuddle it close because I know at some point I'll have to put it down, and the closer I cuddle it the easier that is to not know.

But I do know it, and once the porridge is ready, Mother moves the pan to the back of the stove and takes the lamb away from me. She starts to take it outside.

I ask her to wait, but she just says, 'Eat your breakfast. The lamb belongs with its Mother,' and she's out of the door.

I sit with the empty spoon in my hand, watching where she disappeared outside. *Its Mother.*

Mother means creator. But Mother didn't create the lamb, the sheep did. Which means that the sheep is also a creator, which means that the sheep must be like Mother. Which means that maybe the lamb is like me.

For days and days I watch the lamb. When I finish my chores or when I'm on my way to fetch water, I stop to look at it, but I don't get to cuddle it again. It skips and jumps around the field. Sometimes it drinks milk from the sheep's tummy, and its long fluffy tail wiggles till I start laughing. When it's tired, it cuddles up to the sheep. None of what it does is like me and Mother. Sometimes at night when I can't sleep, I hold a picture of the lamb in my head and try to find ways we are the same. But I can't, except that we both have dark eyes.

*

All the cold has gone from the sky. We stop waking up to frost and darkness.

In the mornings, the grass is covered in tiny drops of water that make the bottoms of my trousers heavy when I go to the stream. All the brown things start disappearing, till the plants are green and noisy. There are so many birds. I ask Mother where they all came from, so she says when it gets too cold, they fly away to look for somewhere warmer to live, and then when it's warmer here, they come back. I ask why we don't do that, too, but Mother just tells me not to be silly. I wonder what it must be like, to be able to go somewhere else whenever I feel like it, and not just sometimes, like when I went to the mountain. I wonder if I would miss the farm.

*

While I stir air into my hot porridge, Mother says it's time to plant the vegetables again.

Planting is my favourite part. I love the way the little seeds disappear as if we're tucking them up in bed, but without even their heads poking out of the covers, so that when we're finished it will just look like trays full of soil or an empty field. I like the way the seeds aren't vegetables yet, but just pictures in my head.

Mother says that's silly. She likes it when the vegetables are finished and we can pull them out of the soil, and she can count them out and turn them into days left alive.

We stand in the yard with the trays balanced on the wall, pushing the carrot seeds into the soil with our pointing fingers. As I plant them, I talk to them so quietly that Mother can't hear. 'Grow,' I say. 'Grow. Grow.'

*

A lot of the time when I'm with Mother it's like I'm not with her, because both of us are inside our own heads. On some evenings, when we're sitting by the fire and working on something that means we don't need to talk, I try to remember all the things I've forgotten. It's difficult, because I don't know what these things are, but I know they must be there because of the soft woman and the clock, and the pictures my head made when we went to the Clinic.

Mother doesn't like to remember things from a long time ago. Whenever I ask her about her life before she made me, she goes quiet and only talks in small words.

So I keep my remembering inside my own head.

I always start with the soft woman, even though it makes me feel all prickly like there's a wolf-dog watching from the dark. I think of me and the soft woman as if we're in a clear circle on the bridge, surrounded by the kind of thick white fog we sometimes get at the farm – as if inside the circle are the bits I remember and outside are all the bits I might remember but I just can't see yet. I try to make the circle bigger, so I will be able to remember before I was on the bridge with the soft woman, or what the bridge looked like after she fell, or getting down from the railing without her, but there's nothing except the circle and us being there and then her falling, and the harder I try to push into the fog, the more I get the horrible prickly feeling, till it's as if there's a whole pack of wolf-dogs watching, or like I'm hiding from the dead people in the cold room in the Clinic, and I have to stop. Sometimes I think I should just leave the circle where it is.

All through summer we plant vegetables and pull them up and plant them again. Some of them we cook and eat, but some Mother boils in vinegar and puts in jars so they'll keep till winter. We use the long days to look around different parts of the City. Sometimes, I wonder what will happen when we run out of new places to search, but the City is so big that we never do.

*

When the larder is so full I think it won't fit any more food, Mother decides we should explore together. When I ask her what 'explore' means, she says, 'It means not knowing what you're going to find.'

'And that's a good thing?'

'It's a dangerous thing.'

The fire is still just a heap of embers from last night. I think about when I can't remember anything outside the circle in the fog, so I never know what I'm going to find, as if I'm exploring inside my own head. I pull my coat closer around me in the early morning cold of the kitchen. 'Can a dangerous thing be a good thing?'

'No, Monster.'

I look at Mother and she's afraid. She sits in the comfy chair by the kitchen fire, putting on her boots and rolling down her socks, and she is afraid the whole time.

I try to remember when I was afraid. I am always afraid of the wolf-dogs, but that's different because you can see and hear the wolf-dogs and so you know they're there. Mother is afraid of not knowing. She is afraid of there maybe being something there, or maybe not. I don't understand this.

When I climbed the mountain, I was not afraid. What I mean is, I hadn't learned how to be afraid of things that were only pictures in my head. What I mean is, I think I might be braver than Mother.

She stands up and puts her arms through her empty backpack. 'Ready?'

I nod. I wonder if maybe we will find more animals, like when Mother found the sheep, but I don't say anything.

223

'OK then.'

It's still dark outside, but I can see a line along the edge of the world where the sun always comes up. Everything looks different to how it looks in the day. The chickens are locked in their shed during the night so the wolf-dogs and the foxes don't eat them, and the yard looks empty without them. The big pots with purple flowers in look like animals, curled up and sleeping, but ready to wake up and snap at Mother or me. But I know that they are just pots, and that if I turned my torch on I could see the little flowers in them, waiting for the day to start.

The stones in the yard are shiny and clean, like little bits of grey light that match the grey sky, and I can see where to walk. Once we're out of the farmyard it's easy because we just follow the road.

As always, Mother goes first, and I walk behind her. To start with it isn't very interesting because this is the direction we always walk. But when we get to the bottom of the road we turn the other way, away from the City.

At the end of the next road, Mother stops, looking around her, trying to decide which way to go. She looks like the chickens in the farmyard, the way they bob their heads and hold one leg off the ground when they're listening for danger.

I say, 'This is the road that leads to the mountain.'

'Which way?'

I point to my right.

'OK.'

Mother sets her shoulders as if her empty backpack is heavier than it really is, and walks up the road to the left.

I stay where I am. 'Can't we go to the mountain?'

'No.'

I want to sit down in the road. I want to make us go the other way. I want to show Mother what I found up there. But

I don't want her to explore new things without me, and anyway, I don't think she would understand it even if I did show her.

I follow her in the wrong direction, away from the mountain.

Once the sun is up and everything looks light and normal again, Mother decides to leave the road and go through the wood at the side of it. I don't understand why, because walking on the road is easier than walking through trees, but when I ask Mother she doesn't tell me.

We climb over the wall, trying to be lighter than we are, because if we put all our weight on the stones they might slip and tumble over and we could trap our fingers or feet in them. It's good that our backpacks are empty, because if they were full we'd have to take them off and put them over the wall separately, and then one of us would have to hold them while the other person climbed over, because the grass is still wet from the morning ground-water.

It's darker under the trees, but it's a little bit warmer as well. I think this is because of all the wood around us. That's why we always put wood on the kitchen fire – because wood has heat stored inside it the way you can store pickles in a jar, or the way the lamb has its own warmth that lives in jumpers. When you put the wood on the hot embers, the heat comes out as fire, but even if you just walk through lots of trees you can still feel a tiny bit of that heat, like some of it is leaking.

We walk through the wood for ages. There isn't a path, so sometimes when the trees and bushes get too thick we have to turn around and look for another way through. I don't know how to get back to the farmhouse from here, but Mother says she can remember the way. Once, we stop and drink some of our water. Then we keep walking.

I get tired of the dark. The trees are so big and thick that not enough light gets through the leaves. I start wishing I could just chop the tops off all of them, as if we're trapped walking for miles underneath the farmhouse kitchen and then someone could lift up a floorboard and let all the light in. I say this to Mother, but she just tells me not to be silly.

My feet are tired and it feels like we've been walking all day, but I'm only just hungry so it's probably not even lunchtime yet.

I blink. I blink twice. I think I can see the sunlight. I think I can see the edge of the wood.

I run out of the trees into a wide grassy area, and suddenly I can see for ages, all the way to the sky in both directions. Across from me is the most beautiful building I've ever seen, made of glass, with thin white wood connecting the panes. The way it glitters, it's like a cobweb on a cold morning, and I catch my breath. How could we have been so close to something so beautiful and not have known about it?

I'm running towards it. I hear Mother shout at me from the trees, but I don't care. The glass building is shining so brightly.

Up close, the glass is less clear. It's covered in green, and the wood is cracked and grey. Inside is some kind of garden.

I walk around the edge of it until I find the door. I have to rip off the leaves growing over it and shove it with my shoulder, but then I'm in.

It's warm inside, as if somebody's been having a bath. It smells of soil and of green things. There's a stone path that twists and winds, and on each side of it are bushes and trees. It's strange seeing trees inside a building, like someone has trapped the outside under a glass, the way Mother sometimes does to spiders. I wonder how they got here. Did someone grow the trees and then build the building up around them, or was the glass building already here and someone brought

226

the trees inside? They're not a kind of tree I know. A short hard trunk like the willow twists we grow beans up, and a big round bush balanced on top. Bright orange balls hang from the branches.

The door creaks behind me. Mother, her face sweating and eyes wide.

'What is it?' I ask her.

Mother is quiet, looking around at the strange garden. She picks one of the bright balls from the tree and holds it to her nose. She closes her eyes and breathes in, and the glow from it lights up her whole face.

She picks another and gives it to me. It sits heavy in my hand, firm but soft underneath. Its skin feels like candles. I bring it to my face to smell it, as Mother did. It smells sweet and sharp, as if the whole air has been boiled down to this one small fruit. It tastes bitter on the tip of my tongue.

'Like this.' Mother plunges her thumbnail through the skin and peels it away.

I copy, and the skin gives way to soft fruit that's sticky on my thumb. I try one of the pieces. I have to close my eyes just to take in the taste of it. The juice tingles on my lips and where it dribbles from the corners of my mouth.

Mother tells me it's called an orange, like the colour. She says that this place is an orangery. The trees need the glass building to help them grow.

We sit on the winding stone path and eat four oranges each. Then we pack our rucksacks with as many as we can carry back to the farmhouse.

*

We eat oranges every night till they're gone. We sit without talking in the kitchen with darkness at the windows, eating our beautiful orange fruits by the beautiful orange fire. When they're finished, I want to get some more, but a storm comes and blows the roof off the chicken shed, so we have to stay near the farmhouse to fix it so the chickens don't freeze in the winter, and then we have to wash our clothes and clean the rooms and go to the City and do all the other normal things, and then the days are too short for the long walk. So we stay at the farm and I collect the eggs and help Mother chop the wood and dig up potatoes and carrots. Sometimes, when I pull them from the ground, I imagine for a second that the bright stick of orange is a fruit and I will taste that sweet, beautiful taste again.

*

I start to think about the dead people and what it must have been like before they were dead. I try to make pictures of it, but all I can think is that it must have been very noisy with all of them speaking and walking about at the same time, and they must have had to fight for food because it's hard to find food just for me and Mother and the chickens and sheep, and there are so many more dead people. I wonder how they all remembered each other's names.

I ask Mother what it was like, but Mother just puts another log on the fire and says it's a good thing that all of the dead people are dead.

'Why?'

'Better we don't exist.'

I try to understand this, but Mother doesn't always make very much sense. Mother cannot like humans very much, but Mother is a human and I am a human, so maybe she only means the dead people. I think Mother is selfish, the way she sometimes tells me I am selfish. What I mean is, I think she finds it easier to hate things than to want them.

Sometimes she says to me, 'A survivor does not want things, she only needs things.' But Mother is not a survivor, she is a creator. I am the one whose name means survivor, that's what she says, and I do want things. I mean, I want things that I don't need. I want the shiny woman back. I want eyes like hers that are as warm and wet as milky tea. I want more sweet and good things in the larder, like jams. I want to stand on top of the mountain again. And I want more humans who are not dead people. I want someone to talk to who isn't Mother.

*

The sheep that Mother calls a ram has started standing on the backs of the other sheep. Mother says this means we might get more lambs next year and I want to say that I know, but I don't. I just pick up a stack of wood and follow her inside, and I don't say anything at all.

Every day we have to come inside earlier because of the light. Some days it stays so dark it doesn't feel like daytime at all, but more like night pretending, and when I go out to fetch water from the stream I have to be careful where I put my feet so I don't slip down the muddy bank.

I start to get used to it again. Some bits of the day are longer than before and some bits are shorter, but the pattern is still the same, like the pattern of straight lines on the blanket that goes over my bed, where the order of the colours never changes.

We go to the City. We look after the chickens and the sheep. We cook. We eat. We wash. Everything happens in straight lines which means we can survive.

And all the time I carry what I want inside me, the way I carry the soft woman and the memory of the shiny woman. I work hard to keep all these things on the inside, but sometimes I wonder if Mother can see them on the outside, too.

I look at Mother. She's standing in the yard pushing seeds into the black plastic trays so we can try to grow vegetables on the window-shelf in the kitchen. Her back and shoulders are round like the top of the hill as she bends forward. She handles the seeds gently, like she is one of the chickens covering its delicate chick.

Mother says that when human people are first made, they are tiny. She says they're smaller than a marrow. They are called babies.

Once I found a baby. It must have been a baby because it was smaller than me or Mother, but it was one of the dead people. It was only bones, lying on the grass outside the City, next to some normal-size human bones. It must have been ground bugs that ate it and not the wolf-dogs, because the bones were all still in their right places. Most of the baby's body just looked like the chicken bones that Mother crushes up to sprinkle on the vegetable plants to help them grow, but its head bone looked like a human head bone, only smaller.

I picked it up. It sat in the middle of my hand, just the right shape to fill it, not heavy, more like holding a turnip or one of the round metal bowls we use in the kitchen. It made me remember lying on my bed and filling my hand with the round bump of my chest, and how my skin felt warm and like a shiver, like I was hot and cold at the same time. The baby's head bone wasn't hot, just cold. Once I suppose it must have been warm, when it was a real baby. The head bone was thin across the top, like it hadn't had time to get its proper thickness yet. I ran my fingers across the thinnest bits, careful not to accidentally break it.

But then Mother called me away from the next road, and I had to put the baby's head bone down and run over to her.

I put it down as quickly as I could without breaking it, but I didn't have time to put it in its right place. At first I didn't mind that it was a hand-space away from the stacked bones of the baby's neck and back, but by the time I got to Mother, collecting more tools from the front of a shop, I only wanted to run back to the baby and move its head bone. I wanted to fix it, the way Mother fixed the door to my bedroom when the handle broke. I want it to be a whole baby again. Sometimes, even when I'm not trying to think about it, I remember that baby with the gap between its head bone and its body bones, and I wish I knew the way back to it.

*

I'm going to grow a baby. Not a dead baby, but a real living human baby, which is going to grow into a person like me or like Mother.

I know this because Mother is wrong. Mother says that there is only us, that one day there will be no people at all, because we will be like the dead people. But there can always be more of something. What I mean is, I can become a creator and grow another person, the way Mother grew me.

I will not tell Mother. Instead, I am going to pack up my rucksack, ready for a journey. I will do this when Mother is outside chopping wood or fixing the wall around the sheep field or collecting water in the red plastic bucket. Then tomorrow night I will wait until Mother is sleeping and I will tiptoe out of the house. I will have to walk down the stairs in my socks and only put on my boots at the last moment so she doesn't hear. I will open the big front door very slowly, careful not to let it say the creaking noises it sometimes makes, and then I will walk quietly across the yard. I hope the chickens will not hear me and start clucking, because then Mother might wake up and come outside to check it isn't a fox, and she'll find me and I'll have to tell her why I'm standing in the yard in the middle of the night in my boots and rucksack.

But if I get across the yard without being heard, I will climb over the stone wall so I don't accidentally clang the heavy metal gate. Then I'll wait until I'm on the other side of the hill before I switch on my torch, just in case Mother is looking out of the window and sees the light. If there are no clouds I might be able to see without my torch.

The nights are long, now. There will be plenty of time to

walk to the City, and I will be back at the farmhouse before Mother wakes up.

Maybe Mother will like having another person to talk to. Maybe the only reason she doesn't want other people is because she doesn't know them yet and that makes her afraid, the way she was afraid of not knowing on the day we explored and found the orangery.

I think this is another reason I am braver than Mother.

*

The next day it rains. It makes loud noises on the windows like someone knocking on the glass with their fingertips. The wind sounds like a great big tree brushing its top branches all over the side of the house.

The sheep cuddle each other next to the stone wall, and when I go outside to check for eggs and feed the chickens, I come back with my clothes and hair stuck to my skin like I've fallen in the stream. It's a cold rain, as if someone has taken the cold from the metal tools when we leave them in the yard overnight and turned it into water and made it sting when it falls. Mother puts a pan outside the back door in the morning and by the time it gets to evening there is enough water for our cups of tea.

It's like the snow, except louder, and we don't go outside more than we have to. We spend the day sitting by the kitchen fire. Mother sorts through all the food in the larder and tries to work out what we should eat when, so that nothing will go bad and we won't run out. I sew bits of old sweatshirt together to make a blanket.

We go to bed without washing, because it's too cold and wet to go to the stream for the wash-water. I pile extra blankets on top of me to keep out the draughts, and I try to sleep listening to the rain making patterns on the roof and the wind shaking at my window. It's too wet to go to the City tonight.

*

It rains all through the night and into the next day. And the next day. And the next.

I wake up every morning and my tummy has this sad flat feeling like someone has squashed it with a boot. When I go to bed, I fold the pillow over my head to block out the noise, and I hope if I listen hard enough to the quiet inside the pillow, I'll hear the end of the storm.

*

We come downstairs on one of the rainy mornings, and the kitchen is full of tiny wriggling things, which Mother says are called silverfish, though they're not proper fish like the ones in the stream. They are shiny grains of rice with two long eyebrow hair stalks that Mother calls feelers, and when they move their whole bodies wriggle from side to side. They wriggle across the floor and the arms of the comfy chair and into the cupboards. Mother goes into the larder and shouts when she sees them trying to get at the food.

We spend the morning squashing them, until my back hurts from always bending over to chase them, and my eyes sting from looking only at small things. Every time I think we've got them all, another one wriggles out from somewhere. I want to leave two of them, a Monster and a Mother silverfish, but Mother says no, so we squash them all.

*

When I went away and then came back again, when I climbed the mountain, before the shiny woman and before I knew I was a bridge, Mother wanted to know where I'd been, and I didn't know how to tell her. I didn't know the words to describe it, because nearly all of my words come through Mother and Mother wasn't there. Even if I did know the words, I don't think she would understand, because Mother doesn't understand the kind of thing I saw – but maybe that is about words as well, because maybe I just don't know how to put the right words together.

So I told her I went to the mountain because I didn't know what a mountain was up close. Which is true, but that is just a little bit of it. Like when I'm doing something really difficult like trying to unscrew my torch to put different batteries in, or remembering a tricky word, and Mother says I stick my tongue out to concentrate. But what she means is that I stick a tiny bit of my tongue out, and most of it is still hidden inside my mouth. That is what I did when I told Mother where I'd been. I told her a tiny bit and kept the rest of it hidden in my mouth.

*

The rain has stopped.

When I woke up this morning, for a moment I couldn't work out what was different, and then I realised it was quiet. I ran to the window and looked out. The sunlight wasn't much because it still had to push through all the clouds, so it looked grey and weak as if it had been watered down, but all the branches and wall stones and roof pipes were covered in little drops that looked like they'd trapped some of the sunlight inside them, so everything shone.

All day, I keep looking up to the top of the hills at the back of the farmhouse, where Mother says the weather comes from. Each time, I think I might see purple in the sky, or a dark-grey smudge that means more rain, but there's nothing. The clouds get whiter, and the sun tries harder and harder to push its way through.

I ask Mother, 'Will it rain again?'

I don't want to say 'tonight', in case she asks why. Even so, I hold my breath in case it starts coming quicker and she realises something is different. My eyes start itching and I want to blink a lot. I try to keep them open.

But Mother is busy clearing the yard from everything the storm left in it.

'Not till tomorrow at least,' she says, and I can't see her face but she speaks quickly so I can tell she isn't really interested. 'Help me shift this branch.'

*

We spend the day clearing the yard and the fields. Mother fixes the log store where the roof has collapsed. I check on the chickens and the sheep.

That night, I sit with my back against the metal bed so I don't accidentally fall asleep before Mother comes upstairs. I wait a long time after I hear her stop moving about.

The night-time animals are making small fidgeting noises in the grass at the side of the road. Sometimes I think it might be the wind, though there isn't very much wind tonight – but maybe that is what not-much-wind sounds like at night – small animals. Mother always says that things sound different in the dark.

Some of the noises come from bigger animals though. I can tell because their noises are bigger. They sound like footsteps or like a person talking in a high voice. As I turn onto the main road towards the City, I hear a fox which sounds like someone coughing.

Even without the water falling on me from the sky, everything is wet. My trousers are damp up the inside of my leg from where I climbed over the stone wall. The stones were dry but the moss holds water like a towel, and when you touch it, it lets the water out. Mother says if you get thirsty you can drink it, but she says it's hard work and doesn't taste very nice.

I'm trying to keep on the road and not step in any puddles. I don't want to walk all the way to the City and back in wet boots. I zip up my jacket all the way to my neck.

Night is always cold. Even when the sun has been shining all day, it doesn't stay warm the way the embers stay warm after the kitchen fire has gone out. When night arrives, it's as if everything just forgets it was ever daytime.

The first time I spent a night away from the farmhouse, when I went to the mountain, I slept under a blanket with my back against a wall. When I lay down the grass and stones were warm, but I woke up later when it was still dark and the grass had gone cold. At first I thought I was lying on the big stone slab in the larder, and I had shivers all the way through my body. When I remembered where I was, I got up, packed up the blanket and started walking. Mother always says that moving makes you feel warmer.

I slept again during the day when the sun was still shining so the ground wasn't as cold.

On the second night I found some trees that still had their old leaves underneath them. I pulled lots of them into a pile so it would be a bit like my mattress at the farmhouse, and that helped.

Tonight, I don't stop. I keep moving, which keeps me warmer, although that is not the only reason I do it. I have a picture in my head which I didn't put there, of Mother sleeping in the big bed, under the spotty blanket, then waking up and coming through to my bedroom to tell me it's the morning, and my bed being empty.

If Mother wakes up and my bed is empty, I think she will be angry because she knows I am a bridge and that I can separate us, and maybe she will think I have left her for ever. Or maybe she will be a little bit sad. Or maybe she will realise she is a bridge as well, and think that she separated us, and that would make her even sadder.

So when my eyes start closing or I can feel a blister rubbing the back of my foot, I let that picture into my head and I force myself to keep walking. I have to be back at the farm-house before Mother knows I'm gone.

I think so hard about moving and about staying awake, that when I look up and I'm in the City, I almost can't remember how I got here.

The City at night is darker than anywhere else. It's as if the buildings and the roads with holes in them and the rusty cars soak up the little bit of light that gets through the clouds. Maybe they are like the moss, and they soak up the moonlight during the night-time, then throw it all out again during the day, and that's why the glass buildings all shine so much.

I switch on my torch. The light looks small in the big darkness, much smaller than when there are two torches, mine and Mother's, but I keep walking. I get to a part of the City I've never been to before, but I should be able to get to the Clinic quicker if I don't have to go round by the vegetable-growing building or the house with the bats in.

I try to notice things I walk past, so I can remember the way back. A tower. An upside-down car with its wheels in the air, like a ground bug on its back. A crater, which I have to clamber down and up the other side. A tree with all its wet brown leaves underneath it. Once, I see a wolf-dog a few buildings ahead, but it slinks away with its back low to the ground.

The Clinic appears as if it's been walking towards me while I've been walking towards it, and we both turned the corner and are surprised to see each other.

Being here on my own is different to being here with Mother. With Mother, she's always the one who decides what to do and I just follow her, but now I'm here because of what I want instead. I followed what I want like following along a road without any places to turn off, the way Mother sometimes says one word leads on to another and then another and that's how a sentence gets made.

But without Mother it's like the Clinic lights are even brighter, and they make me feel open and looked at, the way I was warm and full looking at the shiny woman, and then Mother opened the door and all the cold air rushed into the room and I wanted to hide under the blankets. But I've come all the way here in the dark, so I can't just turn around and walk back to the farm.

To push open the doors, I have to take the piece of metal out of the handles, where Mother pushed it to stop the foxes and wolf-dogs getting in, but it's harder on my own, and I can't get it out.

Mother always says that if we can't do something, we need to look for tools that mean we can, like the metal to get us into the vegetable-growing building, or the board to scrub our clothes against in the washtub. I look around for a tool that will help me.

By the side of the road, a few steps away from the Clinic, is a pile of stones. I choose the biggest one that will still fit in my hand, and try to hit the metal out of the handles. Instead, the metal just bends so it's even more stuck, and in my head I think the sound of one of Mother's words that she says I'm not allowed to use – but I don't say it out loud in case there's an animal waiting somewhere.

I think about the vegetable-growing building, which has the door we use and a smaller door on the other side that we always keep closed. I take my stone and start to walk.

The Clinic is big. I'd forgotten how much of it there is. I walk around it till I can't even see the road back to the farm, and all the time there's that feeling at the back of my neck as if there's a wolf-dog watching. Not a real wolf-dog, but the same one that watches me whenever I try to remember something before or after the soft woman on the bridge.

The door on the other side of the Clinic is really two doors pretending to be one. They're made of glass, so more like windows than doors, and I can see through them into the little dark room on the other side.

Next to the window-doors is a number box like the kind

we sometimes find in the shops. I take out my plastic card and run it down the side of the windows the way Mother taught me, but nothing happens. I try again. I smash one of the window-doors with the stone.

In the quiet city, the noise hits me like a head-butting ram. I stop and listen the way Mother taught me, in case there are wolf-dogs near who have heard me, but there's nothing new – only the broken window-door where before it was all in one piece. I smash the sharp edges till there's a hole big enough for me to fit through.

The dark room on the other side is so quiet I can hear a ringing sound, like when you hit a glass with a spoon, and I can't tell whether it's the room making the sound or if it's just inside my ears. I drop the stone and it crashes on the floor.

In my head, I make the picture of that cold cold room again, with the woman who wasn't Mother. Then I make a picture of it from the outside so I will know which room it is again. I pull together all the things Mother told me and all the things I know on my own or from the dead people, like gathering different kinds of vegetables into the same bucket. I go deeper inside the Clinic and deeper inside my head, and the night-time feels big and heavy around me.

*

Back outside, the air smells different. Air always smells different at the end of the night than at the start of it – more like grass and like water.

I walk back past the tree with wet brown leaves, and the crater, and the upside-down car, and the tower, until I'm in a part of the City I know, and I can get home without thinking too hard. My feet want me to stop and sit down, and my whole body feels heavy from not sleeping. My trousers rub between my legs, but I make the picture in my head of Mother waking up and me being gone, and I make myself keep walking. I think the sky is already lighter.

By the time I get to the hill behind the farmhouse, the edge of the sky is pale and grey, and I can see the road without squinting. By the time I clamber over the farmyard gate, the birds are twittering and starting to fly out from under the barn roof. I open the big farmhouse door, slip into the kitchen and listen. Nothing. No sounds from Mother. Just the birds outside, and the embers and hot ash making their breathing noise in the grate. Mother will be downstairs soon to put book pages and dry twigs on the fire and blow it back into a flame.

I take off my boots and hurry upstairs. I climb into bed. The sheets are cold from not sleeping in them all night, but it doesn't matter. I think I fall asleep before I've even thought about falling asleep.

*

I wake up to Mother's face. She's leaning over my bed and frowning. For a moment I think she knows and she's here to tell me off, but then I see that she's holding a bowl of porridge and a weak cup of tea.

'Morning,' she says, and her frown turns into half a smile, then back to a frown again.

Outside, the sun is already bright and high up in the sky, and all the clouds are gone.

'How late is it?'

'Late morning,' she says. 'You were so fast asleep I didn't wake you. Here.'

She hands me the porridge, which I eat sitting in bed. As soon as I take the first spoonful I realise how hungry I am and I gobble it up like a chicken gobbling up grain.

Mother watches me eat. 'Are you OK?'

I nod, my mouth full of porridge.

'You don't feel ill?'

'No.' Can Mother tell that I didn't sleep all night? Do I look different?

She pauses, her hand resting on my stripy blanket next to my leg. 'We'll take it easy today.'

Mother takes my empty bowl and leaves me to get out of bed. I don't have any wash-water, so I wash between my legs with tea, then put on clean clothes and go downstairs to Mother.

There are still things to be mended and cleared away, but Mother lets us leave it for now. We spend the day doing ordinary jobs. We check the chickens and the sheep, and tie new bits of ribbon to the poles in the field to keep the birds off the vegetables. Then Mother helps me carry up water from the stream, and I stack the wood as she chops it, so the log store is full again.

All day I carry the night before inside me like a precious breakable thing which Mother cannot see, the way all day a chicken carries around the egg it's going to lay the next morning. Sometimes it feels so big in my chest that I might explode with it and tell Mother, because she can't stop me doing it any more. But then I remember how she said that humans shouldn't exist, and the way her voice was flat and hard like a spade as she said it, and I'm afraid to.

So I just work with Mother, and when we finish the logs she says we should call it a day, so we go inside and sit quietly by the kitchen fire and I try not to think about the City at night and the Clinic full of cold and rooms and corridors, in case Mother sees what I am thinking about.

*

We work next to each other in the field or the barn or the house, but we don't say very much. When we walk into the City, Mother goes first and I follow her, holding the Clinic inside me the way I can hold my breath – or sometimes we walk side by side but with our steps all at different times. When we're at the farm, it's like we're both at different farms, even though we might be close enough to touch each other.

Mother's words carry only what they need to so we can get the jobs done and survive.

'Shut the door. Stay right.'

I pull the heavy barn door closed so this sheep we're chasing can't get in, and hurry to stand at the side of it with my arms out, making myself as wide as possible. Mother walks down the last bit of the lane clapping her hands, and the sheep runs into the farmyard ahead of her. She shuts the big metal gate. It screeches like a night bird and when it clangs into place, the sheep makes short, sudden movements like it doesn't know which way to go. Mother keeps walking behind it and I stand with my arms out saying 'Hey hey hey' to stop it getting out the other side of the yard, and slowly we push it towards the barn. It kicks its back legs and turns in little bits of circles, till it's squashed right up against the stone wall and we are close enough to grab hold. It takes both of us to stop the sheep wriggling, but once it's still I can put my legs on either side of its body so I've got it with my knees as well as my hands, and it can't go anywhere. The sheep's wool is soft and warm through my trousers.

'Got it?'

I nod.

Mother crosses the farmyard to get the bowl and the knife. I can feel the sheep trembling. It feels very big and round for an animal with such thin legs, and its trembles run all the way through me so I have to keep holding hard to the sheep's body till Mother comes back. The sheep tries to fidget away from me, but I'm stronger.

'Hold back the head.'

I pull back the bottom of the sheep's face so it has to look upwards and its neck is long and open. There's a group of small grey marks on the back of the sheep's head that makes me think of Mother's wolf-dog bite. I try to count them, but I keep getting lost and having to start again. Mother puts the bowl under the sheep's neck.

Sometimes, if Mother's wearing shorts or working with her trousers rolled up, I can see the pink mark on her leg where she says a wolf-dog bit her a long time ago. She doesn't talk about it much, unless I keep asking her, and then she either speaks only in small words or stops speaking altogether. 'It's in the past, Monster. Let it go.'

Mother has always told me to let things go, as though thoughts were objects I could hold and then not hold, like watching something fall from very high up till it's too far away to see where it lands. I do not know how to let go of thoughts like that, like the thought of the soft woman falling from the bridge, or the thought of Mother smacking my face and taking the shiny woman away.

I used to think Mother might have let go of some of her thoughts, but then I noticed the way her face looks like a shut door, or the way she sometimes touches the wolf-dog bite when she thinks I'm not looking. I think when she touches it, it means she's holding on to the thought instead of letting go, like when I touch the tally marks on my bedroom wall to count the days, except Mother's wolf-dog bite is like touching a bit of the past, and my tally marks are always counting forwards to something that hasn't happened yet.

Later, Mother tips the bowl into the stream and I wash the mess off the cobbles in the yard. We take the woolly skin off the sheep's body and chop the sheep-meat into bits, some to cook and some to rub salt into so we can keep it in the larder. Mother says the meat might be tough because the sheep was too old for milk or lambs, but she says eating it will make us stronger.

While we work, I think about the sheep's body after Mother made the cut, the way it twisted and jerked between my knees and made me think of the kitchen clock – how I can hear it tickerting when nothing else is making a noise, and how it's sometimes faster or slower, but always with a sort of silence in between.

*

It goes like this:

I do not tell Mother until I'm certain it's worked, until I can feel the seeds I planted sprout and start to become shoots that will grow into arms and legs and fingers and toes, until I can feel them turning into a baby.

On the day I'm finally sure, when I can feel my baby's small head through my tummy like a round stone, I sneak down the thin stairs before it's light. I screw up paper for the grate and blow on last night's embers to make them flicker and burn again. Being careful the pans don't clang and wake Mother, I pull together the ingredients – flour, salt, some of the baking powder from the tub in the larder, water, leftover eggs from yesterday morning, a bit of the fat from when we killed the sheep. I know Mother won't mind me using all these precious things, not today, because this is a special day and I'm making it as a surprise.

It's nearly light by the time I've finished working, and when she comes downstairs rubbing the sleep from her eyes, the kitchen is full of the warm smell of fat and baking biscuits.

'What's this?' she asks, as she lowers herself into the big chair by the fire.

I hand her a cup of tea, brewed dark, just the way she likes it, and sit opposite her. 'It's your favourite,' I say, 'for a surprise. I have something very special to tell you.'

So I tell her. I tell her about the Clinic and how I remember that we used to live there. I tell her about the cold room, and how I watched the woman who wasn't her, and how I remember the hard pair of hands that weren't hers either, that taught me where the seeds went even when it hurt. I tell her how I pushed the seeds into myself. And because I know now that it's worked, I tell her I have a baby growing inside me and it won't be just us any more. Now we have another human we'll be able to talk to and be with. I tell her how wonderful it will be once the baby is born.

Mother's face goes all light and shining. She's already warm and glowing from the firelight, but when she hears that we won't be alone just the two of us any more, it's as if her skin isn't just *in* the firelight, it *is* the firelight, like her whole face is a candle flame and it's the brightest thing in the room.

And Mother smiles. And I smile. And we're both candles now, both so bright and happy that it doesn't matter that the sun isn't up yet because we're our own warmth.

'That's wonderful,' says Mother, taking hold of my hands. 'You're wonderful.' And she draws me into her arms and hugs me and holds onto me as if she might never let me go, and her body is warm from the fire as she says again, 'Monster, you're wonderful.'

That is how I think it will happen. That is what I plan.

I like to hold these pictures in my mind when I lie awake on top of the covers, trying to pretend it isn't cold. I spread my fingers like spider legs across my belly and wonder if I really do have a person growing inside me. I can't feel anything yet, but if I close my eyes I can picture the seeds I planted, like I am the soil protecting it as it grows. I can picture it sprouting, little arms like shoots, a sapling of a girl. I want to ask Mother how long it will be before I know for certain if it's worked, but then I would have to tell her about the Clinic at the same time, so I don't.

I wonder how big my baby will grow, and how I'll get her out. When Mother digs up potatoes she uproots the entire plant, and when she does this she turns the earth inside out.

I wonder, when my child is born, will I be uprooted like the plant, or turned inside out like the soil?

Perhaps she will burst out of me the way the hen-chicks break out of their eggs. Perhaps I am not supposed to survive. Perhaps that is the rule: to create a person you must lose a person. I will split and break apart as she bursts out of me. I think there's a sort of balance to that, like when Mother weighs ingredients for cooking, something being created and something else disappearing. I wouldn't mind becoming one of the dead people if it meant creating a new person – though I will be sad if I never get to see my baby.

But I don't think that can be right. Mother says I am a survivor – that is who I am and what I'm good at. So I don't think I will become one of the dead people. I will become a creator like Mother. I will live with my child and plant potatoes and the chickens will lay eggs and we will collect cans and clothes from the City. I am a survivor, and my child will be a survivor, too. Mother says hoping is dangerous, but I lie on my bed with my hands on my belly and hope.

*

I wake in the half-made light before the sun comes up. My face is cold and I can see frost on the inside of the window, but the rest of me is hot and sticky under my blankets. I swing my legs out over the bed. Even before my feet touch the floor, my insides are bubbling like hot water. I throw up my tummy into the empty wash bowl.

I get out of bed. I throw up again.

I keep on throwing up until there's nothing left inside me to throw up. Then I wipe my mouth on the back of my hand.

I wonder if Mother is the same, throwing up her tummy in her bedroom. Perhaps there was something wrong with the soup-tin I ate last night. Perhaps this is the Sickness that Mother sometimes talks about, the one that made so many of the dead people. Maybe it was still at the Clinic after all and we never noticed, and I brought it back with me on my clothes, or accidentally planted it in myself, like the flowers we have to pull up from the vegetable field because Mother says they're weeds.

Mother is already downstairs, stoking the kitchen fire. I tell her about my Sickness and she rests the back of her hand on my head. Then she pours me a mug of hot water and wraps a potato to cook in the fire. She tells me the potato will be good at filling the empty space in my tummy.

She sits down beside me and looks at me for a long time.

I look away so she doesn't see the Clinic and my walk to the City at night, because if I did plant the Sickness inside myself there, then maybe I am not a survivor like Mother says. Maybe I am not a creator either. Maybe I am not anything,

255

like all the dead people who don't have names any more. I do not want Mother to hate me like she hates the dead people. I drink the water slowly and all the time her eyes do not stop looking at me.

Once I have drunk the water and eaten the potato, I feel a bit better, and we get on with the pattern of the day.

I dream about the soft woman. She stretches out her hand to my face, and as she touches my skin I wake up, breathing hard, the blanket scrunched tight in my fist, as if that's what I've been chasing – as if I've finally caught it.

But what my dream catches hold of isn't the blanket but a question: where was Mother?

In the Clinic when I hid from the dead people and their big hard hands, where was Mother? In the city with the river and the high bridge leaping over it, when the soft woman sat me on the railing and we dangled our feet over the void, when I let go of her hand and she fell into the gully alone, where was Mother?

If Mother is my creator, if I grew inside her, then why do I not remember her? Why was she not there to save the soft woman or to keep hold of me?

I look at Mother where she crouches now, toasting bread over the fire, watching the eggs tickerting in the pan. She's sharp and cold, like a packet of nails. Her body could never be soft or deep enough to grow a child. And she does not bleed.

Before the shiny woman, I did not think about words very much. What I mean is, I thought about them only as rucksacks to carry the meaning of what I wanted to say. And what I wanted to say was always true. The words were like containers for my thoughts. I never looked closely at words. I never thought about the volume of what they could carry, how some words carry more than others, how some carry more than they pretend to, how some do not carry anything at all.

I never understood that Mother's words might not carry her real thoughts. And I never realised that Mother could be a lie.

*

Another morning. Another Sickness.

And another.

It pushes itself into my days and settles there. Again and again it pulls out my insides into the wash bowl or the bucket or onto the ground outside the house. Again and again Mother washes it away down the river for the fish to nibble. Then she pours me a mug of hot water and cooks me a potato on the fire.

Mother does not say much about it, she just does these things without talking, but when she does talk she says it must be the Sickness.

'Is this what the Sickness looks like?'

She hands me a blanket for around my shoulders. 'I don't know, Monster. I just don't know.'

*

The day is closing in around us as we make our way back along the lanes from the City. The yellow flowers are back at the edges of the road, but I don't pick any this year because I don't want Mother to think everything is the same as last year, and I don't know how to tell her that it isn't. And because if Mother's name is empty then maybe the yellow flowers are empty too, and maybe there's no point trying to make the farmhouse feel as though it's full of sunshine when it isn't, because that's also a kind of lying. So I try not to look at the yellow flowers. I fiddle with my bag strap and try not to look at Mother either.

Our bags are full of food – biscuits, cereals, even a packet of powder that Mother says works a bit like milk powder and will turn into soup if we mix it with water. Mother insisted on packing all the jars and cans in her own bag so mine wouldn't be too heavy because of the Sickness. Maybe that's why she walks next to me instead of her normal few steps ahead, because she's struggling with it all. But maybe not, because she did it on the way to the City as well, when our bags were empty.

'Mother?'

She hitches her bag higher on her back as she looks at me.

'What does your name mean?'

She frowns. 'You know what it means – it means "creator". Your name means "survivor".'

I have to look away from her. I concentrate on kicking a stone along the lane instead. 'Why?'

'Why what?'

'Why does your name mean creator?'

'Because I created you,' she says, and I can hear in her voice that she's smiling her special just-for-Monster smile – the smile which says she's older and knows more than I do.

I kick the stone in front of us and it bounces over a hole. 'No.'

'What?'

'No.' And I tell her what I know, that she isn't my creator, and that her words aren't true, and that her name is empty like a cup that's leaked all its water away.

Mother goes quiet. Our footsteps and the clatter of the stone are suddenly very loud – so loud that when Mother does speak, I almost can't hear her. 'How do you know?'

I don't know how to answer this without sharing the soft woman, which I don't want to do. I just say, 'It doesn't matter,' and watch my feet landing one after the other on the road.

Mother slows, so I have to slow too if I want to hear this new quiet voice: 'I said it the first time without thinking . . . and . . . I liked it.'

I kick the stone so hard it flies off into the long grass and yellow flowers at the edge of the lane. I take longer, quicker steps, until I'm ahead of her and she's following behind, watching me walk away from her and not being able to talk to me or touch, the way I always used to be with her.

Mother's words are like snow. They cover all the good things with a thick blanket, full of shifting grey shapes I can't quite see. Except when I pull away Mother's words, the good things underneath them are gone, and the City and the fields and the farm are empty.

*

I think about the seeds that I pushed into my belly, and how they won't be able to grow into a child now. A child is like a plant and Mother says plants can't grow in sick soil.

I've stopped bleeding.

It's the Sickness, Mother says, upsetting my body and breaking up its rhythm. Every day I check my knickers for blood but nothing comes.

I think about all the other patterns of my body that the Sickness could break up. The pattern of my fingernails growing and being trimmed, the pattern of waking up and going to sleep, the pattern of my breathing in and out again. What would happen, I wonder, if the Sickness broke my pattern of breathing out? What if I just kept on breathing in and in and in, and none of the air inside my body could get out again, and I just swelled up till my body was as big as the farmhouse? Would I keep on getting bigger, or would I burst?

I ask Mother, but she is busy chopping up wood in the last light of the day. She says I would not breathe in and in, but out and out, so that there was no air left inside me at all, and my body would shrink because I would be empty inside. But that won't happen, she says.

I tell her I am already empty inside.

She blows on her hands to warm them and tells me not to be silly.

I tell her my tummy can't hold anything any more, not water or potatoes. I tell her how it can't even hold a baby.

Mother goes very still. She rests the metal bit of the axe on the chopping block and leans on the end of the handle as she looks at me. Sometimes when Mother looks at me like this, I feel as if she's looking right into the back of my head, where the soft woman and the shiny woman and my walk to the mountain are stored.

She asks me what I mean.

So I tell her about the seeds, how I tried to plant them inside my belly but how I didn't realise I was sick. I tell her about the long corridors and cold cold rooms, how I knew where to go and what to do even though she never told me because I remember from the Clinic and from the dead people and from before Mother was there. I tell her how I wanted to make a child, to be a creator like the other woman wanted, the one in the picture in my head, who I thought was Mother but wasn't.

I talk for a long time. I tell Mother everything about it that I can think of so that she can understand it all and what I did. All the time I am talking, she stands very still, her hands leaning on the axe handle.

At last I run out of things to say, and it's quiet. Mother carries on watching me.

'Mother?'

She tucks the axe away in the log store, as carefully as she tucks me into my blankets at night. Then she picks up an armful of wood and walks back to the farmhouse. She doesn't look at me. She says nothing.

I watch her long legs and wide back as she walks away. I watch the back of her head. There's a piece of moss stuck in her hair where she's bent too close to the log store. It flaps and waves in her jolting steps.

I watch her until she closes the farmhouse door.

The sun left the edge of the sky while I was talking to Mother. The night draws tight around the little farm and there's a cold wind. I can feel a shiver starting somewhere in the middle of my back. I pull my coat-sleeves down as far as they will go. It will be warm and yellow by the kitchen fire, but I do not want to go inside. I don't want to think about the way Mother looked at me, right before she stopped looking at me, when she learned about my emptiness – the way my emptiness seemed to leak through me and into her, so that behind her eyes she also looked empty.

I put my cold hands inside my coat and spread them on my jumper over my belly. I imagine I can feel the deep blue emptiness there, like a night sky before the stars come out. I make a picture of it yawning inwards and inwards, so far inside me that it would take days to get to the end of it – only to realise that it was not the end, but a cliff edge, a bridge over an enormous gully, with more emptiness running deeper and further beyond. And I make a picture of myself, tumbling into my own emptiness and becoming lost, and Mother opening the farmhouse door and seeing me gone.

Somewhere a long way away, a wolf-dog barks. Something screeches nearer to the farmhouse.

I pick up some of the logs and slowly go inside.

*

Mother does not speak to me or look at me for six days. I count them on the tally I use to count the days between bleeding. It has been sixty-one days since the last time I bled.

I think I may be like Mother now. I think the Sickness has created this emptiness inside me and the emptiness has swallowed all the blood in my belly, and now like Mother I cannot bleed.

When Mother finally does look at me, she acts as if the silence never happened. She does not mention it, she does not name it, and so neither do I.

It's lunchtime when it happens, but I am cooking nothing because I do not want to feed the emptiness. Mother is cooking a tin of tomato beans on the fire. They smell sweet and thick, like something turning bad, and the horrible sweetness of it hits the back of my throat and travels right down to my belly. I want to throw up again. I don't know how to be in the same room with it.

I tell Mother I'm going outside to chop some more logs.

I think she will ignore me the way she has ignored me for the past six days, but this is when she looks at me. She looks at me over the tomato-bean tin cooking on the fire, and there's something like weather on her face, like a fight between clouds and maybe a storm about to break.

Then it clears and she says, 'Don't.'

I look at her with that sweet thick smell in my throat and I want to wait and say nothing and see what she'll decide to do next – but I can't just stand here with the Sickness building inside me, so I say, 'Don't what?'

'Chop the wood.'

'We need more,' I say, which is sort of true, because we always need more wood because the kitchen fire is always hungry.

'Don't,' she says again. 'You shouldn't. I'll do it – after lunch.'

'Why?'

She's quiet again, looking at me, and I look back at her, trying to breathe through my mouth so I can't smell the tomato beans. We look at each other for a long time, or at least it feels like a long time, and I think maybe Mother is going to not speak to me again for days and that this is going to be our lives now, unless the Sickness takes me and makes me one of the dead people – until at last Mother very quietly says, 'It's dangerous for you, chopping wood. The strain. It's dangerous when you're pregnant.'

'What's pregnant?'

'Going to have a baby,' she says. 'Carrying a child in your tummy.'

I'm sad then, because Mother is wrong and doesn't know it yet.

'But I'm not,' I tell her. 'I can't. I'm empty and sick and I haven't bled since more than thirty days ago so I can't make a child inside me.'

Mother smiles. After days of not talking, she smiles and she comes over to me and puts her hand under my jumper to touch my tummy. Her hand is warm and sticky from the fire heat and the tomato-bean tin, and the feeling of it there travels right up to the Sickness at the back of my throat so I have to struggle not to let it out. Mother spreads her fingers so her hand sits across my belly.

'I'll help you,' she says, and she puts her other hand on the side of my face. 'We can raise the child together.'

And that horrid thick smell rushes into my body and I can't hold it back any more. I throw up on the kitchen floor at Mother's feet. I throw up over and over and when I'm done throwing up her hand is gone from my belly and she's sitting me in the big chair and pulling back the hair from my face. And I have to lean close to hear what she's saying, which is, 'It's OK, I'm here, Monster, I'm here, it's all going to be OK.'

*

Sometimes, when I don't want to talk to Mother but I don't want to think about not talking to Mother, I think about the mountain. I like to think about it as if I'm there.

It's hot. My legs feel heavy like sheep's meat, like there's too much of me to climb so high. When I breathe, the air I take inside me gets heavier too. I can feel it falling down my throat and catching on the sides.

Every bit of me is helping to pull me up the side of this mountain. I can't remember why any more. I just grab onto it with my hands and the bottoms of my boots, and I pull till I can't feel the rock any more. My hands are hot and sticky, but also cold, and I can't feel where me ends and the mountain starts. It's like the harder I try to climb, the heavier I become, till my body starts to turn into stone. What I mean is, I've been climbing for a long time and I'm tired.

I pull myself over the last bit of rock where the top of the mountain stretches out like our kitchen table and I fall on the earth.

There's grass on top of the mountain. It isn't the green grass we have in the fields by the farmhouse, which smells sweet like the apple tree. This grass is thick and brown. It pokes the side of my face like an animal with sharp fingers. As I lie there on top of the mountain, I start to realise it's poking the rest of my body too. My hands stop being made of stone and start to feel the small things again. Then my arms and my chest. Last, my legs. I can feel the spiky grass through my trousers.

Eventually I can breathe again, and the air stops scraping when I pull it inside me. It stops making so much noise.

I sit up.

All around me is the world. I look as far as I can and there's no edge. It just goes on and on, for ever. It is green and brown, and the sky is bright, bright blue. I have never seen so much of it. I feel as if I might fall into it off the top of this mountain and be lost.

I can't see the farmhouse, where Mother will be feeding the chickens and taking water from the stream to pour on the vegetables so they don't get too thirsty. I can see the hill that is outside my bedroom window, but the farmhouse and my bedroom are hidden behind it.

Close to the hill I can see the edge of the City. The City is all grey. From up here where everything is green and brown and blue, it looks like a smudge of ash from the kitchen fire, like someone has put a big sooty thumb over the fields.

On the other side of the City there is just blue. Like the sky but darker, less empty. The sea is enormous.

Sea . . .

I make the shape of the word in my mouth, a hissing sound and a smile. Like *see*, only somehow deeper, even though it sounds the same. *Sea.* It isn't one of Mother's words, so I can't think how I know it. It just appears, like when I make pictures of things in my head but without me needing to try. When I make a picture of the word *sea*, it's more water than I know how to make sense of. It's more than the bathtub or the puddles in the farmyard. It's all the water that was ever rain, that ever smashed into my bedroom window during the storm, that ever rushed away from me in the stream behind the house – and in that water are fish, like the ones in the stream only bigger, and the water is always moving, up and down and over and over.

I let this picture of sea sit in my head, this thing that is all mine and not Mother's. It feels strange, having this word and not knowing where it comes from. All my other words have something around them, like the way the walls of the farm-house connect all the rooms to each other, and then connect the inside to the outside, and then everything outside is all connected to everything else outside through the fields and the walls and the lane. So everything fits together and I can fit all of my words into that everything.

But *sea* doesn't connect to anything. It just sits on its own in a big empty space. And I don't know how it connects to me.

I wonder if this is what it's like to be Mother, to be afraid of things that might not be there or might not be connected to anything else. I wonder if I am afraid.

I try to feel around the edges of this new and not-new word, but there's nothing except the sound of the word itself and the picture it makes in my head. It's like at night when it's so dark I can't even see the moon and it feels like my bedroom isn't there any more – it's just me in my bed and nothing but dark all around me, and it isn't frightening, it just is. I decide it's the same with the word *sea*.

I make my eyes narrow to try to see the other side of it, to see if there is a wall or a fence or a hedge where the sea finishes and the sky starts, but I can't see anything. So I look at the line between the sea and the ground instead. It twists and wiggles like the road from the farm into the City, like the sea and the ground can't decide where to put their own edges so it's all different in different places. I follow the shape of it with my finger.

I stop. My finger is still pointing at the line between the sea and the ground, but where my finger and the sea and the ground all meet, there's a tiny curl of smoke. Except that it's quite far away, so really it must be a big curl of smoke.

I watch it till my eyes hurt, in case it goes away, but it

doesn't. It just keeps curving from the ground up to the sky, then disappearing into nothing.

Smoke comes from fire, and to get fire you need either me or Mother, because fire can't just happen on its own. But I'm here so it isn't from me, and I'm sure it isn't from Mother because she's at the farm and anyway I don't think she knows about the sea and the smoke is right next to it. I try to make a picture in my head of fire without any hands to make it happen, where the flames just make themselves out of nothing, like the word *sea*, but it's too hard. I can't work out how to start the picture off without me or Mother in it, without a match or a lighter or the embers from the kitchen grate. I try to find different ways into making it, the way Mother says to find different ways of getting past a problem by using tools. I try to start with wood opening into a flame, or with a built-up fire, or with a lighter waiting for someone to flick its little wheel, but it all needs hands, and I screw up my face and stick the end of my tongue out because I'm thinking so hard. I think harder and harder, until I'm thinking so hard my head is full of pictures of hands starting fires – and that's when I notice the noise.

I notice it so suddenly it makes me jump, like I've heard a loud crash, or a howl – the kind of noise that makes me think there might be wolf-dogs near – though it isn't a crash and it isn't a howl. It isn't any noise I recognise.

I stand on top of the mountain and listen as hard as I can. I try to make a picture in my head as if I'm pushing my ears out, all the way to the edges of the world, but there's nothing. And I realise the noise is silence. The silence is enormous, like the sky. It goes on and on and on and I'm standing right in the middle of it. Like the whole world and all this great big silence belong to me.

Mother tried to explain it to me once, the sound of not

having noise. She said, silence is what happens when things end.

'What sort of things?'

She said, 'Anything. People, animals, days. It's the noise a fire makes after the ash is cold.' When I still didn't understand, she said, 'The noise the dead people make.'

I thought about this when we killed the chicken to cook the meat. I listened for the silence, but all I could hear was the scratchy twitch of its body, then the soft *phut* as Mother pulled out its feathers, then the bubbling and crackling as we put it in the big metal cooking pot over the fire.

But then, on top of that mountain, when the wind stopped and I held my breath inside me, I heard it. The sound of hearing nothing. I listened and listened and the silence was so loud it shouted over everything else.

Mother thinks that silence is a sad thing. She thinks that silence is all about endings, but it isn't. All the other noises are about endings, because they start and then they stop, but silence just keeps going and there isn't a way to know how long it lasts. It just is. I can hold it in my head like I hold the picture of the shiny woman, both of them not changing. I think the shiny woman is a kind of silence too.

Sometimes, when Mother is sad, I want to take her to the top of that mountain and let her listen to the silence, but it wouldn't work, not really. You can't have silence with more than one person, because other people have a beginning and an ending and that is a kind of noise. Even the dead people have noises – they have buzzing flies or the little bits of air that squeeze out of them, or they are just made of bones that rattle and crunch. You can only hear silence when you're on your own.

And Mother is afraid of the dead people so maybe Mother is afraid of silence. But what I learned on the mountain is that silence is beautiful. Silence is like smoke, filling the space till it is everywhere. It is not the sound of endings and dead people the way Mother thinks it is. Silence means beginnings and things carrying on. It means not just me and Mother, but other people who are not dead people, too. It means another moment and another and another, because in silence there is no start and stop, just the kind of always that Mother calls hope.

I listened till the silence was so loud I had to make a noise. I shouted as loudly as I could, and a rabbit ran out of the long grass towards its hole. A breeze came and lifted my small neck hairs. The silence disappeared.

Once the silence had gone, I started to look for the other city, the one with the bridge. I turned around and around, trying to look hard in every direction, but it was nowhere. Only the City and more hills and mountains, and a forest, and a few stone walls and buildings like the barn, and the smoke curling up to the sky, and next to it, the sea.

The world is big. Maybe it goes on for ever.

The farm is turning green again. Mother stops letting me do things. She says I have to think about the baby, but the way she says 'baby' is like she can't stop all her angry thoughts from pushing to the front of her mouth and tumbling out, like the word 'bridge'.

When I look at the separate trees and fields and bushes, it's as though nothing is changing, but then if I stand at the top of the hill behind the house and look at everything at once, I can see the way all the bits of the world are suddenly brighter at the same time. It makes me think of the kitchen fire in the mornings, how it's all grey ash and just a couple of sparks, till we blow on it just right and hold the bits of book paper to it, then suddenly the whole thing catches fire and is bright and warm and beautiful.

Sometimes, I can feel my baby moving and fidgeting inside me. I imagine her pressing the insides of my belly with her small hands, trying to feel the edges of her small dark world. Sometimes when her arms or legs kick out, it feels as though she sweeps through my whole body, like summer, like stepping out of the shade. When I rest my hand there, I picture her leaning her head into my palm, like she can feel the extra warmth from my touch.

I will not let that warmth disappear. I will not let Mother be the bridge that pulls me and my child apart.

My belly is bigger now. I've burst out from all my spikes and angles to become round. Mother says round like the moon, but I think my body glows brighter and warmer than that. I think I am round like the sun.

*

Every morning, there are so many birds outside my bedroom window that I have to hold my pillow tight over my head to not think about the noise.

All the little flowers have appeared at the side of the stream. Outside the gate, the long grass is full of colour and flying bugs. The bigger my belly grows, the more ground bugs and tiny animals there are, and the louder the air is. It's like the noise and the plants are all growing with me – as though the farm wants to be like me, the way I wanted to be like the shiny woman, which is sort of beautiful, but sometimes I just want all the noise to stop.

I keep remembering the orangery. Even more, I keep thinking about the oranges inside it, sitting in the trees like brightly coloured birds. Sometimes all I can think of is picking one of those oranges, peeling back the hard skin, and the sharp sweet taste of the fruit. I wake up thinking of oranges, and when I try to sleep my mouth goes dry with needing them.

After two days of this, I announce, 'I want to go back to the orangery.'

'No.' Mother is kneading dough into bread on the slab in the larder and doesn't turn to look at me.

'Why not?'

She pushes and presses with her knuckles. 'You're too big. You can't climb over walls in that state.'

'But I need oranges.'

'No.'

I can feel her 'no' fizzing inside me the way our apple juice fizzes when it's gone bad. I go back to the kitchen and stuff my feet into my boots. I have to sit in the chair to tie them up because it's difficult to bend over my belly. Then I find my coat and my backpack. It's late to set out for the orangery now, but I don't care. If it gets dark before I get back, I'll use my torch. I've walked at night before.

'What are you doing?' Mother has come out of the larder. She stands in the doorway, sleeves rolled up to her elbows, her hands red and shiny from kneading the bread dough.

I jut out my chin the way she does when she's arguing. 'I'm going to get oranges.'

'You can't.'

'I can,' I tell her. 'I am.'

She looks as if she wants to say something, but doesn't know what. I wait, but she just stands there looking red and angry, so I turn around and start to open the door.

'Wait!'

I turn back to Mother. Something else comes through her anger, like worms wriggling up through the soil after it's rained.

'Don't go,' she says.

'I need oranges.' And I do. I don't just want them, I need them, and because I am a survivor I know the difference.

'Then I'll go. Not today,' she says quickly, 'but tomorrow. I'll go first thing tomorrow and bring back all the oranges I can find.'

I hesitate. Tomorrow is a long time to wait, and if Mother doesn't leave until tomorrow morning then I won't have oranges until tomorrow night. But Mother is right. Sometimes my feet ache just walking around the house. I'm too big and heavy to climb over walls and walk all the way to the orangery and back. So I say, 'OK.'

I put my backpack in its place by the door, then sit in the comfy chair by the fire. Mother waits till I've kicked off my boots, then she nods and goes back to her bread. I close my eyes and lick my lips, and try not to think about slices of orange bursting with sweet juice.

*

The house is quiet with Mother gone. I make a picture of her in my head, walking through the trees that block out nearly all the light. It's warm. She stops to take her water from her backpack.

I think about the time she found the sheepfold, how she left with a full backpack, ready for a journey, and I don't know if she came back because of me or because of the sheep, or maybe just because she realised she had to.

Mother won't try to leave this time. I know this because Mother is not a survivor like I am. What I mean is, she is good at keeping alive, but she is not good at being away from the farm. Away from the farm, things have a different pattern, and Mother is always afraid in case she becomes one of the dead people. In the picture in my head, she drinks her water and puts the bottle back in her bag, and she never stops looking behind her for something in the dark that isn't there.

After I've fed the chickens and collected the eggs, I sit by the kitchen fire and feed it with wood to keep it burning, because even though it's warm outside, the kitchen gets cold without the fire. When I get hungry, I cook a tin of meat soup. I try to finish the blanket I'm making, but my fingers feel too fat for the needle and I can't concentrate. So I just sit in the comfy chair and watch the flames.

I think about my child and what she will be like. Will she be beautiful like the shiny woman, or a different kind of beautiful like the soft woman? Or will she be sharp and small like me? Maybe she'll be big like Mother, with her arms and legs all looking like separate animals.

I try to picture her face. I wonder if it already looks like her face, or whether she hasn't grown into one yet. I don't like this picture of my child without a face, with just a sheet of skin where her eyes and nose and mouth should be, so I decide that she does have one, and that this is the face I will see when she comes out of me and I hold her for the first time. I make a picture of her with a tiny nose, a small bump like the end of my little finger, and cheeks that bunch up and shine when she smiles. I imagine her smiling a lot.

I imagine stroking a finger along her pale eyebrows, so thin and soft because every part of her is so small, even her eyebrow hairs and her eyelashes. Her eyelashes won't be dark and prickly like mine, but beautiful, and if she blinks they'll flutter against the back of my hand like the dandelion clocks in the field.

Her eyes will be brown like the worn floor by the kitchen fire, and they will look at me the way I remember the soft woman looking at me. They will look at me with so much warmth and joy that we will want to stay with each other for ever.

This is how I imagine my child. I won't tell this to Mother – it is a private thought. When I put my hands on the bare bump of my tummy, I pass these thoughts through them to my child, silently, without words, so it's just between the two of us. I imagine she can hear me thinking this way, and I wonder what she thinks about, and whether she imagines I can hear her thoughts, too.

I sit like that in the comfy chair by the kitchen fire and I feel something like silence. Not the silence from on top of the mountain, because I can hear the fire and the clock and the chickens clucking in the yard, and the creaks and tapping that the farmhouse sometimes makes when everything else is still. It's a different kind of silence, like the silence is inside me, because it's just me and my baby and we can think to each other without using sounds.

And in that sort-of silence, I realise how to spend the afternoon while Mother is gone.

*

First I take some cans from the larder and pack them into the bottom of my backpack. I add a packet of biscuits that hasn't been opened. Then I clamber with it up the stairs. In my bedroom, I pack all my clothes and the spare blanket from the drawer. I will need more than this, but it's a start.

As I pack, I think about possession, about what Mother said when she taught me that something could be mine or hers – and how something could also belong to nobody, because nobody could just do what they like with it. Mother says the towers in the City are nobody's, that once they belonged to somebody but now they belong to dead people. She thinks the Clinic and everything inside it belongs to nobody too.

I think she's wrong. I think it belongs to me now, because possession does not mean you can do what you like with something. Possession means knowing. I think my arm belongs to me because I know the details of it, the hard bumps and bulges, the soft dark hair covering it. And I think the field and farmhouse are ours because we work them and care for them together. And the Clinic with its shut doors and cold tubes of seed is mine, because I have climbed into the belly of the building at night and have pushed those seeds deep into myself. The same way the mountain and the silence at the top of it are mine because I have stood in the middle of it and Mother hasn't.

I belong to my child and my child belongs to me. Together, we could make everything ours. We could walk away from Mother and the small belonging of the farmhouse, out past the City to the edge of the land where it butts up against the sky. We will be like the wandering packs of wolf-dogs, my child and me, and we will go wherever there is food and shelter and wherever there is new ground to learn and claim. And if the smoke I saw from the mountain is still there at the line between the ground and the sea, and if the hands that made the fire are really other people's hands who aren't dead people, but alive like me and Mother and my baby, then maybe we can go and find them, and I can teach them everything I know about how to plant vegetables and collect eggs and find food in the City. And maybe these other not-dead people have different words to me and Mother, because they're not connected to the farmhouse like we are, so their words can't be either. Maybe all their words are unconnected, like when I stood on the mountain and thought the word *sea*. It must be frightening, to have no connections at all. If I find them after my baby is born, maybe I can teach them some of our words too.

And if I really am a survivor, and if my child is a survivor too, I will plant more seeds in my body and become even more of a creator. I will create enough children to fill all the spaces left in the world by the dead people. They will all belong to me and I will belong to all of them, and it will be so much better than living with Mother who is a bridge and full of lies and can't belong to anyone.

After I've packed my rucksack, the journey feels real, almost like a thing I could touch. My skin tingles, which might mean I'm excited or might mean I'm afraid. I can't tell the difference.

The light is getting bluer, so I gather the chickens and lock them up for the night, and then I go back to the comfy chair and put another soup tin on the stove top. I put more logs on the fire, and from the slopes of the wood and embers I can make pictures of mountains and valleys, of little streams and crouching cities. In my head, I can make pictures of me and my child exploring them together.

These pictures burn so brightly inside me, that when Mother comes home I barely notice her in the dark doorway.

She comes and stands in front of the fire. For a long time she says nothing. She watches me, as if she knows I'm keeping something inside me, but she doesn't ask. She just sighs. Her face is closed again, like crossed arms, and her bag looks empty.

'Did you get the oranges?'

She rubs a hand across her forehead. 'There weren't any.'

I don't believe her. Mother didn't want me to have oranges. I would have walked for them myself, but she said no, so I let her go without me, and now I have no oranges.

'Why not?'

I make a picture of the orangery in my head, filled with bright fruits and that smell of hot earth, and Mother standing in the middle of it, deciding not to bring anything back – but I can't make the picture stick. So I make another instead, where there really are no oranges. I make a picture where the stiff glass door is open, and instead of oranges, the branches are covered with the green ends of twigs, as if more hands than I know how to count have reached up to pick the fruit and carried it away. And in this other picture, Mother goes from tree to tree, searching, touching her fingers to the green bumps on the highest, most difficult to reach branches where the oranges used to be. In this other picture, a small breeze makes Mother's hair lift and wave like long grass, and there's the smell of smoke from the fire by the sea.

'Why not?' I ask again.

She watches the kitchen fire flickering. Her hand shakes. She says, 'I don't know,' but her eyes are like the stones in the field that clang against our tools and won't let us dig past them.

Even now her words still carry lies. Mother says lies are something you can fall for, and I know what she means because Mother is empty and emptiness is something you can tumble into. She is not my creator. She is not kind. She is not even brave enough to say whether the pictures in my head are real.

I can feel myself getting angry, but I hold on. And what I hold on to are the bright thoughts of my child. I hold on to our journey to the mountain and then to the edge of the land. And I hold on to the rucksack in my bedroom.

So when Mother speaks again, when she says, 'Monster, listen . . .' I just shrug and turn away from her. And she knows that's the end of the conversation, because she sits down on one of the hard chairs and closes her eyes till her hand stops shaking, and that is how Mother's second silence begins.

*

Mother is silent for weeks. Not silent the way the mountain was silent, or the way she went silent when I told her about the Clinic. Mother is silent on the inside. I can see the silence through her eyes. She doesn't say very much, but when she speaks it's as if her words have nothing behind them, as if everything that was Mother has dropped away. I think what I can see in her is the emptiness.

And I'm glad I can see it, because it helps me remember that it's there.

*

Every day I can do less before I need to rest. On days Mother goes to the City, I stay at the farm and think about leaving. I take everything out of my rucksack and put it in again in a different order.

On the other days, it's as though one of us is the sea and one of us is the ground, and there's always this twisting line between us. Mother digs up food from the field and plants the summer seeds, like cabbages and lettuces and other green things. More and more, she stops working at small noises, or even at no noise at all, and she looks all around as if there might be a fox or a wolf-dog coming, but there never is. Sometimes I stand next to her and pick the vegetables up from the ground or pass her seeds to plant, but mostly I stay in the yard, or somewhere else close to the house where I can hear the stream. I like how the sound of it never stops. I like how it's as if it's trying to speak and cover up Mother's shaky new silence, but how it never says any actual words.

When it's too hot to be outside or in the kitchen by the fire, I sit in the barn with the door open so I can see the chickens in the yard. Even when it's sunny, the inside of the barn is dark and cold and smells a bit of chicken mess, even though the chickens don't live in here any more. I like the way the dark means that I can look right at things and not be able to see them properly, but then if I look right at something else, all the things on the edges suddenly have shapes again, but not always their proper shapes, so I can make pictures in my head where everything in the barn is the shape of a baby waiting to be born.

*

In the evenings, I sit by the fire and try to feel my own bigness. I try to work out if I feel heavier than yesterday.

Mother sits on my cushion on the floor, and her body is like the string we use to tie the bean poles, all pulled tight.

*

On the afternoon that it rains, fat heavy drops splash noisily in the yard. I want to stand outside in it, with my head back and my mouth open, but Mother says no. So we sit separately in the kitchen, and I watch her fixing the edge of a sheet in the window-light. Her hands are always busy now, always making something or mending, as if they have their own minds and she wants to keep their minds distracted.

I rub a hand across my big round belly.

'Is it kicking?' Mother's voice is as tight as her body.

'She's just getting herself comfortable.'

She looks at my belly and her eyes are like a foggy morning. She looks far away and forgotten.

For a moment I want to walk over to her, to stand between her and the grey window-light, lift up my shirt and say, Look, here it is. Here's my belly. Here's my child. I want her to put her rough hand on my glowing belly and I want to hold her there till the baby moves. I want to tell her, You are a part of this. I'm the soil that this child grows in, but you're the rain and the sunshine and the coloured ribbons that flutter from the post to scare away the birds. And even though your words are empty, you're my Mother and I'm your Monster.

But that is not the promise I made to myself, and Mother is not like Mother any more.

The baby kicks. Her kick sends that warmth rushing through me, right from my big toes to my elastic chest, up to the roots of my hair. I think it spills into my eyes, too, and makes them shine like torches, because Mother's own fog-filled eyes turn back to her sheet.

I make myself remember the top of the mountain, how the

world from up there was so big that I could explore it all and never run out of new things to know, that feeling that without Mother I could fly across it like a bird or walk on quiet paws like a wolf-dog.

But there is one thing I still need her for: 'Mother? What happens when the baby's ready to come out?'

She looks up, the fog clearing a little, as though she's found a way back through to the sun – my sun.

I try again. 'What I mean is, how?'

Mother lays down her sheet so all her attention is on me. For a moment it's like it used to be, when she would teach me words and how to peel and boil potatoes and how to eat with cutlery and wash myself. Then the fire spits and Mother makes a small jumpy movement at the noise.

'You'll push the baby out,' she says, and she isn't looking at me but at the bit of wall behind my head. 'It will come out of your belly through your vagina.'

It isn't a word I know – it sounds soft and flabby, like a flap of plastic blowing in the wind.

'The bit between your legs.'

The bit between my legs – where the shiny woman looked at me, where I pushed the seeds to plant my child inside me, where my child will squeeze out of me to begin her life by my side. All the things that pull me apart from Mother. All the things that make me different. I didn't know it had a name, but I suppose everything has one.

I put my hand there. It seems too small to let a child pass through.

'Will I die when the child comes out?'

Mother says, 'No,' but she says it quickly, like she's trying to stop another word coming out instead.

I pick and pull at the hole in the comfy chair.

'I'll help you. I won't let anything happen to you.' She does this little smile that's more sad than happy and doesn't really unfog her face. 'You're a survivor, Monster.'

I decide Mother is telling the truth. What I mean is, I think she's saying that she hopes nothing bad will happen, and that she'll try to help me as much as she can, even though she doesn't know how much that is.

'Will it hurt?' I ask.

'Yes.'

'OK.' I look back at the fire, trying to imagine the kind of hurt that comes from a child pushing through the space between my legs.

Mother has a thing she sometimes says, which is, 'No pain, no gain', which means if you want to make something, you have to be OK with it hurting, like when we had to rebuild the chicken shed and everything ached at the end of the day.

So I'm glad that it'll hurt when the child comes out, because it means I'll be creating something all of my own. It doesn't matter what Mother says – I won't just be a survivor any more, I'll be a creator. I'll be a Monster and a Mother, both at the same time.

I sit apart from Mother and think these silent thoughts to my baby.

*

Whenever Mother goes to the City, she likes to pack her rucksack the way she taught me, with the things she needs closest to the top. But after I went away to the mountain and then came back again, I learned to pack all the heavy things in the middle, so the rucksack fits against my back and doesn't pull as much on my shoulders. What I mean is, I pack my bag by weight instead of by need.

I come upstairs one night and the rucksack under my bed feels wrong. When I put it on, it drags and rubs against the bottom of my back. Even before I open it, I know Mother has been through it. I make a picture of it in my head, of the rucksack open and all the things inside it laid out on top of my blanket, and of Mother's big hands moving across them.

I watch Mother's hands chopping carrots with the small knife while I peel the skins from three onions. Her fingers are bony and covered in small marks. She doesn't look up till I've finished cutting the onions into small pieces on my own board, and even then she only looks as far as my hands.

She waits. Then she reaches across and takes hold of them.

Mother's hands feel rough in mine, like something from outside. She is here and not here, like the clock when the swinging metal circle gets stuck, and the quiet it makes by not tickerting is just a different kind of noise, the way not speaking can sometimes be just as loud as saying words. Mother has mostly been not speaking since she came back from the orangery.

'It's all changed,' says Mother, in a quiet voice that makes me think of ash settling in the grate. She says it to my hands, as if my hands aren't part of me and might have changed things by themselves. Then she goes back to chopping the carrots, slowly, with her hard, grey hands.

*

Later, Mother sits on the cushion against the wall with her arms folded and face crossed and her eyes almost closed. I watch the shapes in the kitchen fire and think about the soft woman. I try to push at the edges of what I remember. I think about the emptiness inside Mother, and I concentrate on the thought of her not being there.

The back of my neck prickles like wolf-dogs are watching, but I'm ready for it so I can ignore it. I make a picture in my head of me standing on the bridge with the soft woman, before she puts me on the railing. In the picture, we're inside the circle which is inside the fog, and the fog is all around us. Then I screw up my eyes and try to make myself see through the fog because then I might remember what comes before this. What comes before the railing and the bridge and the soft woman and me? I try and try, but the fog just gets thicker, till it's almost solid like the windows we sometimes find in the City, made of glass but painted white so we can't see through.

Mother's breathing gets louder and slower as she falls asleep. A log tumbles in the grate, sending up sparks.

I shut my eyes and make another picture, of the circle in the fog and of me sitting on the railing in the middle of it, alone, after the soft woman has fallen.

The bridge and the railing are bigger without the soft woman, and the me in the picture is smaller. The railing is cold and my hands hurt from holding onto it so tightly. I sit there for a long time, with a lump of something in my throat like I've swallowed without chewing, too afraid of falling to try to get down.

The fog disappears. The me on the railing is trembling right through my body, and the me by the fire is too, because even though I know there are no wolf-dogs watching, it still feels as though there are. The back of my neck is prickling and I can hear my heart thudding like a gate in the wind – and then there's a voice, deeper than my voice or Mother's voice. A man's voice. I don't know how I know it's a man's voice, I just do, the way I knew about the sea and the Clinic, but it says some things I don't understand, and the picture-in-my-head me tries to speak. I open my mouth and my spit makes a gargling sound at the back of my throat and I can't think of any words to say so I shut my mouth again, and I don't open it, and I can feel my words leaving me already – though maybe that is just the memory and not how it really was.

Two hands grab my chest. They lift me up off the railing. Suddenly I'm hanging over the gully and it's too far down even to see where the soft woman landed, and the hands are going to drop me but they don't – they lift me back over the railing as if they're going to put me down on the bridge, but they don't do that either. The hands pass me to another pair of hands, and these ones are bigger than the first pair and harder and covered in thick black hairs. The hands are tight around my chest and I want to wriggle away but I don't want them to throw me over the edge and my voice has forgotten how to shout. Then the hands become arms and the arms are around my middle and squashing me against another chest, and this chest smells of sweat and not washing and something sharp like chicken mess, and everything inside of me is wriggling and I can taste something like sick that I force back down – and the second man says something and laughs and the chest and the arms around me rumble like thunder and my heart is thudding thudding thudding and I think the men are wolf-dogs and I can't speak and I don't think I can breathe—

I open my eyes. I stare at the shapes in the fire till my head hurts from the brightness of it. I make a picture of the bridge over the gully covered in fog, so all I can see is the clear circle where the men are holding me. I try to push the men out of the circle so they're back in the hidden part of my head, but they won't go. I try to pull the fog in so that it covers everything in the picture, but I can't do that either. I don't know how.

I sit for a long time, watching the flames.

I think about how they took my words away, how the soft woman fell from the bridge and my words fell with her, or how maybe the men squeezed them out when they grabbed me with their big hard hands. There must be so much I don't remember. Maybe it's like when we killed the sheep, and Mother said we had to not let it see the knife, so it wouldn't be afraid. Maybe it's better I don't remember, because I couldn't change it anyway. But even when the sheep couldn't see the knife, it still knew what was going to happen and it was still afraid.

I think instead about my baby. I think about her growing in my belly like a carrot seed in soil. I think about the small circle of her world, how that is all she needs for now. I think about the bigness of everything outside of her, and I put a circle of fog around us.

Mother is still asleep on the cushion on the floor. I look at her and then I look away from her. The fire is quieter now, but I can still hear the clock tickerting and even though it's not any louder than it was yesterday or the day before, it won't leave me alone. I feel like I'm inside a snail shell and the clock is one of the small birds picking me up in its beak and bashing me against the window-shelf over and over, and even when I put my hands over my ears I can still hear it, like it's inside my head with the picture of the men holding me in the circle of fog on the bridge. And suddenly I know what Mother means when she looks at the clock and says the time is wrong, because the clock keeps on saying its small noises as if time is always something to talk about, but sometimes time just is, and there are no words to fill it with because sometimes it's better to leave a circle empty.

I get up from my cushion and walk over to the clock. Inside its glass cupboard, the metal circle is swinging from side to side to side to side. The noise over here is even louder, as if it's supposed to stay inside its little cupboard but somehow it's managed to get out and is shouting about it as loudly as it can.

I reach up to the little people on top of the clock, the man and the woman that look as though they would snap if I dusted them too hard. I pull at the little man figure, but the wood must be thicker than it looks, because I can't break it. I open the cupboard door and grab the metal circle. I push it backwards into the hole it sometimes gets stuck in before Mother sets it going again, and I shut the cupboard door.

The noise when it's not tickerting is even louder than when it was, but it's a different kind of noise. It's the kind that's so loud it lets my head feel empty, like I don't have to make pictures to fill it with. I sit back on my cushion and let this new loudness sit inside me, like it's growing strong and beautiful in my head the way my baby is growing strong and beautiful in my belly. I watch the fire without making the shapes in the flames into pictures, and I think about the top of the mountain. I put my hands on my belly and feel my baby moving inside me.

*

The sky is bright and dry, but the sun isn't burning as hot today. I take the blankets outside to sit on the big rock at the edge of the vegetable rows and watch Mother work.

She looks small against the huge field. She's all angles and thinness. When she bends over I can see all the bumps of her backbone through her jumper. I never noticed her getting smaller. I wonder if she's always been like that.

I stretch my hands across my big thighs and press into them. If I do this it stops them hurting so much. They don't hurt like a sudden hurt, like cutting my thumb on the knife or banging my foot. It's a quiet hurt, one that's always there now, like the quiet that now lives in the kitchen where the noise of the clock used to be.

When I breathe in, the air is thin and wet. It smells like the ground. I close my eyes and go on breathing it until it feels like Mother is a long way away. I think I fall asleep. I don't know what dreams I have, but when I open my eyes the sky looks grey and everything inside me feels flat and shaky.

*

I grow even bigger. I grow till I feel as if I'm too big for my own skin, and everything feels too heavy. My belly and chest grow rounder, like they're trying to fill the space that Mother's emptiness has left behind.

My baby moves and stretches as if she can feel the edges of her little world, as if she's decided it isn't big enough and she needs to be outside.

Mother says it won't be long now. She says it in the same hidden voice she used when she told me the oranges were gone, which says she doesn't want the baby to come but knows there's nothing she can do to stop it.

I pack more food into the rucksack hidden under my bed, then I take it all out and put it back in again. I spend my days fidgeting, counting each one off on the tally on my wall.

They're long, these days. Long and empty, and they prickle at me like wearing too many blankets. My skin is always hot and itching. I start to understand why waiting has the word *weight* in it, because it's heavy, this long time of nothing happening. It takes a lot of effort to move, as if my arms and legs are made of blocks of wood too fat to lift. I wait. I weight.

*

It starts like this.

I'm getting ready for bed, washing my face and under my arms with the warm water from the wash bowl. The baby's kicking, but the water feels smooth and soft, like a blanket after I've slept in it all night. I wash twice, to feel that soft water again, and as I rub my face in the towel to dry it, that's when my body kicks back at the baby.

I drop the towel and grab the big roundness that's now my belly as it kicks in at the baby again.

'Mother!'

Her feet are up the stairs, fast, and I can feel my heartbeat right through me, fast to match them. Mother's in the doorway. She looks at me once and says, 'Downstairs. Now.'

I'm heavy with all the days of waiting, and so close to curling up in my comfortable little bed and letting myself sleep.

But Mother grabs the blankets and bundles them up in her arms. 'It's starting. Come on.'

So we go downstairs, Mother in front to keep me from falling, both of us stepping one careful step at a time.

I'm standing in the kitchen, now, just inside the door. It's warm and yellow. The fire's still flickering in the grate, and it almost feels as if everything is normal. I try to think these thoughts to my baby. I spread my hands over my belly and make pictures in my head of warmth and fire and comfy chairs. Then I try to think of these pictures flowing like the stream in summer, quiet and calm, from my head, down through my neck and shoulders, along my arms to my hands, and then into my belly so they can be pictures inside my baby's head, too. Like this, I tell her, 'It'll be OK, it'll be OK, it'll be OK, it'll be OK.'

'Monster.'

My trousers are wet. I feel all the wetness fall out of me like blood. It soaks down the insides of my legs, and I want to tell Mother that I'm sorry, I didn't need the toilet, I don't know what happened, but she's already bent in front of me, helping me peel off the wet clothes, till I'm standing in the kitchen wearing nothing, and even with the fire and my belly still hurting I feel cold.

'Here.' Mother helps me into a big T-shirt, then leads me to a space in front of the fire, where she's pushed back the chairs and made a kind of bed out of a pile of blankets on the floor.

As soon as I lie down the kicking at my belly starts again, harder and harder, till it's not like kicking any more but like the baby's grabbing the bits inside of me and twisting and tightening and I cry out, and Mother kneels down beside me with a small towel which she dips in the wash-water on the stove and dabs against my forehead, but the water's been on the stove too long so it burns and I jerk away from it.

I don't know how long we stay there.

Mother puts more wood on the fire to keep it burning. The pain in my belly comes and goes, and all I want to do is sleep. But the floor is too hard, and if the baby's going to come out then I can't sleep, so I just lie there trying not to cry out every time it hurts.

I think about the mountain, how the silence at the top of it made it as if time didn't exist. This is the same, lying here, even though there's the fire-crackle noise, and me, and Mother, because there's no time now, just hurt and wait and more hurt and weight until the baby's ready to force her way through me into the outside world.

*

'Push,' says Mother.
I say, 'Fuck.'

*

'Push!'

'*Fuck.*' I spit the word out like a sharp stone, like Mother when she's angry but worse. I spit out this word of Mother's and I'm claiming it. I'm owning it, sharp and brutal, feeling it through every little bit of my body. 'Fuck!' I scream. 'Fuck fuck fuck!'

'Push,' Mother urges.

I push. I push so hard it feels like my body's going to rip apart.

'That's right,' Mother says.

I push.

I push till I don't even know any more if I am pushing, if I'm doing it myself or if the whole big round sun of me has vanished and now I'm just outwardness, I'm everything pushing and reaching – I don't exist any more – I'm just push and force and pain, and when I scream Fuck! again and again I don't even know if I can hear it, if it makes a sound or if my voice has been pushed out of me and there's none of it left. I'm a tree, my thick branches are pushing up, my roots reaching down, all pushing out and I'm empty inside, there's nothing there. I'm a kettle, I'm steam and it's hot and it hurts and I'm an egg exploding and Mother's hands on my arm aren't there any more or if they are I can't feel them. I'm smoke, I'm water, I'm a thing that can't be held, I'm all force—

'Push,' says Mother, and I scream, 'I am push!' or at least I think I do, I'm not sure, and I turn myself into everything straining, like a fire trapped in a grate, like pushing up a chimney, I push and I feel the toilet parts tumble out of me and I think is this it, is this my baby, but it isn't, and then

302

the smell reaches my nose and it's rich and sour and suddenly I know I'm still here, still human and not one of the dead people, I can feel my body again and the baby still inside me.

And Mother says, 'Push,' and I push and it hurts – fuck it hurts – and it's out, or I think it's out – but Mother says it's just the head and for a second I think she means my baby's just a head with no body, but then she says, 'Just one more push,' and I do, even though I think I can't any more, I push and my baby is born.

My baby is born.

My breaths are short and loud and everything hurts, but I have a child, and I'm trying to sit up so I can see her between my legs, but Mother's there, she's in the way, she's already a bridge between us. Then Mother picks up a knife and sticks it in my baby and I scream.

She's holding my baby – there's blood, they're covered in it – and I think I might still be screaming, but then I see the red stub at my baby's belly, which is what Mother must have cut, because my baby's small face is screwed up and it's her who screams. She opens her little mouth and she lets out this big scream, and it's like she has claws, and with that scream her claws take hold and she pulls me towards her. And I want her, I've never wanted anything more. I want to hold her and press my nose to her and learn every little bit of her.

'Here,' Mother says, and she hands my baby to me. 'It's a boy.'

For a second I'm distracted by this new word. 'A what?'

'A boy. A baby man.' She places my baby in my arms, so my hand is behind her small head, like the baby's head I picked up in the City but softer, warmer, mine. There's a little flap of skin between her legs, and she has a wrinkle at the top of her nose. Her tiny fingers and toes curl and uncurl against my

T-shirt. When her eyes are open, I don't know if she's looking at me or past me, but it feels as if she's looking at me, because everything in me goes warm and happy, even the tired parts and everything that hurts.

Mother lifts my T-shirt so I'm holding my baby against my chest, and she helps me move so my baby's mouth is next to the red-pink bump there, which Mother says is how I'll feed her, the way the sheep fed the lamb.

'When?' I ask.

'When he's ready.'

I try to make sense of these words that are different for a baby man.

Mother watches my baby's mouth making bubbles against my chest. 'What will you call him?'

He. Him.

I hadn't thought about how I would have to give my baby a name. How can I name her when I don't know what she'll be – what he'll be?

I look down at this tiny person I've created. This baby man. This him.

I want to give him something, so that even though my baby's now outside of my body, even though I won't always be holding him like this, he can still have something from me to keep us connected. I think of the blanket I made, with all its tiny pieces, but wrapping him in it feels like putting a layer between us, and not the right gift. I think of the rucksack under my bed. I think of the smoke next to the sea and the other not-dead people who might be there, who we might be able to find. I make a picture of them and suddenly in the picture they have big hard hands, and their hands are covered in little black hairs and they're holding my baby so tightly and pouring their strange unconnected words into him the way Mother poured her not-true words into me – and there are wolf-dogs in a circle of fog all around us, and the strange words are a layer between us even thicker than the blanket, thicker than the fog, and they're so thick in the picture that I can't even see through them any more to my baby.

My baby wriggles a bit in my arms and I cuddle him closer. His little mouth finds the red-pink bump on my chest and he closes around it and sucks, and I can't help smiling. It's as if this is his way of talking to me, not through Mother's words or these new him-words, but through his mouth and my chest, as if every suck is telling me he wants to stay here with me, to keep being a part of me, no words, no other people, just my big sun-body and my baby's tiny fragile one. The warmth from his sucking spreads through me like an egg yolk on hot toast, like we're sinking into each other or rising around each other, and I don't know where we separate, because for the moment we don't. And the moment feels like it could go on for ever, like it doesn't have any walls or fences around it, it just is, and nothing outside of it exists.

Me, sitting on a heap of blankets in front of the fire. My baby, his mouth pulling me out of myself through my chest. This is everything I need, everything there is.

I hold his small weight against my skin and the journey disappears. The rucksack under my bed shrinks till it's just a picture in my head, and then isn't even that, and the men on the bridge in the circle of fog are a long way away. I look at my baby's wrinkled face, at the creases across his tummy, and wonder how I ever thought that I would need to leave.

I look across at Mother, sitting apart from us against the comfy chair, and I smile, because even though she is still empty, that doesn't matter when everything else is full. I think about how I am a creator now, how I wanted my baby and so I made him become real. But then I remember how I thought pushing him out of me might turn me into one of the dead

305

people, and how maybe it would have if Mother hadn't helped, and I know I am also a survivor. We are both survivors, Mother and me, and we are both creators. Really, I think that Monster just means Monster and Mother just means Mother. I look at her, and my head is filled with pictures of my baby's scrunched-up eyes, his delicate body.

I say, 'We're going to stay at the farm.'

We will stay here, all of us. There will be the farm to keep us safe from the other not-dead people, and there will be me and Mother to keep my baby alive. We will be the same and not the same, Mother and me, like we are two separate sides of a gully and there's no bridge to separate us. Instead there's my baby, filling the gully up and joining our two edges together.

I try to think this to him, through my chest and his small pink mouth. He doesn't have any words yet, so I send him a picture of the Clinic where the seeds were stored, and the carrots in the field, and of things growing. I send a picture of the farm filled with people, and the City filled with people. Not the other not-dead people who made the smoke, or the men in the circle of fog on the bridge, but me and Mother and my baby and maybe new people. My people – mine because I will know them, because I will create them. This is what I'm going to give you, I think, except I try to think it in feelings not words – a feeling of pushing outwards and over-flowing like a full cup.

Everything, I think. *Everything.*

*

Light comes slowly through the kitchen window. There is another day, a day for me, and my baby, and for Mother.

I am not afraid the way Mother is always afraid, of things which might or might not be there, or of things which are there but we can do nothing about. I know what is outside the farm and the fields and the City, and I just decide to leave it there. I smile again at Mother, and Mother half-smiles back at me. Already the gully is less deep.

My baby's eyes start to close. He breathes small breaths that make his whole body move.

I tell them, 'There will be so many days.'

*

My baby sleeps, and wriggles, and sucks milk from the red-pink bumps on my chest. The parts of me where I pushed him out start to hurt a little bit less.

Mother says I'm healing. She says this means getting better, like when my bedroom door handle broke and she fixed it to make it the way it was before. But I'm not going back to the way I was before, and anyway I don't think that's what healing really means, because Mother says her wolf-dog bite is healed, but she still has pink marks on her leg, so maybe healing really means making something different. Maybe getting better doesn't mean going back to how it used to be, but moving forwards instead – like when Mother taught me how to build up the walls around the field or how to look for tools in the City, and I learned more and more till Mother said I was better at it.

I want to explain this to my baby, but even if he knew what words meant, he could never understand healing because there was never any before for him, so how can he know what I mean by after? So I show him the things that are now instead. I show him things that are here.

*

Mother goes to the City to collect more food. I stay at the farm and feed my baby. Every day he gets a little bit bigger. He makes small noises. His tiny fingers learn to grab and hold on.

*

I stand in the yard with my baby wrapped in a blanket and held up against my chest, and I show him the chickens and their scratting. I make clucking noises in his ear. He looks across my shoulder and I show him the barn, where in the winter we store food and sheep. The days are already getting shorter and colder. I cuddle him close and teach him about warmth.

In the kitchen, Mother is making something she calls an automaton, where she'll be able to turn a handle and a little model of a chick will peck at a little model of a seed. She says she's making it for my baby.

I put my face to his neck, where he smells of me and milk and sour things. I lean him back so he stares up at me from my arms. His eyes are warm and deep like full cups of tea. Ever since he was born, I've felt like I'm falling.

'Look,' I say, as I show him the place by the fire where Mother kept us alive as I pushed him out of me and he became not just a picture in my head. 'This is where we made you real.'

Mother looks up from her tools and painted bits of wood. She looks at me and she looks at my baby, and her face is a bit less like crossed arms. I smile. My baby's lips make bubbles and his fingers curl at the blanket.

He makes me think of the mountain – how the noise stopped and there was no start and no ending, but just one big everything and being able to see right to the edges of the sky. How I could go anywhere but at the same time be happy right there. How there would always be more time.

'I've thought of a name for you,' I tell him.

My voice is quiet and at the same time is the only thing in the room.

He looks at me till the words disappear because between us we don't need them, because words can be empty and everything about my baby is full. I look at him and he looks at me, till we grow into each other and then out, till there's nothing but my baby and my baby is everything, the farm and the fields and the City, and Mother and the sea. He goes right to the edges of the world, and the world keeps on going for ever.

I say, 'I'm going to call you Silence.'

Acknowledgements

There are so many people flitting invisibly through the pages of this book, and huge thanks go out to all of them. To Lucy Luck at C&W, whose unfailing energy and positivity have kept me writing: thank you. Thank you to Jo Dingley at Canongate, for having faith in Monster and in me, and to Megan Reid for insightful comments on the manuscript. Thank you also to the rest of the Canongate team, for supporting me and making me feel welcome right from the start.

The creation of this book has been a journey which I would not have set out on without the support of Penguin Random House and the WriteNow scheme. Thank you to Tom Avery for seeing the book's potential when it was still just a sliver of an extract, and to Siena Parker for supporting my development as a writer. Thank you as well to Jacob Sam-La Rose at Flipped Eye for first flagging up the opportunity.

My thanks go out to the rest of my WriteNow family, for the shared joys and for the support during moments of midnight anguish. Thank you to Nelson Abbey, Nazneen Ahmed, Charlene Alcott, Emma Smith-Barton, Christine Brougham, Elizabeth-Jane Burnett, Manjeet Mann, Emma Morgan, Rebecca Pizzey, Geraldine Quigley and Ben Wilson. Thanks also to Polly Atkin, for her willingness to celebrate good news over drinks and a pizza.

For being critical fans and sympathetic readers, I have to thank Jessi Rich and Elizabeth Mann – also for encouraging me to write the book when I was teetering on the brink of beginning. For this, thanks are also due to Zosia Wand and her writing group at the Reading Room. Thanks also to Zosia for cake and coffee, and for making toast when I arrive having not had time for breakfast.

Continuing the theme of food and hospitality, thank you to Supal Desai and Lara Trela for putting me up on numerous trips to London, and to Stephen Hyde and Nicky Godfrey-Evans for lending me their phone line and space at their kitchen table.

My final thanks have to go to Mum and Dad. I couldn't ask for more supportive parents, or for more patient neighbours. Thank you for almost thirty years of advice and hugs and stories. Thank you for the thousands of miles of lifts, and for being an equally encouraging audience at book festivals and school concerts. For always believing in me, and for teaching me to believe in myself: thank you.